Of a Feather

Of a Feather

DAYNA LORENTZ

HOUGHTON MIFFLIN HARCOURT
Boston   New York

hmhbooks.com

The text was set in Caslon 540 LT Std.

Library of Congress Cataloging-in-Publication Data
Names: Lorentz, Dayna, author.
Title: Of a feather / Dayna Lorentz.
Description: Boston : Houghton Mifflin Harcourt, 2021. | Audience: Ages 10 to 12. | Audience: Grades 4–6. | Summary: A baby great horned owl, Second, so called because his sister, First, is already out of the nest, is reluctant to hunt for himself, but when his mother is injured he is forced out into the forest; Maureen is a human girl pulled out of her grandmother's violent home and placed with an aunt—but her Aunt Beatrice is involved in falconry and runs a mews where injured raptors can heal, and it is here Maureen and Second (now called Rufus) meet and learn how to heal each other.
Identifiers: LCCN 2019042999 (print) | LCCN 2019043000 (ebook) | ISBN 9780358283539 (hardcover) | ISBN 9780358378587 (ebook)
Subjects: LCSH: Great horned owl—Juvenile fiction. | Wildlife rescue—Juvenile fiction. | Wildlife rehabilitators—Juvenile fiction. | Falconry—Juvenile fiction. | Aunts—Juvenile fiction. | Brothers and sisters—Juvenile fiction. | CYAC: Great horned owl—Fiction. | Owls—Fiction. | Wildlife rescue—Fiction. | Falconry—Fiction. | Aunts—Fiction. | Brothers and sisters—Fiction. | LCGFT: Bildungsromans.
Classification: LCC PZ7.L8814 Of 2021 (print) | LCC PZ7.L8814 (ebook) | DDC 813.6 [Fic]—dc23
LC record available at https://lccn.loc.gov/2019042999
LC ebook record available at https://lccn.loc.gov/2019043000

Manufactured in the United States of America
DOC 10 9 8 7 6 5 4 3 2 1
4500816340

 *For* EVIE & JOSH

and all the other members of the Owl-Human Alliance

Prologue

THE VOLE STICKS ITS TWITCHY LITTLE NOSE OUT OF THE shadows and tastes the air with its whiskers. It thinks that no owl is watching.

Think again, vole. *This* great horned owl has his eyes on *you*.

I can picture it perfectly: The wind will ruffle my feathers as I dive, I'll feel the fur beneath my talons, and then —*SNAP!* Breakfast.

There's a crash and the tree branches shiver with the impact. It's my sister, First. "The sun's been down for an hour and you're still in the nest?" she squawks.

I don't know why she's here. She fledged last week. Mother twittered with pride, watching First's silhouette disappear into the trees. I tried not to notice Father glaring down his beak at me, like he doubted I'd ever fly off on my own.

"Shouldn't you be somewhere else in the forest?" I hoot in reply.

"Doesn't mean I can't flap by to check in on my favorite runt."

"Actually, it does mean that," I grumble. "You should be claiming territory—some *other* territory."

First narrows her eyes, rouses her feathers. "Who says I haven't?"

This owl says. I can tell from the low angle of her ear tufts, from the grumble in her hoots, that she hasn't. I feel a little bad for her, want to give her a bit of a nibble on the beak, but then she lifts her tufts and chirrups, "At least I'm not shivering in my feathers at the thought of hunting my own food."

That's the First I grew up with, always pecking you right between the eyes, where it'll hurt most. I contemplate slashing her with a talon. "I am working on a plan."

"Planning is for prey. You're a great horned owl. You hunt. You catch something. Or you don't and try again."

"You have your way, I have mine." I turn my eyes back to the vole hole.

First bobs her head, widens her eyes. "Care for a game of Talons?"

Now I'm suspicious. Talons is a game Father invented for us, to prepare us for "the real forest," he said. We start in trees on opposite sides of a clearing, and whoever forces the other one to the ground wins. First *has* fledged—she's in the "real" forest. How bad must things be going for her to want to play with me?

Gah, who gives a hoot? This is First. She'll figure it out.

"Not now," I twitter, and pull my feathers into my body, hunker my head down between my wings. "I'm studying."

Need I say that I was not the greatest player of Talons? Need I mention that First, being the first to hatch, is bigger and stronger and—perhaps this is unrelated to our hatch order—ruthless?

"What?" First tweets. "Is baby Second afraid of stepping a toe out of the nest?" She blinks her eyes: top lid down, then clear guard-lid across.

When I don't answer, she flaps off the branch.

Even owls have a hard time hearing other owls. Our feathers are so fluffy, they melt into the wind, become a part of it, so nothing—not our prey, not ourselves—can hear our approach. So it's only when First slams her talons down in the center of our nest—a wide circle of sticks Father stole from a red-tailed hawk back in the dead of winter—that I realize she hasn't left for good.

She grabs a clump of molted feathers from the nest and

drops them on my head as she wings off. She's not taking no for an answer.

I take a tentative step out onto a branch. "First?" I hoot quietly. "Are we starting? Should I fly out to the clearing?"

The ripples of wind from her wings hit me just before she bops me on the head with her feet. "Already started!"

Great Beak! I stumble, miss a talon, and am off the tree and flapping through the night. I weave between the branches, twisting with the air as it curls around obstacles. The forest gives way to grass and I scan the stars for First.

She's already swooping down toward me.

I flip my feet forward but too slowly, so I duck my head and dive, and she misses.

"That's cheating!" she cries, carving through the night to make another pass.

I'll try this move I saw Father use on an eagle who attacked our nest. I pull my wing in a bit and dip it down. I should flip over, so that my talons are where my back would be, then swirl back around. But the air current tugs too hard. Instead of a graceful twist, I flop over onto my back in midair and begin to drop, upside down and with no way to flap. "Help!"

First snatches my feet in her talons, drags me back up into the nest. "What was that supposed to be?" She drops me like a piece of prey onto the sticks.

"It's a special flip technique I'm testing out," I chirp with as much dignity as I can muster.

First blinks slowly. *"Planning, testing,"* she hoots. "Maybe you should stay in the nest, brother. Out in the forest, you either do it or you're prey." She lifts off and disappears into the darkening blue.

It's full dark by the time Mother returns to the nest with a rat, which she lays at my feet. "Was your father here? I thought I heard hooting."

"No," I answer. "It was just me. Practicing."

Mother nibbles my tufts. "My little perfectionist, even practicing his hoots."

I bob my head away from her beak. "Mother," I squeak, then try again in a decent hoot. "Mother, should I—am I —do you think . . . ?"

She tilts her head as if trying to locate the rest of my hoots inside me. "Every owl fledges in their own time." She pushes the rat toward me. "Eat something."

I look down at the rat, then back at the vole hole. *You either do it or you're prey,* First had squawked.

I push the rat back toward Mother. "You eat it," I hoot. "I'm catching my own breakfast."

Mother twitters softly, then flaps off into the night.

She left the rat.

I manage to ignore it until the sun pinks the edges of the sky, but then I gobble it down before closing my eyes to sleep.

1

Reenie

I CAN ALWAYS FAKE A SMILE, *ALWAYS*. EXCEPT TONIGHT, my face just won't cooperate.

For sure, tonight wasn't great. Gram's mean boyfriend, Phil, let his usual simmering stew of anger boil over. He and Gram were yelling loud enough to keep me awake. Loud enough to wake the neighbors, too, because one of them made a big deal of everything and called the police just as Phil started throwing plates as punctuation. Now, the social worker is lost trying to drive me to some stranger's house, her car smells like feet, I have mud on my pajamas, and I cannot make my mouth bend into a smile.

The car swerves hard onto a side road, and the wheels bump as the road turns from pavement to dirt. I lean forward, pressing my chest to the seat belt, to get into the social worker's peripheral vision. "Should we maybe go back to my gram's house?" I say in my nicest kid-trying-to-help voice. It's the one that works best on adults in these kinds of situations.

The social worker yawns, gulps a swig of coffee from her thermos, and smiles sleepily. "We'll find it." She looks back at the road. I think her name is Randi. Yes, Randi with an *i*. I pull my backpack onto my lap, reach inside, and wrap the matted fluff of the marabou string Mom gave me tight around my fingers.

"Ah!" Randi stops the car in front of the driveway of a ramshackle farmhouse built too close to the curb. "Here we are," she says with forced cheer.

The headlights pick out shadows along the house's patchy and peeling white paint. The curtains are drawn across the bay window and no light shines by the green front door.

"Who lives here, again?" I ask. I've never been here before.

Randi-with-an-*i* has to look at her folder. "Your great-aunt. Your grandmother's sister?"

"I didn't think Gram had a sister."

She flips pages. "Your father's mother. Her sister."

That explains why I don't know her. I unwrap my fingers, tuck the marabou away. "Okay."

Randi squeezes my knee. "This isn't the end of things, Reenie."

"Maureen."

"Right. Maureen. Sorry." She glances at the folder. "It's another step in the path, that's all."

I pull the handle and pop open the door. "Sure."

There isn't much ceremony in my transfer of custody. The social worker gives the alleged aunt the thick folder and some paperwork. I can guess what the folder has in it: the whole story of me and Mom. How I've been living with my gram all summer, ever since Mom's sadness got so big, it pushed everything else out of her. It's not the first time this has happened, so we all knew what to do: Gram got Mom admitted to the psychiatric ward at the hospital, and I camped on the futon in Gram's junk room. Why'd Phil have to mess everything up? Why'd the neighbor have to be such a light sleeper?

The alleged aunt signs some papers, hands them to Randi-with-an-*i*, keeps others. In less than ten minutes, Randi's back on the road, and I'm standing on the warped wood floor of the wide foyer of a potentially falling-down house with a total stranger who's supposed to be my replacement parent.

"I'm Beatrice," the alleged aunt says. "Beatrice Prince." She's tall and old. "You can call me Beatrice." She's got long gray hair strapped back in a braid with scraggles poking out. She's wearing men's flannel pants and a T-shirt so faded I can't make out the words, only the letters R and T in a few places.

"You're Will's kid?" she says after a minute of me saying nothing.

"I guess." My dad has never been around.

She gives me the up and down with her eyes. "You look like him."

"I've seen pictures."

She considers me for a moment more, then says, "Huh." She turns and walks toward the back of the house. "Come on," she says, beckoning from halfway down the hall. Clearly, Randi woke her from a deep sleep.

I follow her. The floorboards groan and shift beneath my sneakers. The foyer narrows to a hall alongside the stairs, then opens into a kitchen. There are jars and bowls everywhere. A breeze slithers in through the open window, carrying a stink that's wild and musky and rank.

"What's that smell?" I ask, pulling my T-shirt over my nose for emphasis.

"I keep birds," she says, stopping beside the counter and taking a sip of water from a mason jar. "This is the kitchen. You can eat whatever you want. That over there is the living room." She points to the room next to the kitchen. "I don't have a TV." She says this as if daring me to complain about the fact. "There's a dining room, but I don't use it for dining."

"What do you use it for?"

"My birds." She walks toward me, back to the front of the house. We stand there, facing each other in the narrow hall. I don't feel like moving.

She raises her hand, pointing behind me. "I'll show you your room." When I still don't move, she squeezes around me, then turns and heads upstairs.

I follow her up the steps to a landing. Right leads to her room at the back of the house. Left leads to my room at the front. Between them is the one bathroom in the house.

"The blue towels are yours," she says. "I also found an extra toothbrush and hairbrush. I wasn't sure—" She stops midsentence, scratches her scalp near the base of the braid. "I'm sorry about your mom going to the hospital. I didn't know—"

My fingers claw the canvas of my backpack. "It's been two months," I say. "I'm over it."

The alleged aunt takes a moment, then nods. "I'll leave you to get yourself to bed."

I must look unusually awful for the aunt to feel the need to start in with the "I'm sorry about your mom" stuff, so I poke my head into the bathroom. It's clean enough, with a pedestal sink, a rickety-looking shelf over the john, and a claw-footed tub with a white curtain hanging from a circular bar above it. The window looks down the road, back south where I came from.

There's a mirror over the sink. My brown hair is a snarl on top of my head. There are circles under my brown eyes and the whites are bloodshot, some of those "signs" adults like to point to when identifying the "troubled kids." I splash a handful of water on my face, dry off on one of the blue towels, crack open that new toothbrush, and brush my teeth. The toothpaste tastes too minty, but too minty is maybe a good thing. At Gram's house, there was only one bathroom and four adults—Gram, Phil, Mom's brother Tony, and his girlfriend, Lisa—plus me, so I didn't have a lot of chances to brush my teeth. Not that that was a big deal—I mean, I didn't even have school. But your mouth begins to feel fuzzy after a while. Here, there's a little metal stand for the toothbrushes. I drop mine in and it jingles. It doesn't have to act so happy.

Back in the hall, I approach the closed door identified as "my room." "My room" is huge. The walls are yellow—not my color, but whatever—and there's a round rag rug made of all different-colored strips in the center of the floor. On one side is a desk with a chair; on the other, a big old bed with a quilt and two pillows. The closet is a cavern of empty hangers.

I open my backpack and take out my two T-shirts. I hang

them. They spin listlessly in the vast space. I hang my jean shorts, my four clean socks, and three pairs of underwear on the remaining hangers. I unzip the hoodie I'm wearing and hang it, too. The closet still looks empty. The clothes drift around like they're looking for someone.

My backpack lies on the floor, split open like a skin. The marabou hangs out over the zipper. Mom splurged on it one night as we checked out of the Dollar General. We went home and had a karaoke party, taking turns wearing the marabou string as a boa, dancing and belting out Taylor Swift until the neighbors banged on the wall for us to stop.

That familiar buzz crackles up from my belly button and prickles the inside of my ears. Words fizz out of it: *afraid, stranger, alone.* The buzz careens around inside of my skull and the words flash like lightning and my fingers start to tingle and I can barely keep the tears from trickling out, but I do. I take a deep breath. Suck it all back in. Squeeze the buzz down to a tummy rumble. Lock all those words up tight.

"Good night," I hear from the hall. The strip of light beneath my door goes dark.

I could say something back, but I don't.

The floorboards squeak under my feet as I cross the room. There's a night table next to the bed. The shallow drawer has a nub of pencil in it, some old hair bands, and a wrinkled paperback book, *My Side of the Mountain.*

I'm in someone else's room. Or what was someone else's room. So many questions, but I have to wait until the alleged aunt is asleep to begin a proper investigation. I mean, she got a whole file on me. It's only fair.

I dig out the paperback. It's about a kid who runs away to the middle of nowhere because his house is too crowded. I hate it when books make it seem like kids have a choice about this stuff. It's like, *Where's this guy's Randi-with-an-*i*?* But whatever—the story keeps me awake.

Finally, the grumble of a snore rattles across the hall and it's go time. Creeping downstairs, careful not to squeak any floorboards, I first head for the "bird room." I'm hoping for a menagerie, but no; it's just a mostly empty room with shutters over the windows. What do these birds do in here? Boring.

I sneak into the living room. There are bookshelves and then more books stacked like end tables next to the couch and the overstuffed chair which huddle around the wood stove. I flip through a few—mostly mysteries with gray-haired ladies surrounded by doilies on the covers. Head-lights from a passing car scan over the room, catching me like a thief in the act. I freeze; they pass; I search on.

In a second bookcase near the front window, I hit the jackpot: a photo album. There's a wedding photo—the alleged aunt was married. The guy looks nice enough. Here's them hiking, here they are in a canoe. Here's them with a baby. A little girl. A postcard from the girl: *Dear Mom, Dad's new house is nice. Mindy is nice, too. I miss you. Love, Ava.* It was mailed from St. Louis. Ten years ago.

So I'm in Ava's — the kid's — room. The aunt's divorced. The kid lives with her dad. Did she have a choice? Is this a clue or just what happened?

A stair creaks.

I shove the postcard into the album and the album back into the bookcase and scramble toward the kitchen.

"Maureen?" Beatrice asks, flipping on the hall light.

"I just wanted a glass of water," I say, grabbing a glass out of the cabinet.

She steps into the kitchen, turns on the overhead light. "It's your house now too."

I fill the glass. Take a sip.

"Maureen," she begins, "I'm not your mom, but I —"

"No," I say, interrupting, "you're not." And I'm not her replacement kid. I put the empty glass in the sink and walk past her.

"Good night," she says as I tromp upstairs.

I shut myself in my room. She stays in the kitchen washing that glass for a good ten minutes after.

2
Rufus

I SUCK THE COOL AIR IN THROUGH MY BEAK. SMOOTHING my chest feathers, I align my facial disk, twitching each tiny feather, coaxing the night sounds toward my ears. Silence blooms into patterns of noise: the wind in the branches; the sharp scratch of a late summer leaf against its neighbor; the prickling of tall, dry grass in a nearby field. Bugs thump and chitter inside the dead bark of a neighboring trunk. Heartbeats dance in the darkness.

I'm going for it.

I lift my wings, spread them wide, and drop silently off the branch. I think there's a vole . . . just there . . . maybe?

Yes, a vole. Or a vole-ish creature somewhere in that pile of grass.

I glide toward it. Bob my head, try to lock on to the heartbeat. Where was it? Which tussock?

Now I'm too low.

I flap.

Something skitters near the tree. Mine! I swerve, stretch my talons, crash down into the grass like a stone, and —

Nothing. I've got a footful of straw.

"Forget it," I say, and flap back up to the branch. We've been at this all night, have flown far from the nest to a strange part of the woods, and every single hunting strategy I've come up with has failed. I hunch my head down between my wings and fluff my feathers, laying my ear tufts flat back.

"Second," Mother peeps softly. "Quitting is not an option."

I burrow my head deeper between my shoulders. I know she's right. But it's not my fault. I'm doing everything she says. "My ears are broken," I squeak.

She hoots softly, "Second." Even my name is an insult: second egg to hatch, forever destined to be behind. Mother nips my feathers and steps closer on the branch. "It takes time to learn how to hear the world."

"First got it on her first night."

"First was a week older."

"First fledged three weeks ago." Tonight, Father flapped away to hunt on his own. Mother stayed. But for how long?

She clacks her beak at me. "Enough of this feeling fluffed. You're a great horned owl, master of the night forest. You own the darkness. And you will catch that mouse, so help me." She tromps down the branch, opens her wings, and disappears into the shadows.

It was a mouse? And I was so sure it was a vole! An entire moon's worth of studying and I still can't tell a mouse from a vole . . .

I clack my beak back at her. It's not as if I *want* to be a bum owl. The only owl in the history of owldom who can't find food in the dark.

Far off, a saw-whet *tooh-tooh*s. Even that tiny bug of an owl is having better luck hunting.

I have to stop feeling sorry for myself. I am a great horned owl. Master of the night forest. *Master.*

I bob my head up and down, turn it, bob again, do a full circle, am beginning to feel dizzy, but I still can't pinpoint where in the grass around the bottom of the tree the mouse is rustling.

I go for it anyway.

I swoop, glide on a warm current of air, then drop, talons out, wings folded.

Gah! Leaves! Nothing but dead leaves . . .

"They're too fast," I screech, flapping up from the dust.

"I need some slower food to hunt." But then a better plan hatches in my mind: we could hunt as a team! Why does hunting have to be a solo effort? Who says owls have to live alone?

"Mother, I have a new plan! Let's hunt as a team, in a pack, like the coyotes. Maybe you catch something and then leave it for me to finish off? You know, maybe only half kill it, or stun it a little. What about that plan?"

I land on a branch. "Mother?" I twist my head around first one way, then the other. Her silhouette must be hidden in shadow.

Or she left me.

She wouldn't have left me.

Would she?

"Mother?" Fear grips my beak and my hoot comes out as a warbling squeak.

Something coos from a nearby tree. Not something —Mother.

Mother is perched a swoop or two away near a space in the woods. I can almost feel her frustration from here. She's cooing softly because she doesn't trust me to hear her heartbeat on my own.

My feathers begin to fluff. I *didn't* hear her. I couldn't. Because I am broken! My ears are full of down and I'm never going to catch a meal ever and—

"Calm, Second," Mother coos. But she doesn't fly to me. She doesn't hoot anything more.

She thinks I can do this.

No.

I *can* do this.

I breathe in the cool air again. Let it calm the frustration and anger building in my gizzard. My feathers smooth. Realign. The noise map of the darkness flickers back to life. Mother has stopped cooing.

She believes I can find her.

She believes I can survive.

I stretch my wings down and back, prepare for flight.

But there's a new noise. A rumbling, coming closer, fast.

Mother hears it, she has to, but instead of waiting to see what it is, she dives from her branch into the clearing in the trees.

"Second!" she screeches. "I caught two mice! They were just out in the open, eating an apple core!"

Two mice! We haven't eaten yet today—Mother's been trying to use my hunger as motivation and won't let herself eat until I catch a meal. But two mice out in the open? That is too good to pass up, no matter if it ruins a night's worth of educational starvation.

I open my wings to swoop down to her, but blinding light blazes over the crest of the small hill. The low rumble I heard is now a deafening roar. I screech, "Mother!"

I see her lit in the brilliant light: wings out, ready to fly away.

But the rumbling monster is faster than even her. There's a thump and a snap of bones breaking.

Mother screeches.

"What's happening?" I squeak.

The rumbling monster squeals, stops. Its side flaps open like a stumpy wing and a smaller creature—long-armed and -legged, and thin like a young tree—comes tumbling from its belly. The lanky creature clicks on a small light, yelps, and tries to pick up Mother.

Mother flaps, but one wing lies still. She stumbles, escapes the lanky creature's grasp. "Second!" she cries.

"Mother!" I shriek. My talons seize the bark.

"Fly away!" she screeches. "Save yourself!"

"No!"

The lanky creature throws a thick skin over Mother, muffling her cries. The creature picks her up inside the skin, carries her to the back of the huge hollow monster, lifts its tail, and places Mother in its belly. The lanky creature then scrambles to the open wing, climbs into the belly of the beast, closes the wing, and rumbles on, faster now than before.

"Mother!" I shriek, regaining my voice. I fly after her, blindly flapping through leaves and sticks. "Mother!"

The beast is too fast for me. It kicks up dust, blinding me, filling my lungs. I cough and sputter.

It races away toward distant bright lights. Mother told me to never go near those lights.

I collapse onto a branch. I clack my beak and pant, flap my wings to free myself of the monster's dirt.

Mother's been eaten.

My heart pounds, drowning out all other noise in the night.

She's gone.

The wind rushes through my feathers, reaching my skin. I shiver. I'm alone outside the nest. For the first time.

Alone in a strange forest.

I creep along the branch until I hit the tree's trunk. I huddle down inside my feathers, which are all out of place after crashing through the brush. What does it matter? Father warned of predators—other owls, eagles, hawks, coyotes, even skunks—but he never described anything like that monster. And now I'm left alone in its forest?

Alone, alone, alone. *Aloooooone,* a coyote cries.

The cold moon glares down. Shadows crawl. The darkness crackles with things on the hunt.

With monsters. Hungry monsters.

"Oh, Mother," I chirp.

But Mother is gone.

I close my eyes tight. Shut my ears to the noises. Maybe if I keep perfectly still, maybe if I turn into nothing more than another patch of darkness, into nothing at all, all the evils of the night will slither by me. Maybe then, I'll be safe.

3

Reenie

"MAUREEN!"

The aunt is up awfully early for a Sunday.

I meander downstairs to the kitchen. Beatrice is standing with her mason jar of water and car keys.

"Where are you going?" I ask, picking up a piece of toast from the plate on the counter.

"I have to take you to Rutland."

And then I remember. I have "visitation" with my mom on Sundays from nine in the morning until noon and after school on Tuesdays and Thursdays.

"I need to get dressed," I tell her, dropping the toast.

When I come downstairs, Beatrice is already in her pickup truck, which is parked in the dirt driveway that runs alongside the house. I slide into the passenger seat.

"You ready?" she asks.

"Fine," I say.

At first, "visitation" meant driving to the hospital. Then, after Mom was moved to a treatment house, she'd come over to Gram's. Today, we pull up in front of a coffee place in Rutland.

"Want me to come in?" Beatrice asks.

"No." I slam the door before she can object.

My mom's alone at a table. As I walk inside, I make a quick assessment of the situation: Hair is brushed—*good sign*. Clothes look clean—*excellent news*. Bags under eyes—*warning*.

She sees me and waves, her foot jiggling. She stands and gives me a weak hug. It feels so good, tears sneak out the corners of my eyes. I pretend to wipe my nose on my sleeve and scrape them away.

"Beatrice's house is nice," Mom says. "I saw it once."

"It's nice." *It's not home*, the buzz whispers. I smile hard until it stops.

She releases me, sits. "You're okay?"

"Yeah." I sit in the other chair.

"I can't believe Phil—" Mom stops. Her foot jiggles

harder. "I'm so sorry about all this, Reens." Her voice cracks
—*alarm bells.*

"Don't be sorry," I say. I can't let things fall apart in the
first five minutes. She wipes her eyes—oh man, I can't let
her cry. "It was my fault," I tell her. "I knew Phil and Gram
were in the middle of something, but I had to go to the bathroom. It was just bad luck that Phil threw the plate at that
exact second."

Mom's face has gone white. Her cheeks melt down, her
mouth opens. "He hit you with a plate?"

Now I've done it. "No, really, Mom, it's fine. The plate
hit the wall. I was barely scratched." I lift a hunk of hair
behind my ear to show her where the shard of plate cut me.
"See? It's totally nothing."

Her eyes stare past me out the window.

"Seriously, everything's great." I grab her hand.

Her eyes come back to me.

"They have cards here," I say, pulling a deck from a shelf
and splitting it to shuffle. "Want to play hearts?" It's our game
—we even have a special deck of cards . . . somewhere.

She lifts the corners of her mouth. "I left the magical
sparkle cards back at the residence."

She remembers—*good sign, great sign.* Our cards have
glittery unicorns on them. "Bring them next time?"

Mom nods, and then her face sinks. "Next time," she
says, like it's so far in the future, it may as well be never.

My cheeks start to vibrate; they're working so hard to hold my smile. We play hearts for the rest of the time. I lose, and then she loses; we both take turns letting the other one win.

Beatrice is waiting for me out in the truck at noon. I open the door and climb in.

"How'd it go?" she asks.

"Fine." I curl into the seat, pull my knees up against the seat belt.

She nods. As we pull onto the state highway, she asks, "You want to go see the school or wait until tomorrow?"

"I've been to Rutland Intermediate before."

"Did the social worker not tell you? Well." She wrings the steering wheel with her hands. "I guess it was late."

I let go of my knees and my feet slide to the floor. "Tell me what?"

"I can't drive you to Rutland every day. I've got work, and it's just too far." She says it like we've already had this fight, like she's explained it to me a hundred times.

"I'm not going to my old school?" The buzz cranks up, creeps out.

She glances over at me, looking a lot less sure of herself than she sounded. "I'm sorry, Maureen. I wish I could—"

"It's fine," I snap, because the buzz has filled my whole body like a blizzard. I grip my jeans and dig my fingers down.

This is not a big deal, I tell the buzz. It's not like I had friends. It's not like any of those kids mattered. *It's fine. It's fine.*

We drive back to Branford. The rumble of the road and the smooth voice of the lady on the radio quiets the noise inside. I let my eyes glaze over watching the green streak by the car window and try not to think about having to march into some strange country school tomorrow.

When we park at the house, the aunt pulls a couple of shopping bags out of the truck bed. "I stopped at Goodwill while you were at visitation." She holds out the bags. "Thought you might need—"

"I don't need anything," I say, teeth gritted. "I have clothes at Gram's, somewhere. I'll get them when I go back there." I'm sure my fall stuff didn't get lost when I moved. At least I think I'm sure.

The aunt hugs the bags. "Your gram, she—well, the social worker—"

"Gram can't find my clothes?" Typical Gram.

"It's more complicated than that." The aunt has gone pale and fidgety. "If they don't fit, I can get another size." She holds the bags out.

I cannot handle any more of this conversation. I grab the bags, go inside, head right up to my room, throw the bags into the closet, and flop on the bed. At least before, when I was at Gram's, I could stay at the same school. I had my same clothes. Now, I'm in the middle of nowhere with a stranger and about to be tossed into sixth grade with a bunch more strangers while forced to wear strange clothes that are probably ten sizes too small. I can't even cry because what's crying going to do? I'm trapped in this house, in this life, in this everything.

I try to game out how I can possibly fill the hours until I get to sleep. What I wouldn't give for a television . . .

I try to read, but my mind keeps sliding off the page. I stumble over the same paragraph three times, then give up and stare at the pictures.

I hear a whistle. It's coming from the back of the house. Is the aunt whistling for me now? And then I hear a scratchy screech and see something flash past the window in Beatrice's room.

I sneak across the landing, into her room, to the window. A big old oak blocks half my view. The aunt is standing by some shed wearing what looks like a fancy baseball mitt with tassels. Then I hear that screech again, loud, from somewhere in the oak. I have to get a better view.

I tiptoe downstairs and into the kitchen. The aunt whistles. I press my face to the glass slider that leads to the backyard. The yard's scraggly grass is punctuated with wooden posts of various shapes and sizes. Around the back edge of the wide yard, near where the trees start and spread, are wooden sheds with what look like jail cells made out of narrow pipe stuck on the front. Where's the screecher?

Beatrice whistles again and taps her glove. A shadow shifts on a tree branch and then lifts out into the light, soars, and crashes onto Beatrice's baseball mitt.

When she said she kept birds, I did not imagine this crazy huge bird—bigger than a football—with wild amber eyes and a hooked beak. Red-brown feathers lie smooth on its head, but the longer, fluffier feathers on its chest are white patterned in slashes of red-brown. The bird's long legs —half the bird's body is made up of its legs—end in curved black talons that dig into the leather. Now I understand the glove.

I slide open the door without really thinking, drift across the lawn. "What is that?"

Beatrice startles. "I thought you were upstairs." She straightens her shoulders, clears her throat. "This," Beatrice says, "is Red."

The bird looks right at me. The feathers on the back of its head lift into a crown. It opens its wings like a cartoon villain with a cape and flaps slowly, showing off.

It looks toward Beatrice and gives a little squeak of a call. Beatrice whips her arm and the bird flies away into a tree, and it's like I've been given a gift, seeing this magic flight, a slow swoop and glide over the grass and then flap up to a branch.

"She's a red-tailed hawk," my aunt says, stepping toward me.

"Is she your pet?"

Beatrice snorts as if the word offends. "A hawk is nobody's pet."

She whistles, raises her left arm, and shakes the glove, in which I see there's a dead mouse. The hawk comes soaring out of the shadows. The only warning of her approach is the tinkling of the tiny bells attached to her legs. She swoops up and lands neatly on the glove, light as a bubble, and skewers the mouse with her beak. She swallows the whole thing down, then turns her attention to the stranger in her yard.

Red looks at me, through me, inside me, like she knows everything about me. Like there's no such thing as a secret.

She doesn't look away.

"Do you like birds?" Beatrice asks.

The word *bird* seems too plain for Red. Imagine if, when Snow White or Cinderella whistled and sang, instead of twittering little nothing birds who folded ribbon and sewed skirts, she got this dragon of a bird, big enough to rip an evil queen's heart out.

"I like her," I say, reaching a hand out to touch the feathers, like scales . . .

Beatrice grabs my fingers in midair, wrenches my hand down. "Never touch a hawk's face."

Anger flashes up like fire. I jerk my hand back. "Fine," I snap.

Like I need this bird. Like I need anything. *Alone, alone . . .*

I turn to go inside. The buzz is a strangling roar in my throat.

"Wait," Beatrice yelps. "Maureen," she says, voice calmer. "Let me show you. Please."

I peek back over my shoulder.

"Like this," she says, and rubs one finger on Red's chest. "You try."

The buzz whispers, *Don't. Dangerous.* But Red—her feathers glow in the sunlight. I can't resist.

I creep back, stretch my finger, and touch the soft feathers. It's like she's made of cloud.

"It's almost passage bird season," Beatrice says. "I'm planning on catching a passage red-tail. I'm going to need help feeding the birds and cleaning the mews."

"The what?"

"These aviaries." She points to the sheds. "They're called mews. I hope to catch a hawk and I could use your help taking care of it. If you wanted to help."

I look at this beautiful bird. "She's trapped here?"

Beatrice shakes her head, relaxes her shoulders. "Red's an imprinted bird. I bought her as a chick from a breeder for the falconry school. She's never lived in the wild—never could, either." She swings her arm and Red soars away into the top of a tall pine. "I do plan to catch a wild bird using a trap, but even that I don't think of as trapping. The world is a tough place for a hawk. Humans have encroached on their forests with power lines and rat poison. And Nature herself was never easy on birds of prey. Most first-year birds won't make it through the winter. So by catching a passage hawk and training it, and also keeping it fed and warm in these mews, I am taking something wild for myself, yes, but I'm also helping it survive a world that's hard on the young and vulnerable."

She whistles and Red swoops down from the branches, bells tinkling in her wake. It's all a blur, as my eyes have teared over. It's not like I don't know about the world being hard.

Beatrice goes on. "I've trapped passage hawks for a number of years now. Seen every one through to the spring, watched them fly off into the rest of their lives. I like to think that at least for some of those birds, I made that possible for them."

She slings her fist and Red flies off again, flapping deeper into the surrounding trees. "Falconry is not about trapping. Once a bird's trained, they fly free on the hunt. If the bird wants, it can take off for the hills."

"Why doesn't she?" I ask, eyes searching the shadows for Red.

Beatrice glances at me. "Because falconry is about trust." She whistles and Red emerges from the branches, wings wide, circling and then diving back to Beatrice's glove. "Red knows I'm here to keep her safe and healthy. She trusts that I won't put her in danger on a hunt and will rustle up enough prey to keep her happy.

"Like I said, a hawk's not a pet. She's a partner."

A *partner* . . . And suddenly I'm soaring above the clouds on the wings of a dragon bird, *my* dragon bird . . .

Red squawks, and Beatrice feeds her another chunk of meat. "I could teach you."

"Falconry?" I ask, sounding way more hopeful and excited than I would normally allow, seeing as she sprang it on me.

She nods, smiling like she knows she got me. "As a master falconer, I can train an apprentice."

My eyes are practically popping out of my head.

"I can't officially register you," she goes on, establishing the limits of the fantasy. "You're too young for the license. But we can do something unofficial."

I nod, afraid to say anything because I'm not even thinking in words, but in exclamation points.

"You can touch her again," she says, "if you want." A

smile flickers at the corners of her mouth. She turns Red's rust-striped chest toward me.

This could all be a trick, some help-the-foster-kid plot, but then I lock eyes with Red and I decide it doesn't matter. My fingertip touches the smooth outer feathers, the fluff of down beneath, then hits the breastbone.

Red squeaks and promptly poops on my sneaker.

Beatrice smirks. "We're going to have to get you some boots."

I don't even care. My fingers are already reaching again, running along the ridges of Red's feathers, imagining how it's possible to soar on such wisps.

4
Rufus

DAY PASSES, NIGHT TOO, BUT I STAY HUDDLED INSIDE MY feathers against the rough bark of the evergreen tree. The thick thatch of its branches is like a nest, almost feels like home. But then I remember that Mother is gone—I see her shadow in the growling monster's lights—and I feel like there will never be a home for me again.

A little after dawn, something snuffles in the leaves around my tree's roots. It doesn't matter. Let whatever it is pass.

But it doesn't pass.

The tree shivers as claws scrape the trunk.

I crack open my eyes, bend my head around. I can't see the climber, but something breathing in raspy breaths is definitely hitching its way up my tree trunk.

I shuffle away from the trunk but get tangled in the web of branches. I slash at them with my talons, break a twig.

There's a high-pitched yip followed by a growling grumble, and snot sprays my wing that's closest to the trunk. I dare to turn my head.

Great Beak! It's a giant rodent covered in sharp spines. The spines bristle and flex—this animal has the most dangerous fur ever imagined: owl-piercing fur! This is the nightmare beast First used to hoot about, the Revenge of the Rodents! And I'd thought she was just making things up to scare me out of my skin. Alas, no!

The gargantuan rodent opens its mouth, bears its beak-like orange teeth. I don't wait for it to strike. I burst through the thicket of branches and escape into the misty morning air. I fly, but my wings feel wet and heavy. A dizziness clouds my eyes.

How long since I last ate?

I sink on a cool draft of air and find the nearest branch.

I'm tired, so tired.

I sleep.

A loud noise growls to life somewhere nearby.

My eyes crack open to a gray dawn—a half day, as

Mother used to call them. There's a monster in the field that stretches out in front of my tree. Its lights cut through the mist. It's bigger than the one that took Mother. It has a mouth of claws that spin and slash, cutting the tall, sweet grass that grew happily in that field.

The monster's growling drowns out all other noise, but in the dim light, I see movement between the stalks. The ground undulates, like the dirt itself is fleeing the monster. As it gets closer, I see that it's not dirt, but mice and voles and rats and . . . FOOD!

I swoop down, talons extended and ready to grab whatever they can. As I get closer, I can hear the heartbeats: a roar of life nearly as loud as the thrashing monster. My foot feathers sense a vole beneath me. My claws snap.

I caught it!

I don't bother to try to carry it someplace more private. I tear with my beak and gobble a bite.

A rat squeaks as it crashes into me.

And then a mouse clambers over me like I'm just a lump of feathers.

I should fly away to escape being trampled by the crowd of angry vermin, but my gizzard is growling and they're everywhere, the little meals-on-feet. I can't decide between snatching another mouthful from my vole or stretching my talons to catch a second breakfast. It's too much! I try to do both at once, bending in half to grab a bite while reaching my other claw at a passing mouse, extending my wings to balance.

A screech from above cuts through the noise. A talon pierces my shoulder.

"Poor little owl," the goshawk says, beak right against my ear.

Cold terror silences all other sound. I swivel my beak around and slash at the goshawk's face. She screeches, digs her talons in deeper. I drop my vole, fold in my wings, and roll onto my side, slashing at her with my talons. But her grip is too strong. She flaps and screeches, lifting me up with her. I scream and slash with my feet, flap my wings, anything to get her off me.

I land a talon in her leg and she shrieks. It's enough to get her to loosen her grip, and I jerk hard away from her. It's like I'm tearing my own wing off, but suddenly I'm free and I flap as hard and as fast as I can for the cover of trees and darkness.

Once on a branch, I nibble my wing with my beak, feeling over the feathers. The pain is blinding. I stretch my wing out—more pain. I nip at the hurt, but that makes it worse. I shuffle along the bark until I'm against the trunk, then huddle into myself, fluffing my feathers, and hope that my wing stops hurting.

A squirrel chitters angrily from above.

I roll my head and look at her. "Go away."

She shrieks, flicking her tail and bristling her fur. Her squirrel nest is in the upper branches.

"I'm just resting," I hoot. I have no interest—or at least no energy—to bother her nest.

She has the nerve to throw a nutshell at me.

I pull in my feathers, lift my wings, and prepare to show her who says where a great horned owl can roost, when my wing sends lightning bolts of pain through my body. I wince.

The squirrel senses an opening. She launches another nutshell and hits me right in the beak.

"I'm going!" I stretch my wings as far as I can and glide away from the branch, landing on a stump in an open space between the trees.

Never roost in the open, Mother's voice chides.

But my wing won't let me fly.

A crow flaps down from the canopy. "Owl!" he caws. "Owl! Owl!"

Soon other crows call back, "Where? Where?"

"Owl!" this crow barks, hopping around the base of my stump.

"Leave me alone," I hoot, fluffing myself up and raising my ear tufts.

"Here! Here!" the crow shouts, and now more crows answer, "Owl! Owl!"

I have to keep this crow quiet or I'm going to have a swarm on me. I spread my wings, stuff the pain into my gizzard, and pounce on the crow.

"Help! Help!" the crow shrieks.

He flaps and hops and shrieks some more, and I try to get a good grip on him, but my talons keep slipping off his oily black feathers. I'm so tired, I barely have the energy to stand.

He pecks me hard in the shoulder and the pain causes me to topple against the stump.

I drop onto the leaves and walk—actually *walk*—my talons across the ground toward the nearest tree. It, too, is just a stump.

"Owl!" the crow caws loudly, hopping along beside me.

I shuffle my feet faster through the leaves, creating a thunderous noise nearly as loud as this crow and his screaming. I snap my beak at him and he flaps off, up into the trees. Above, the crows are swarming, getting into a frenzy of cawing as the crow I just let escape tells them how I attacked him.

"Mean! Mean!" he caws. "Bites! Bites!"

I reach the dead tree. I dig my talons into the stump and hop and drag myself, beak over claw, up the rotting bark.

"Owl! Owl!" the crows shriek, filling the sky with their noisy cawing, their black wings like a storm swirling around me.

I haul myself to the top of the ragged stump, turn my body, and get a glide going. I manage to get one flap, two, and I lift slightly higher. I spot a tree with a good-size hole in it. It's too close to the field, too open, but I can't fly any farther.

Please let it be empty.

I land my talons on the edge of the bark. The hole is empty and cold but dry and small and snug. I drag myself into it, filling the space with my feathers, and hunker down into myself.

My wing throbs. Almost as painful is knowing that I have just been driven off two perches, first by an angry squirrel and then by a murder of filthy, foul-beaked crows.

There has never been a worse great horned owl in the history of owldom. I am he: The Absolute Worst Great Horned Owl Ever.

5

Reenie

I WAKE UP MONDAY MORNING WITH *THE FALCONER'S Apprentice* under my head on the pillow. It's all about hawks and falcons and how to care for them and train them for use in falconry. Normally, these kinds of books bore me to death, but I need to know this stuff for the passage hawk I'm going to catch. To be honest, I couldn't put this book full of statistics and facts and words like "flying weight" and "tidbits" and "creance" down—which is why I have a crease in my cheek from my pillow buddy. I slam off the alarm clock and drag myself out of bed.

Monday is orientation at my new school. Beatrice and

I listen to classical music as we drive past thick forest broken by fields of weeds, some with a home plopped in them, and within ten minutes we turn onto the state highway, entering the crowded store-and-apartment-block part of the town. We're not talking city; it's two blocks of three-story hundred-year-old buildings and an inn that was last popular when my great-grandmother was born. Branford is the refuge for hipsters who work in Rutland. That's how kids at my old school talked about it.

We park in front of this giant brick building into which crowds of little kids clutching parents' hands are pouring.

"Are we in the right place?" I ask, hugging my backpack to my chest. In it, I had put the falconry book. It's my good-luck charm.

"This school is grades K through six," Beatrice says. "Orientation is for kindergartners and new students."

She leads me into the cavernous lobby, where a woman with a nametag and a plastered-on smile points us down one of the long hallways.

"Welcome to Otter Creek Elementary," she says, all singsong and happy. It's making me suspicious, how happy she's pretending to be.

We find the sixth grade orientation classroom, and Beatrice stops at the door.

"You coming?" I ask.

"You're on your own from here."

I freeze, look around. There are only a few other kids. Beatrice is still waiting in the doorway.

"It's a half day," she says. "I'll be back at noon."

I nod. I walk to the closest desk. I sit.

We play a name game, some get-to-know-you activity. You're supposed to give your name, where you came from and why you moved, and your favorite thing about your old town. Most of the others have normal stories: divorce, Mom's new job, to be closer to grandpa. Easy stories. My story has never been easy.

This is the first time the state has officially gotten involved, like with courts and lawyers and stuff, but it's not the first time Mom and I have had to live apart. The first time she went away to get help, it was like I'd been torn in two. I stayed in the junk room at Gram's house all winter. By spring, Mom was back, and we found our own place to live. The second time she had to leave, we had lost that apartment and were already living at Gram's house, so it felt more like Mom went on a long vacation without me. By the third time, I'd learned how to get by without a parent. Even when she's home, the sadness can take her from me. It's just easier to not expect anything from anyone, to take care of myself.

When the teacher gets to me, I don't feel like explaining, so I make something up.

"I'm Maureen L'Esperance. I'm from Burlington. I like boating on the lake." I took a school trip to Burlington once.

All I wanted that day was to be one of those people out boating on the lake.

The teacher checks her sheet. "Oh, uh . . . lovely," she splutters. "Thank you, Maureen."

We then have to talk about where we live here in Branford and something we're excited about in our new home.

This is easy. When she comes to me, I describe the old farmhouse in the woods on the other side of Route 7. "My aunt is a falconer, and she has a real red-tailed hawk."

The other kids stare at me.

"How interesting!" the teacher exclaims.

The class moves on to talking about schedules, where stuff is in the school building, rotating "days" and moving from class to class. Then we're given a tour, which ends outside at the school's ginormous playground. We're told to "go play." The place is so big, the five of us new kids just kind of hang by this wooden pavilion, taking it all in.

"Isn't falconry, like, from olden days?" one girl says.

"People still do it," I say.

"But it's hunting, right?"

"Yeah, I guess." I'm not really focused on the hunting part. How can anyone focus on the hunting part when I mentioned a real live red-tailed hawk?

"Hunting is mean." This girl—Peyton, I think—crosses her arms.

"Are you vegetarian?" I ask.

"No."

"Then somebody's hunting your meat for you. So I guess you're mean, just once removed."

Her face curls into a scowl. "That's not very nice."

The other girls look at me like I've called Peyton a mud-sucking pig. When she slinks away, they follow her toward the swings. It's not like I wanted to be friends with them anyway. I mean, I'm here for a couple weeks, a month maybe.

"I hunt." The only boy in our group sits at the table under the pavilion. He's the one who moved because his parents got divorced. He's wearing a camouflage shirt and Carhartts with grubby sneakers. I think his name is Jaxon.

"I don't," I say. "But the hawk is pretty cool."

"I've seen one up close once," he says. "My dad's a game warden back in St. Johnsbury. He brought home a hawk who'd been hit by a car."

He seems a little too laid-back about something as egg-crackingly awesome as having a hawk in his house.

But then he hitches up a corner of his mouth, half smiling, and says, "I held its wing while my dad examined it."

And I see that he gets it, that he knows.

I want to grab him by the shoulders and have him tell me what kind of hawk and hit where and did he get to have it perch on his glove — basically everything about his hawk. I want to tell him everything I've learned about hawks. To scream with him about how amazing it is to just be near a hawk!

But the buzz crackles: *Dangerous.*

I know better than to let my feelings out. I decide not to get into it.

"Cool," I say.

He nods. "Yeah."

And we sit there in the shade, not talking, until the bell rings and we all file back into the classroom.

"See you tomorrow," he says to me as we grab our stuff to go.

I glance up at him through a frizz of hair, nod a little, and shuffle out the door.

Beatrice takes me back to work with her. She's a vet technician, which means she gets to pet a lot of animals from what I can tell. I hang out in the back of the office with the dogs and cats left for medical stuff or boarding. They all kind of look how I feel, like they're full of questions and a little lost.

It's weird how Jaxon saying he'd see me tomorrow kind of deflated me. Shouldn't a person saying they'd see you tomorrow, speaking to you at all in a friendly way, make you feel good? But he was being friendly to the half girl I pretended to be. The quiet one who enjoys sailing on lakes and has never had to beg a gas station attendant for an extra hot dog. That's who he wants to see tomorrow. Not like this should surprise me. No one looks at the whole me and sticks around.

Mom tried to do a fancy friends' birthday party for me in kindergarten at one of our old apartments. One of the kids' moms called social services after finding bugs swarming some dirty dishes in our kitchen. That ordeal was the first time I remember Mom locking herself in the bathroom for a night. Next day at school, no one sat with me at lunch. *Cooties*, I heard whispered as I passed. I was about ready to lock myself into a bathroom stall, but instead, I smiled. Teeth bared and blinding white, I walked right past that whisper and every other one I've heard since.

Friends are dangerous. But no one can hurt you if you don't let them see you, if they only see the smile.

One of the dogs whimpers this pathetic little yowl. I drag a chair over to his crate, pull out the hawk book, and read him the biological facts of the red-tailed hawk. *Crop, gizzard, mantle, crown, primary feathers, secondary feathers.* The dog quits yowling and starts snuffling at my neck. I pet his wet nose. He licks my finger like he's hungry.

I'm definitely getting hungry.

Beatrice slides open a pocket door and sighs. "I think we're done here."

I hop down and slip the book into my bag. "Red's probably getting hungry."

Beatrice's eyebrows rise slowly. "Oh?"

"Definitely," I say. "Her gizzard's growling."

She snorts a little laugh. "I've never heard a gizzard growl."

"They do," I say with authority.

"Then I guess we need to get a move on dinner."

When we get home, I start poking through the pantry. When I live with Mom—even Gram, some nights—if I'm hungry, it's up to me to figure out something to eat. On Beatrice's shelves, I see cans of beans and jars with vegetables floating in them. What am I supposed to do with these?

The aunt appears like a ghost behind me. "Do you eat soup?"

I shrug.

"Soup it is." She scoops up two cans and three jars. An hour later, she serves soup. It's not bad.

"How was school?" she asks me.

"Fine." I try to avoid all personal questions as a matter of policy.

"Meet any nice kids?"

For a hot second, I think about Jaxon, but the buzz warns, *Dangerous.* "A few," I say. This is the kind of vague response that stops adults from further prying.

It works like magic. The aunt doesn't ask another question. I feel only a little bad about it.

We eat in silence. A clock somewhere ticks. A car drives by. A bug outside starts grinding its wings.

"I'm done," I say, standing. I put my bowl in the sink. "Can you start teaching me about Red now?"

Beatrice's eyebrows crimp like she's calculating something, but then she's up and tugging on her boots.

She shows me how to clean the aviary, how to cut up the dead mice—*gross*—and how to clean the leather gloves. Then she hands me a new glove, kid-sized and everything.

"Thought you might need this," she says. "It's called a gauntlet."

I slide it over my fingers. It's thick and heavy. It must have cost a fortune.

It's mine.

I probably should have talked more at dinner.

"Thank you," I say, finally.

She smiles and nods in response, then calls Red down from a nearby tree. The hawk swoops and lands on Beatrice's glove, snaps up the tidbit of meat from her fingers. Then Beatrice turns to me.

"Lift your arm, straight and strong."

I lift it. Try to be strong.

Beatrice moves my wrist into position, holds my glove against Red's legs, and then it happens.

Red steps onto my glove.

She's feather-light, but the weight of her—not the "pounds" weight, but the power she gives off—nearly sends me sprawling.

It only lasts a moment. Red realizes pretty quick I'm not Beatrice and flaps off to a perch. But that moment.

I don't think I've ever felt so special.

The sun has made the trees all golden, and I have that feeling they use to sell packaged cookie dough: like I've come home. I let myself soak it in it for one whole second before ripping the feeling off like a Band-Aid.

I can't be sucked in by this. This whole life is a placeholder. I have to remember that. No matter how nice, no matter if the hawk lets me hold her, this home is not mine.

⌣

Beatrice wakes me up early so I can make the bus. I must look as happy about school as I feel—which is *not*—because she offers me a gift: "This weekend," she says. "We'll start this weekend."

I pause midbite of my cereal. "Really?" I say, mouth dripping milk.

"Do you need a napkin?"

I wipe my face on my arm. "We can start trying to catch my—*a*—passage hawk this weekend?"

She smiles. "Season opens September first."

My heart revs right up to full throttle. "What do I need to do to get ready?"

Now Beatrice is actually laughing at me. "Nothing," she says. "I have everything we need."

"So I just have to wait?"

"Falconry is eighty percent waiting."

I jam my spoon back into the bowl. "I know," I say.

I've been reading. I got barely six hours of sleep because I was up so late reading the new falconry book I found in the living room alongside the apprentice manual—I have to keep switching between the two just to fill in all the stuff I am completely clueless about. There isn't enough time in the day to learn everything I want to know about hawks.

"I'll pick you up after school," she says, standing to put her bowl in the sink.

"I can take the bus." I don't need special treatment.

"You have visitation," she says.

"Oh."

All the excitement drains out of me like someone pulled the plug in a bathtub. What kind of terrible kid am I that I'm more excited to catch a wild bird than I am to see my mother?

"We can feed Red when we get back." Beatrice continues shuffling through her morning routine as she talks. It's cool that she's not all over me, trying to make me feel good about things that there's nothing to feel good about. Gram would be barking at me to stop frowning, that I'm lucky to have a mom at all, and can't I show some gratitude for everything I've got by doing a load or two of laundry?

"Okay," I say, and slurp the last of my milk.

School is school. In the cafeteria, I grab lunch and take my tray to a table in the corner. I brought the paperback novel from home for company and start to read. Sam has stolen a baby peregrine falcon from its nest. I'm half horrified and half jealous.

"Can I sit here?" A girl with straw-colored hair and green-brown eyes hovers over the seat opposite me.

"Whatever," I say, and keep reading.

I get another paragraph in—Sam's calling his falcon Frightful—before the girl interrupts me.

"Are you new here? I've never seen you before. My name's Jamie Hendricks."

"I'm reading," I say without looking up.

"Oh," Jamie says. She eats her sandwich from a fancy insulated lunch box with her name embroidered on it. She probably lives in a mansion with a golden retriever and parents who tuck her in with a lullaby every night. I scoop the last of my stew into my mouth, shove my book into my pocket, and get up to dump my tray.

"I'll see you in class," she says. Her words are like hooks, catching me before I can escape.

This girl does not take a hint. "Yeah," I say, and run out the doors to the playground.

I find a bush near the school wall and sneak behind it. I'm only half surprised to find that Jaxon's already shoved himself back there. He's using a pen to scratch a piece of wood.

"Hey," he says, not even looking up.

"Hey," I echo. Then, "Whatcha doin'?" escapes before I can stop my mouth.

"I whittle," he says. "But you can't bring knives to school."

"Yeah," I say, though I've never really thought about it.

"Pen does an okay job," he continues, "if the wood is soft." He pulls out some plastic knives. "These help with the bigger cuts."

I pick up a knife. "From the caf?"

He shrugs, half smiling. "Use what you find."

He pokes around under the bush and pulls out another hunk of wood. He holds it out to me. I take it.

I fish a pen from a pocket and begin scratching at the wood. It makes a small gouge. I try the knife; a long chip peels off. And that's how we spend the whole of recess. Scratching the wood, alone, together.

Jaxon's piece looks like a lizard.

Mine's going to be a hawk.

After school, Beatrice drives me down to Rutland. She listens to public radio, some talk show about a tax bill in the legislature, and I scratch at my wood. It's not good, but it does look kind of like a bird. When we get to visitation, I hand the wood to my mom.

"I made this," I say.

She takes it in her fingers like I've just handed her a bomb. Her eyes tear up and her lip trembles.

"I'm sorry," I say. "I know it's awful. It's supposed to be a hawk, but—"

She wipes her hands over her face and fake smiles back. "I love it, Reens. It's beautiful."

Nothing I do is right. Even my gifts make people cry. "Do you have the sparkle cards?" I ask, trying to move on. And then Mom is crying even harder, mumbling that she forgot, she forgets everything, how could she be so stupid?

I tell her it's nothing, not to worry, because it *is* nothing, it has to be nothing, even though a tiny voice inside asks, *How could she forget?* But I crush that voice and grab a deck of cards from the shelf like they're a life raft. We play a bunch of games of hearts. I let her win every hand.

In math on Wednesday, the teacher has us turn our desks around to work in pairs, and I discover Jaxon behind me. "Hey," I say.

"Hey." He pulls his pen and wood out from the desk as though the whittling and not the work sheet is what's been assigned. But then I notice he's already finished the work sheet.

"You can copy," he says, not looking up.

"I don't do that," I say.

He smiles. "Good."

I hunch over my paper; he hunches over his wood. The briefest glance at my school file would reveal that I am not a great student, particularly in the math department. This algebra? Algibberish . . . When I get stuck on the second problem, Jaxon—without appearing to even look up from his whittling—says, "You forgot to subtract the six from the other side."

"I don't need help," I snap. Jaxon hunches farther down and keeps whittling. I feel a little bad but also a little freaked out. Do I look like I'm having *that* much trouble with this work sheet?

And then it sinks in: I have no idea what six he's even talking about.

"What six?" I finally allow myself to blurt out.

Jaxon puts aside his pen and wood. "Here," he says, pointing farther up on my paper. "You just left this part out."

It takes a second, but I see it. That rat of a six was hiding all the way over on the other side of the equation! This odd calm comes over me as I get to $x = 2$. "Thanks."

Jaxon nods. "Sure."

At lunch, I scarf down my food before anyone can ask to sit with me. I rush outside and find Jaxon behind the same bush. My whole body kind of sighs with relief as I sink down next to him.

"Hey," he says, already whittling.

"Hey." I pull out my book and read.

After school, Beatrice and I work on this bal-chatri trap. It's a safe trap that won't hurt the bird, Beatrice promises. It looks like an upside-down colander with a mouse stuck under it, and it's covered with wispy little strings. The hawk's feet get tangled in the loops of string when it flies down to get the mouse in the trap, but nothing else will happen. The trap has weights around its edges so the hawk will be grounded once its feet are caught. Even the mouse will be okay because it's protected by the wire mesh.

Beatrice has an old trap that we're fixing. We're using new wire to patch some holes in the mesh and then we have to add more weight—Beatrice said that the last time she used it, the hawk was able to fly off with the trap, which is how the mesh got kind of beat up. And then we have to make all the loops out of these tiny little strings to tie onto the trap.

"I need a break," Beatrice says, putting down the roll of fishing line.

I shake my hand, trying to untangle my fingers from a failed attempt at a knot. "I'll keep working."

"*You* need a break," she says, pointing at the deep red dents in my fingers from the pressure of the plastic string.

I shrug. If we take a break, the trap might not be finished in time and then it'll be a whole other week before we can start with my quest for the passage hawk.

"Red needs a walk," she says, and heads out back.

I sigh, drop my failed loop, tie on the work boots Beatrice found for me—she hit a thrift store on her lunch break and came back with treasure—and follow. She's already gone into the aviary. I find her with Red on her fist, standing in front of the little table in the tiny room between the doors leading into Red's open flight space. She holds her fist near this weird contraption on the table: it looks like a scale, except it has a perch instead of a flat plate on top.

"She's good," Beatrice says, marking something in a small notebook on the tabletop.

I know what she's doing from all the falconry books I've read—every bird has its flying weight, which the falconer needs to keep the bird at to fly it. If the hawk is too heavy, it might not hunt. Too light, it isn't getting enough food or might be sick. Falconers figure out what the flying weight of their bird is and try to keep them in that condition. But still: it's a little creepy, weighing an animal.

"Isn't it kind of cruel," I suggest, "to keep Red hungry?"

Beatrice arches an eyebrow at me. "Keeping her motivated by the food is a part of it. But it's not starvation. Think of Red as an athlete. I'm helping her stay in top form." She hands me my gauntlet as she steps out of the tight room and into the golden afternoon. She throws Red off the fist and the hawk disappears, the jingle of her bells the only evidence of her presence.

"Give me your left arm," Beatrice says, and I lift it. She grabs it and curls my gloved fingers into a fist. "Hold still."

Is she . . . is she really . . . ?

"Now, whistle," Beatrice says, shoving a chunk of meat into the space between the leather of the thumb and index finger of my gauntlet.

I do, and Red comes diving down from the branches, her bells warning of her approach. I turn my head and see her just as she swoops up and alights on my glove.

She's never flown to me before.

Red devours the morsel, then stands, peaceful.

"You have to hold these between your middle and ring fingers," Beatrice says, tugging the two little leather strips that hang from Red's legs and jamming them into my hand. "They're called jesses, and they'll keep her from flying off."

I nod, my voice stolen by this magnificent creature perched on my arm. She flew to *me*. My heart pounds. My right hand tightens into a fist, nails digging into my palm, to help keep my left arm still as a branch for Red.

"You can walk," Beatrice says, smirking like I'm being a freak.

But it's a nice smile, so I don't say anything snarky. Plus, I am holding a hawk and that is so freaking cool that every rotten thought just poofs right out of my brain. I dare to step forward. Red glances past my head but stays standing. I attempt to walk.

"Come on," Beatrice says, and strolls down the path into the woods.

I follow, rolling my feet over the rocks and roots to keep from jostling Red as we make our way slowly through the sun-dappled shade. When we reach a clearing, Beatrice stops.

"Now cast her off your glove." She holds her left arm straight out and whips it forward. "Hold onto the jesses until the very last moment."

"Cast her?" I say. "You mean throw her?"

"Birds of prey only fly to eat. They spend most of their waking hours sitting around, watching for prey. So as a falconer, you have to cheat a little." She swings her arm again. "Just throw her into the sky."

I whip my arm just as I've seen Beatrice do it, releasing the jesses just as I would a baseball. Red flies off. The jingling song of her bells tells of her travel into the tangle of branches.

Imagine when it's not Beatrice's bird but my passage

hawk flying toward me. Imagine pulling this wild beauty from the air and making it mine. Then it won't matter that I'm living in a temporary home with a temporary family, going to a temporary school, meeting temporary friends. I'll have one real thing for myself, a dragon bird to soar with, something so majestic and powerful, even I can't weigh it down. Which is why it's impossible to be patient about this whole process.

"It's getting dark," I say. "Shouldn't we get back?"

Beatrice gives me a once-over. "We'll have the trap ready in time," she says. Does this lady read minds?

"Oh yeah," I say. "Sure. I'm not worried. I just . . . don't want to be out late. For Red."

Beatrice snorts air through her nostrils. "For Red." She whistles, and Red flies back to her fist.

At recess Thursday, Jaxon holds out a pen to me. It's a regular pen, but the nib and conical cover over it are metal. A pin pricks inside my gut and this warm, fuzzy feeling burbles up. He thought of me . . . He thought to bring me a pen.

"Thanks," I whisper, taking it gingerly between my fingers.

He nods. "Gives a cleaner scrape."

"Yeah?" I put down my falconry book and pick up a hunk of wood.

"Yup." He runs his pen—same kind—over the wood in his hand and peels off a curling chip.

"Huh."

A pair of sneakers kick through the leaves near our bush. "Maureen?"

Oh, great.

"Maureen? It's Jamie. From lunch the other day." She shoves her way through the branches that protected us. "Oh, hi—Jaxon, right?"

Jaxon flips his face up. "Want to sit?" He scrapes a long line across his wood with the pen.

"Okay." Jamie smiles like she just won the lottery and squeezes down between the roots. There really isn't room for three back here.

She kind of stares at us while Jaxon and I scrape.

Jamie wiggles her sneakers. "My two closest friends moved away over the summer." She picks at the bark of the bush. "How weird is that? Both your friends, moving in the same summer."

"All my friends are back in St. Johnsbury," Jaxon says.

I don't say anything. I don't really do "friends."

"I love crafts," Jamie says. "You guys sculpting?"

"Whittling," I correct.

"Same thing," Jaxon says. He digs under the bush and finds another piece of wood. "Want to try?"

And he pulls another pen from his pocket. The same kind he gave me.

"Wow—thanks," says Jamie.

"Sure," says Jaxon.

And they smile at each other.

So I guess it wasn't so special for him to bring me the pen. I guess this is just what he does. I want to throw the pen back at him. But I don't.

I jam the pen into my wood. Cut out a hunk. I'm going to make another hawk. A lone flier.

After school, I have visitation, and the whole way there, I have trouble working up the energy to act happy for Mom. But then I see her through the window and she flashes me a smile—a *real* smile. Mom's smile is the kind that catches on: my lips can't help but curl up at the edges.

"I ordered us hot chocolate," she says as I sit down.

"Extra whipped cream?" I ask, the warmth already spreading inside me.

"Is there any other way to drink it?"

As we sip our hot chocolates, she tells me about this lady at the treatment center who steals potatoes from the kitchen and hides them all over. It's a real Mom story, complete with silly words she made up and impressions. No one tells a better story than Mom.

"The surprise was dumping a whole bag's worth of tater tots out of my sneaker!" she says.

We both laugh and it's like the sadness is nothing but a bad dream we got stuck in. But it's always like this, isn't it? All my best times are with Mom, until the sadness takes her away.

"Are we going to move back in with Gram?" I dare to ask.

Mom's smile flickers. "You know Gram," she says, and then imitates Gram's scratchy voice: *"Phil doesn't mean any of it—what's the big deal?"* She slurps her cocoa. "So no, we're not going back there."

"Oh," I say. Phil has always been a bum, but that never kept us from crashing there before. "He didn't mean to hit me with the plate," I remind her, because if we can't live with Gram, where are we going to live?

"It doesn't matter if he meant it, Reens." Her smile is gone. "Randi's said we can't go back." So this is what Beatrice was dancing around last Sunday, her explanation for the gift of clothes.

Mom finishes her drink. "Want to play hearts?" She pulls out a new deck of cards, not the sparkle deck, not our cards.

"You forgot again?" The words slip out, the sneaks.

"The sparkle deck is missing a ten and two jacks," she says. "So I tossed it. I'm sorry."

"Whatever," I say, my own smile going back into hiding. I pick up the hand she's dealt me and leave the rest of my cocoa in the cup.

⟡

Friday, at lunch, I see Jamie and Jaxon already sitting together.

I could go over, sit, act all interested in whatever it is Jamie's gushing about. I could be a gusher. But the buzz taps against my gut: *Dangerous*.

I sit somewhere else.

Friday afternoon, Beatrice and I test the trap. Red watches us with a concerned eye from her perch. The mouse scrambles around in the cage but can't escape. And because we added a double mesh, the mouse can't gnaw on the plastic strings.

It's perfect.

I scarf my dinner as if that will make the hours pass faster.

"We're probably not going to catch anything," Beatrice warns, waving a hand in front of my eyes, which stare out into the dark.

"I know," I say, though of course this possibility seems so infinitesimally small as to be meaningless. Our trap is amazing. It will definitely catch a passage hawk tomorrow morning.

I am up with the sun. Beatrice comes downstairs to find me having already made her coffee.

"When did you get up?" she asks.

"Early," I say, practically vibrating with excitement. "Can we go now?"

Red squawks from her aviary.

"Why don't you go feed Red and I'll feed myself."

I take a defrosted mouse from the fridge, drop it into a bath of hot water, and wait for it to warm up, then drop it, wet and steamy, onto Red's dish and carry it outside. It rained last night, and the grass sends up sprays of rainbows in the early sunlight with my every step. It's an omen.

I am *going* to catch a passage hawk.

6
Rufus

COLD. SO COLD.

And wet. So wet.

I discovered why this hole was empty. It's built wrong. It's tipped toward the sky a little, and it lets all the rain in.

All the smart owls figured out this fact.

Only the worst owl in the history of owldom would miss such a crucial fact. Would discover this only because the skies opened and poured waterfalls from the clouds. And they poured right in on my head.

My wings are bedraggled. My horn feathers are slick against my skull. My chest feathers are matted.

Everything is terrible.

All night, I waited for the rain to stop so my feathers would dry. The rain did not stop. So now I'm half sleeping on the edge of this soggy tree hole with my wings stretched a little, letting the sun dry me out. Hoping no one notices me. Especially something humiliating like a thrush. How awful would it be to get attacked by a tiny nothing bird like a thrush?

A rumbling comes from somewhere nearby and then dies. The same kind of rumbling that the monsters make.

I crack open my eyes and peer around my hole.

Nothing. I'm safe. For now.

There's rustling in the grass. Some cries of birds and grunts of deer and buzzings of bugs. Nothing too close. I doze in and out of the world, checking it every so often for danger.

When the warmth reaches all the way in to my gizzard, I test my wing. It feels not great but not terrible. It might fly.

I stretch it out, give it a full flap. The pain is sharp, but I can fly with it. I have to be able to fly with it.

I open my eyes and the light is blinding. How do animals live in such brilliance? The world is white and sparkly and sharp.

Then I hear it.

Squeaking. Not far from here.

Serious squeaking.

I swivel my head and see the mouse. It's just sitting in the grass. Running in circles. Squeaking.

Is this mouse crazy? Why squeak to the whole forest while spinning around in one place? There might be a hungry owl nearby.

There *is* a hungry owl nearby. A starving owl.

I'm off the tree before I think to check my feathers. They're still full of water and I kind of half glide, half plummet to the grass near the mouse. It seems to be trapped inside a spider's web. I hop onto the web, but it's stiff like a twig. I can't get my claws on the little fur ball.

I grab again.

The mouse shrieks and skitters around inside the web.

"Oh, be quiet," I hoot, grabbing and poking with my talons. What is this web made of that I can't get this delicious, tasty, trapped-just-beneath-my-feet mouse?!

And then I feel something slip through the feathers along one of my toes. A slick filament slides up my skin and then grabs.

This is a very strange web. Perhaps this mouse is more trouble than it's worth. I go to lift my leg, but it's caught.

My heart pounds.

I jerk my foot again. Still caught.

"AGH!" I squawk. "The web has me! The web has me!"

The mouse squeals angrily. Like maybe it has a clutch of family that's on its way . . .

I flap and lift off the ground with this shrieking mouse and its web of terror strings, but it's too heavy and my wing screams with pain and I flop down into the grass.

Could the mouse have built this web to trap owls? Could the prey have found a way to fight back? Great Beak, what is going on in this forest of rumbling monsters and vengeful mice?!

"Help!" I cry. "The prey are on the attack! *HELP!*"

Hearing my own squawks, I wonder what owl would even bother to help. How big a failure of a raptor do you have to be to get caught by a mouse in a spider web?

Imagine if First saw me like this. Or Father. Even Mother.

I will not go down without a fight. Even the worst great horned owl is still a great horned owl, as Father reminded me once.

"I will do you proud!" I squawk.

I give my leg one last jerk, confirm I've been captured, and flop still, awaiting the throng of angry vermin that must be on its way, my talons sharp and ready . . .

7

Reenie

"IT'S NOT A HAWK!" BEATRICE YELLS AS WE RUN FROM where we'd hidden in the tall grass.

"It looks like a hawk!"

"It's definitely not a hawk."

Our trap has worked but also failed. The state only lets a falconer trap a passage red-tailed hawk or goshawk. If it's anything else, we have to let it go and then reset the whole trap.

So I'm kind of angry at whatever this thing is that's broken my bal-chatri trap I worked all week to get perfect for my passage hawk. That is, until I see that it's the most fantastically, amazingly beautiful bird I've ever seen in my life.

It's the size of a giant watermelon but brown, with its huge wings open and stretched out along the ground like it's trying to fly. As we approach, its head rotates almost all the way around and I see two enormous yellow eyes rimmed in black, surrounded by disks of coppery feathers. The eyes are on fire, daring me to come any closer, and the deep V of black-brown feathers that stretches from its forehead toward its hooked beak forms a scowl. It screeches, and two feathery horns flip up off its head, adding wings to the V, as if saying, *Are you looking at* me?

It's the ultimate dragon bird, the king of all birds.

"It's a great horned owl," Beatrice says, stopping near where it lies in the grass.

It flaps its splayed wings, then arranges them in this weird upside-down way, fanning out the feathers around its head and body into a wide ruff. It looks like a miniature turkey, all puffed up and angry. The owl stumbles away from us, dragging the trap with it. It gets about five inches before it flops still again.

It's awful to see this bird king dragged through the dirt by my trap. I kneel beside him and he turns his spectacular face to me. Glowing eyes lock on to my heart.

"We have to free him," I say, knowing it to be true: that

no matter how much I want to keep him, this bird is meant to be wild.

"Him?" Beatrice kneels beside me, examining the owl.

"Yes, *him*," I say. He snaps his beak, making this clacking sound, and flops around, trying to get to his feet.

Beatrice gently places a blanket over him, folding his wings against his back and holds him steady as she works his talons free from the trap.

"Look," she says, holding his legs in her thick leather glove. I peer at his glorious little face, which looks like the most malevolent stuffie's, curled in the blanket. "He's not even scratching at me," she says.

A ribbon of cold runs through me. Dragon birds fight to survive. Why isn't he fighting? "What does that mean?"

"He might be sick or hurt," she says.

"Was it the trap?" My voice gets stuck in my throat. *I did this, I hurt him . . .*

Beatrice examines him a bit closer. "No," she says. "Look at his wing. This bird can't go free today."

His left wing sags away from his body and I can see some feathers that are matted with blood. "He's hurt?" I ask. The ribbon of cold turns into a knot around my gut.

"He's also dehydrated," Beatrice says. "And probably starving."

The knot tightens with each pronouncement. "Can you help him?" I ask. *Please don't say he's going to die.*

Beatrice sighs. "We can try. But that's the end of our passage hawk quest for the weekend."

"That's okay," I say. "He needs our help." He starts panting and hissing and snapping his little beak. Still fighting, my dragon bird.

Beatrice smiles down at him. "Yes, he does."

I carry the trap and she carries the owl back to the truck. I put the trap in the bed and hop into my seat. I am completely shocked when I see Beatrice hold out the owl in his blanket to me.

"I can hold him?" I ask, afraid to put my hopes into words.

"How else am I going to drive to the hospital?"

"Shouldn't we tape him or something?" We have painter's tape and a length of pantyhose I call "the sleeve," which we were going to secure our passage hawk in when—if—we caught one.

"I'm not sure he'd last through a taping." She places the precious package into my arms, then flips over the extra material to cover his head. "This will help keep him calm."

"What about the hood?" Falconers put these cute little leather hats called "hoods" on falcons' heads to keep them calm when traveling. We have a couple of different-size hoods that we were going to use on the passage hawk.

"I don't have a hood big enough for that melon," Beatrice says, shaking her head as she starts the engine. She calls someone on her phone. "Hi, Lil? I have a sick owl with an injured wing." Pause — I guess that "Lil" is Lillian Cho, the vet Beatrice works for. "Great — thank you." She hits the gas and gravel goes flying as we head for the animal hospital.

The blanket is thick: fleece-lined on one side and tough canvas on the other — meant to withstand the slash of a talon. The owl is quiet, probably terrified out of his little mind. The truck bucks over ruts and rocks in the dirt road, and I use my legs to brace my body against the seat cushion to keep the worst of it from disturbing him. With each bounce, I scowl at the dashboard, willing the truck to keep still. I'm afraid to breathe too deeply for fear of startling him. He seems like a ghost inside the blanket, he's so light. It's the most shocking thing about these dragon birds — they're all feathers. How can something so fierce also be so fragile?

We arrive at the animal hospital where Beatrice works. She takes the owl from me and carries him in the back entrance. I follow her into one of the rooms, where Dr. Cho waits in her white coat.

"Let's take a look at him," she says, placing the owl on an examining table. She removes the blanket and quickly places a smaller towel over the owl's head. She checks his back, then extends each wing, all while holding his body still. Dr. Cho then folds the wings in and turns him over. She blows on his spotted chest feathers.

"Why are you doing that?" I ask.

"To see his skin," she says.

"If it's scaly," Beatrice says, returning after having changed into a set of scrubs, "he's dehydrated."

"Which he is," Dr. Cho says. "Well, you diagnosed it as far as I can tell. He hurt his wing—it looks like a puncture from a talon. He may have fallen out of his nest while branching and been attacked by another bird of prey . . . though he's a bit old for that."

"Branching" is when a baby bird moves from the nest to hopping around on the branches of the tree the nest is in. It's the bird equivalent of crawling.

"He's had the wound for a day or so. But he hasn't eaten or had a good drink in longer than that." She touches what would be his breastbone if he were a human. "His muscle tone is poor."

"But we can save him, right?" I ask, practically falling off my bench listening to the diagnosis.

Dr. Cho smiles as she places the owl back on his feet. "We can try," she says.

I do not like her lack of commitment.

The doctor stuff starts. Dr. Cho pulls out this syringe with a length of tube off the end of it instead of a needle. She shoves the tube down my owl's throat. "Hydration," she tells me. I cringe, dig my fingers into the underside of the bench. She finally pulls the tube out, then begins working on the wing. While she cleans my owl's wounds, Beatrice retrieves from the back a large dog crate with solid plastic walls. Once satisfied with her work, Dr. Cho puts the owl into the crate.

My owl shuffles and flaps to the back of the crate, then huddles against the back wall, big eyes glaring at us.

"Now it's up to him," Dr. Cho says.

We all look at the lump of feathers with the enormous eyes, and he scowls back at us.

Fight, I tell him, as if our eyes can communicate. *You fight and I'll fight with you.*

We take him home and Beatrice leads me to the dining room. I see now why she keeps it closed off. The room is mostly bare and the windows are shuttered, so it's dim as evening even though it's midday. There's a table on one end and a smallish stained couch on the other. Its upholstery looks like it's been hit by a cheese shredder. In the center of the room is a perch.

"This is my training room," she explains, lowering the crate to the floor near a wall. "If there's too much stuff in it, the hawk gets nervous. Same about exposure to the outside, or light."

"We should feed him," I say, kneeling in front of the crate. My owl is still hunched at the back: a petrified owl statue with great golden eyes. "Maybe some lunch will help him feel less afraid."

"Some lunch will help me," Beatrice says, and walks out of the room.

I drop to my knees and then stretch my legs back so I'm on my stomach in front of the crate. I rest my face on the backs of my hands. It's just me and the owl.

Rufus.

The name just comes to me.

The owl has looked away, his head rotating to inspect the walls of the crate. Did he tell me his name?

No, of course not. That's insane. But I like the name: Rufus. He looks like a Rufus.

"I'm Reenie," I whisper.

His eyes are instantly back on me, staring down my face like just a look from him could kill.

I bet he makes every animal in the forest run screaming with that look.

You are one tough little owl, I think to him. *You can do this, Rufus. You can get better.*

"You making friends?" Beatrice has returned with a plate full of dripping-wet diced meat.

"Rufus needs a friend."

"Rufus?"

"He looks like a Rufus." I scooch up to sit on my butt and reach out a hand for the food. Beatrice hesitates, but then gives it to me. I open the crate door and slip the plate in.

Rufus's eyes don't leave me. He doesn't make a move toward the food, either.

"Do you think he knows what we just gave him?" I ask.

"He knows," she says. She kneels down, peeks in on Rufus. "He might be too weak to eat."

My heart cramps hearing her say that. But this is my owl, and we're in this fight together. "So what do I do?"

"You?" Beatrice's eyebrows lift. She lowers a towel over the crate's door. "Maureen, this is different than with Red. This is a wild bird. It doesn't understand what's happening to it, it's scared, and it will lash out. You need to promise me you'll leave this owl alone, let me handle it."

My jaw clenches down so hard, I worry my teeth might shatter. Who is this lady to get between me and Rufus? "But I can help you. You let me hold him." I give her a Rufus glare.

"Maureen, I'm a licensed rehabber. I can't—"

"*Please,*" I snap.

She considers the situation a moment longer, and then maybe she finally gets that there's no way I'm not doing anything and everything to make Rufus better, because she stands and grabs something from the table at the end of the room.

"Here," she says, and hands me a pair of long metal tongs. "Pick up a tidbit and hold it out to him." She lifts the towel and opens the crate door.

Just removing that metal wall sends tingles all over me. I pinch a bit of meat from the plate with the tongs and hold it out to Rufus. He's looking at me the whole time.

"He doesn't even seem to notice the food." I give it a shake and nearly lose the tidbit from my tongs.

"Imagine if two giant, feathered monsters plucked you out of the grass, stuffed you in a box, and started poking you. You might not want to take your eyes off them for a minute."

She's right. I have to get into my bird brain—my owl brain. What do I even know about owls? He's glaring at me, but when I move, he moves his whole head to follow, not just his eyes—*can* he move his eyes? I wonder if he can even see the tidbit that close. I decide to try something I saw in one of the YouTube videos I watched about training hawks: I rub the tidbit right up against Rufus's beak.

That startles him a little, but he snaps onto the tidbit and gulps it down.

"Good," Beatrice says, kneeling beside me like a coach. "Now try a second bite."

I get him to eat everything on the plate.

He seems sated. At least, his eyes are slightly less terrified and slightly more satisfied.

And I did that.

"See?" I say to Beatrice. "I helped."

"You did," she says, though in a way that sounds like maybe she thinks this was a fluke.

"So I can help you?" I want guarantees.

She glances in at Rufus. "Looks like I don't have a choice." Her mouth quirks up at the corner. She doesn't look or sound angry. She almost sounds happy. Whatever.

"Can I stay with him?"

She flips the towel over the door. "If you want." She leaves.

I peek in through the strip of grating along the side of the crate. Rufus is staring right at me, like he knew I'd be there.

I spend the whole rest of the afternoon just sitting there, watching him watching me.

8

Rufus

THE FURLESS CREATURE HAS FALLEN ASLEEP. ITS BARE face is half covered by the frizz of brown hair that sprouts from its head. It is my chance.

I must escape this cave and find a place to pellet. The cave is larger than any tree hole I've lived in, but that doesn't mean I'm going to foul my nest. There are standards to be maintained. Even for the Absolute Worst Great Horned Owl in All of Owldom.

I creep forward and the cave shifts. Its walls groan and scratch. This cave does not seem to be stable.

The opening of the cave is blocked by some kind of web

—the same web that had protected the mouse that trapped me. My talons are no use on it.

Pellets.

So I am stuck in here? The furless creature is going to force me to foul my nest?

I WILL NOT STAND FOR THIS!

My screech has woken it up.

It pushes aside the skin that hung down over the outside of the web and peers in at me, growls something. It looks away, howls for its mate: the big one with the gray fur tail dangling off its head.

They grumble to each other. I keep up the chatter to remind them that THINGS ARE DESPERATE. They must remove this web.

The one with the gray tail kneels in front of the cave and fiddles with the web. Some agreement must have been reached regarding my freedom. It grabs my feet in one thick, rough paw, wraps the other around my wings so I have no chance to fly, and carries me across what appears to be an even larger cave that my small nest-cave is inside to another small cave in the opposite corner.

So these are my options? Pellet in this nest or pellet in my own? These furless creatures are ruthless. The first chance I get, I am escaping this nightmare.

Once I have expelled my pellet, the gray tail snatches me up and puts me back in my nest-cave. The web is resealed over its opening. The brown-frizz creature resumes its watch.

I've seen animals play with their meals, but these furless creatures are taking things to an extreme. First, I'm poked and stretched and blustered by the smallish one with the black fur on its head. Then these two put me in this cave within a cave. I sense other owls have been trapped in here. Or at least other birds. There are talon scratches in the walls of the cave.

Is this what happened to my mother? She was taken by a furless creature. The shadowy silhouette that emerged from the rumbling monster was the same as these creatures' forms. And now, having been inside a rumbling monster myself, I realize that she was not eaten by the monster. She was . . . or will be . . . eaten by the furless creature.

I wish Mother were here. I mean, not that she should be trapped with me or eaten, but just that, if we're both to be trapped and eaten, I wish that we could have been trapped and eaten together.

This is how bad things are? My one wish is to die with my mother at the hands of these skin monsters?

I huddle as far from the cave's web as I can get and glare at the furless creature. I may be the Absolute Worst Great Horned Owl in All of Owldom, but I am still a great horned owl. I will not be taken down without a fight.

The furless creature has produced a squarish, flat rock that glows like moonlight on water. It taps the flat stone with its featherless wing-toes, the light flashes, and noise comes out of the rock. It sounds like . . . Great Beak, there are *owls* in that stone!

I start chirping quietly. Maybe the furless creature won't notice . . . Maybe the owls will hear me and bring help.

But the furless creature notices. It puts the flat rock down, and the rock goes dark. The other owls cease to hoot. *Pellets.*

The furless creature growls softly, all the while staring at me with its tiny brown eyes. It pinches a bit of mouse in its long, sharp, shiny removable claw and shoves the morsel in through the web.

"No way, Skin Monster," I squawk, clacking my beak and retreating to the back of the cave.

I will not fatten myself up for its dinner. The furless creature can go choke on a bone.

But the furless creature is undeterred. It growls again, puts its face right up to the web. And then it does the strangest thing: It eats a nut. Or at least, something squishy and squarish that smells nutty. And right in front of my cave. I may not be able to smell much, but I can smell that! It chomps away on nuts like some overgrown squirrel that shed its fur like a leaf tree in winter.

This creature is taunting me.

Then again, it seems to really be enjoying those nuts.

Could it be that the furless creature is *not* keeping me here to eat me?

The smallish creature with the black hair on its head did seem to be surrounded by all sorts of animals. I heard everything from a rabbit snuffle to a coyote's snort while in its cave. My wing does feel less hot and stingy after whatever the creature did to it. And the creatures were awfully nice about not making me foul my nest earlier.

Could it be that the furless creatures *help* other creatures? And eat nuts?

The furless creature puts its nuts away. It slips one big, rough paw over its naked little wing-toes and then picks up a mouse morsel. It fiddles with the web and then the web opens a crack. The paw reaches in with the mouse.

The meat does look good.

And I am a bit peckish.

I chance a step toward the paw.

The paw holds still. The mouse beckons with sanguine odors.

I chance another step. The noise of the furless creature's huge heart pounding in its chest rattles my skull. What is it so nervous about?

Stretching my beak, I snap onto the morsel and gobble it down.

The creature gives off an excited squeak. It slips the

paw back out of my cave, grabs another mouse morsel, and slowly, ever so slowly, moves the mouse toward me.

That one bite has got my gizzard screeching. I snap at the paw.

The creature grumbles, pulls the paw back.

Is it afraid of my beak?

I ruffle my feathers, lay back my ear tufts. "Okay, furless creature," I chirp. "I promise I will not bite your paw."

The creature must understand Owlish because it slowly brings the paw closer to me. I let it get right up near my beak and then carefully, not scraping even a scrap of that doofy paw, peck the morsel off the paw and gobble it down.

The creature squeaks again. Its face contorts into this creepy sneer. It looks happy, though. Its heart has slowed down.

This is what it wants? To have me nibble off its paw?

There's a hoot in my head that it is unbecoming of a great horned owl to eat off any animal's paw. But, then again, I *am* the Absolute Worst Great Horned Owl ever. And I am still feeling off—weak and thirsty and hungry as a bear coming out of its sleep cave.

Perhaps eating off a paw is not such a bad thing. Perhaps, given recent events, I don't give a hoot whether it's becoming or not.

The creature grabs some more mouse with its paw and we go back and forth like this, me carefully nibbling off the paw, the creature squeaking with delight at each bite, until I am as full as I have ever been in my life.

When I can't suffer another beakful, I hoot quietly, "That'll be good morning," and shuffle to the back of the cave, where I've scrunched up the thin, nubby matted fur on the bottom of the cave into a bit of a nest. I snuggle down into myself, let my eyelids drift up, and catch the furless creature outside the web snuggling down into itself, its eyelids drooping.

It's nice to go to sleep with another heartbeat in your ears, even if it is the heartbeat of a giant furless beast.

9

Reenie

BEATRICE WAKES ME WITH A SHAKE OF THE SHOULDER. "You slept here all night?"

I wipe sleep from my eyes. "I don't mind sleeping on the floor." I push myself up onto my elbows. Rufus is still snoozing at the back of the crate.

"You fed the owl again?" She picks up the empty, blood-smeared plate I used last night.

"He ate off the glove," I say, the words bringing the excitement back in a wave.

Beatrice does not look quite as pleased. "You stuck your hand in the crate?"

"Only with my glove on." I curl my knees into my chest. "He wouldn't eat off the tongs."

"Maureen, I said you could *help*. Help means help *me*, which means I have to be here if you do anything."

"But he was hungry. And nothing happened."

Beatrice kneels down, looks in on Rufus. "He's weak, so he's not going to put up as much of a fight, but trust me, birds of prey are not pets. If he wanted to, he could do some real damage with those talons." She holds out her arm, which bears a few roundish, talon-shaped scars.

"I'm not stupid," I say. I don't want a lecture. "I thought the whole point was to try to train a hawk."

"A *hawk*," she says, getting a little loud. "Not a great horned owl. Owls are notoriously hard to train. Plus, it's illegal. This is a rehab bird. We make him better and then we release him back out to his wild life.

"I need to know you'll follow my rules with this. You can't just do whatever comes into your head. There's a bird's life at stake here. And your own safety," she adds.

She stares at me and I glare back, but the buzz fires up. What if she sends Rufus away? Gives him to Dr. Cho or some other rehabber? *Because of me . . .*

"I just wanted him to eat something." My stomach has wrenched into a fist. "I won't do it again."

Beatrice's shoulders slump. "I'm not angry," she says. "I just — I don't want you or the bird to get hurt."

"I was careful," I whisper.

She sighs, turns the plate in her hands. "I'm sure you were," she says, and stands. She walks the plate into the kitchen.

I sit there, curled tight, and watch Rufus sleep. It's dark in here, even with the door open a crack. But I can tell from the light in the kitchen that the sun's been up for a while.

"What time is it?" I ask, stretching my legs.

Beatrice doesn't answer. I hear water running. My foot kicks the tablet I borrowed last night to research owls. I tap the screen. It's past nine.

I jump up and scramble into the kitchen. "Don't we have to get to Rutland?" Visitation started fifteen minutes ago!

Beatrice turns off the water. "The social worker called. Your mom—" Beatrice shakes the plate, puts it on the drying rack. "She wasn't feeling great."

"Is she sick?"

"She was . . . she had to go back to the hospital."

I hold my face together, but something inside me wilts. For a whole month at the treatment center, she had been doing better, and now she's back in the hospital? Obviously, this has something to do with me. I should never have told her about Phil and the plate. I've been taking care of Mom for my whole life—how could I have been so careless and let that slip?

I wander up to my room and sit down at the desk. When

Mom's at the hospital, the only way to communicate is by letter. I turn to a clean sheet of paper in my math notebook. I start to write:

Dear Mom,
I shouldn't have said what I said about Phil and the plate. It's totally healed. I don't even think there's a scar.
I'm sorry you're in the hospital.
Please get better. For good this time.

I cross out the last line. Then I cross out the whole thing. I rip the paper and throw it across the room. Then I throw the whole notebook across the room.

I walk back down to the bird room. That's what I'm calling it. Why call it a dining room when the only one dining in it is a bird?

I sit down and face Rufus, who's still snoozing.

I am toxic. Mom is in the hospital again because of me. Beatrice is already tired of me — I can tell from her voice — and it's only been a week. I should probably leave this owl alone before I ruin him, too.

That thought cracks through the others. The buzz sizzles up my spine: *alone.* Tears spring out. Alone, and homeless. Mom told me I can't go back to Gram's. How much longer will Beatrice let me stay here? I give it another week . . .

"I'm sorry," Beatrice says. I didn't even notice her follow me in here.

No, no tears. I strangle the sadness, push it back. "It's not your fault my mom's been locked up." Fine—no one wants me? I can go it alone. Live in the wild like Sam in *My Side of the Mountain* . . .

Beatrice kneels down beside me. "It's not anyone's fault, Maureen." She looks me square in the eyes. "And she's not locked up. She's getting help." Beatrice holds out a Pop-Tart.

The buzz of *alone* bounces around the emptiness inside me. *Who's going to help me?*

I take the Pop-Tart. "Should we wake Rufus up?"

"He'll wake up when he needs something."

I need him to wake up, to give me something to focus on that's not in my head.

"Eat," Beatrice says, laying a hand on my shoulder.

I almost jump out of my skin. It's crazy how nice it is to feel a hand on my shoulder right now.

I take a bite of the Pop-Tart. It's warm and just the right kind of crumbly. In five seconds, I scarf the whole thing down.

I do feel better.

Beatrice pats my shoulder. "I'll get you the other one." She stands and leaves the room.

Rufus coos softly, ruffles his feathers.

What if I save this owl? What if I prove he can be trained? *Imagine if we show her, Rufus.* Imagine when she sees us soaring together. Then she'll understand. Then she'll let us stay.

We'll show her, I think to Rufus.

Beatrice brings me the other Pop-Tart on a plate. I take it, curl up in my fleece blanket, and tap on the tablet.

Search "owl falconry training."

I find listservs, YouTube videos, webpages. I put in my ear buds and start my research.

◡

One thing that's cool about living with Beatrice is that she's not nosy. She moves around her house, doing her own thing, first reading, then cleaning Red's mews. So she doesn't bother me until dinner, when she knocks softly on the door and says, "I made food."

I've sketched out a whole plan for training Rufus. At night, in secret. And then, by the time his wing is healed, we'll be such an amazing falconry team that Beatrice will have no choice but to get permission to fly him as our passage bird this season.

I put the tablet away and stand. My legs are tingly and wobble—I guess I need to move around more. Beatrice is sitting at the kitchen table eating some kind of soup and I join her.

"Rufus slept all day," I say, flopping into a chair.

"He's exhausted," she says, slurping a spoonful. "The injury didn't seem that old, but he was pretty hungry. He was probably stressed and starving for a few days. That would tire out any bird."

I take a bite of soup. She says it like this only happens to birds. I've been stressed and hungry for more than a few days before.

"Red missed you at feeding time." She stirs her soup around the bowl. "What have you been doing all day?"

I worked past feeding time? Yikes. "Um, reading stuff. About owl rehabilitation."

She smiles a little. "My daughter used to get that look."

"What look?" I ask, feigning innocence. There's no way she can know about my secret plans. And then my brain processes the more important fact that was just revealed.

"You have a daughter?" I say, like a person who has totally not been snooping would. She can't know I saw the pictures.

Beatrice swirls the soup. "She's older now. Moved out west with her father after the divorce."

The buzz whispers, *Not your room.* "I'm in her room, aren't I?"

"It hasn't been her room in years," Beatrice says, taking a bite.

The buzz hisses, *Not your home.* "But if she comes to visit?"

Beatrice smiles, but this time it's more of a wince. "She hasn't visited in years."

The buzz fizzles away to nothing. I'm okay for now. Rufus and I have time. Then I notice Beatrice looks on the verge of tears. I can't handle another sad grownup in my life. I scoop soup into my face, clear my bowl, and head back into the bird room.

Rufus is awake. He blinks his great golden eyes at me. He needs to do his business, I'm sure.

"Hey, Beatrice," I call. "I think Rufus needs to barf up that gross lump."

"Casting," she calls back, her chair scraping across the floorboards. Her bowl clatters in the sink, and then she's in the bird room, pulling on her gloves. "Or pellet. An owl *casts* a casting or pellet. He probably needs to do all his business. Course, he's the first bird I've ever rehabbed that got fussy about pooping in his crate."

"Rufus is a gentleman," I say, because he so obviously is. "He would never do something so gross as poop where he sleeps." I open the crate, grateful to see her focused and real-smiling, not fake-smiling. Beatrice reaches in and grabs Rufus around his feet and wings. I grab the dirty towel from the bottom of his crate, snap open a fresh one, and stuff it in.

Beatrice steps toward the second crate but then decides on a different path. "Close the door to the kitchen," she says.

I shut it, careful not to make too much noise.

She holds Rufus out and lowers him to the perch in the center of the room. It's a rubber-coated metal ring on a metal stick standing up out of a heavy base.

Rufus reaches out with his talons and grabs the ring. He stands there, blinks a few times, then begins to teeter. He squawks, lifts his wings, and is about to stretch them straight, but Beatrice lowers her gloves around him.

"He's still too weak," she says. "We can try again tomorrow."

My heart is racing from watching him—he almost perched! He also almost tipped over on his feet. "Try what again?"

"The first step in manning a bird is getting it to trust you and sit calmly in your presence."

Manning. That's a falconry term. "Do you mean . . . ?" I ask.

"I get the sense you're going to train him whether I help you or not." She lowers him into the second crate. "It's probably better if I help you."

This warmth tickles up from my bellybutton. "You serious?" I dare to ask.

"Are you?" she asks me, really digging in with her eyes.

She is serious. She's going to help me do this. I nod my head in a most serious fashion. "I have a whole plan," I begin, then pull out my notebook and show her all my notes.

She nods as she reads. "So this is what you've been doing all day?"

A part of me worries that maybe I didn't do enough, that maybe she needs more proof. "He's already eating off the glove," I say, pointing to the steps in my notes. "Once he's strong enough, I could try feeding him while having him perched on the glove."

I see the corner of her mouth tick up. "Let's see if we can get him standing on a perch, period."

The corner of my mouth hitches up to match hers. "Okay."

That promise—just to try—is enough for now.

Monday morning, I don't open my eyes until almost noon. Rufus had me up all night with his squawking and chirping. Beatrice and I fed him a bunch of tidbits from the glove, though, and he didn't snap at me once. I'm calling it progress.

I scramble off the floor where I'd camped near Rufus's crate. The house is silent, the bird room dark and cool. I find Beatrice sitting in the kitchen, reading.

"You didn't wake me for school?" I ask, bewildered.

"No school," she says, flipping a page of her book. "It's Labor Day."

I pull a chair out, sit. "Oh."

"I thought we could take Red for a walk." She takes a sip of her iced tea, calm and unhurried.

Last Labor Day, there was a crazy loud barbecue at Gram's place. I climbed up into this stubby apple tree with a bag of chips to get away from the crowds of kids running between the trailers. I must have fallen asleep there in the branches. When Mom found me to go home — back when we still had a home — the sky was purple, and my ears rang with the echoes of the party's music. I've never lived somewhere so still, so quiet, as Beatrice's. Against the stillness, the buzz inside me is a low growl. I thought it only showed up when I'm freaking out; I've never noticed it before when I'm just sitting. But there it is: this engine that's always running, always alert. There are some parts of yourself you only find in the quiet.

I take a deep breath, try to slow the buzz. *Alone, alone*, it chugs out.

Beatrice takes another sip of iced tea. The condensation beads and runs down the sides of the glass. She flips another page. Outside, the wind tickles the leaves. A bird calls. In that stillness, I tell the buzz — silently, only in my head — *You can rest*. And for a heartbeat, it's gone. I'm a buttercup soaking up the sun.

A car blasts down the road, blaring music and kicking up a cloud of dust that covers all the front windows. The buzz returns. But oh — that moment.

Beatrice folds a corner of her page, puts down her book. "You ready?"

"Lemme grab a granola bar," I say, pushing my chair back.

She nods. "I'll meet you out back."

After the walk, I go upstairs and find my math notebook in the corner of the room, where I'd thrown it. I take it to the desk, open it to a smooth, clean sheet of paper. *Alone, alone* pulses down my arms, through my fingertips. I focus on the quiet, on the breeze billowing the curtain, on the late afternoon light, warm on my skin. When the quiet reaches all the way inside, I try again.

Dear Mom,
I love you. I miss you.
See you soon,
Reenie

I leave the letter in the mailbox with the flag up.

Monday night is another marathon feeding session with Rufus. Beatrice even goes to bed and lets me feed him on my own. It seems silly to have to keep sticking my glove into his house. I could just let him walk out and stretch his wings. But the buzz fires up and I can't. What if Beatrice found out? What if I hurt him? So I feed Rufus off the glove again until he won't eat another bite and then I just lie there, watching him, and try—desperately, painfully—to be patient.

◄

"Everyone can turn in their homework at the end of the class," the teacher, Mr. Brown, says Tuesday morning, and my brain vaguely recalls that there had been homework. Which is definitely not done.

Oh well. That's one good thing about this life being temporary: my grades won't matter once I leave this school.

"We're going to start this year by looking at what makes our state unique," he continues. "I want you to come up with something about living in Vermont that's important to you. You'll research its history and then interview someone about it. We'll spend class today working in groups to come up with an idea."

Nothing is more terrifying than the Group Project. Especially for the new kid.

People start clumping together like dust bunnies. I shrink into my seat. I'm not sure what would be worse: someone asking me to join their group, or not being asked to join any group.

"Hey." I look up and there's Jaxon. Relief floods through me.

"Yes, definitely," I say, before he even has a chance to ask. I pull the neighboring desk next to mine. "Sit here."

Jaxon sits, pulls out his whittling.

I monitor the remaining students as the clumping slows. Some boys have joined together and are making fart noises with their hands. Jaxon and I are safe.

"Can I work with you guys?"

Or not. She snuck up behind us.

"Sure," Jaxon says, making room.

Jamie pulls over a chair. "Thanks." She smiles her shiny white teeth at me.

"Excellent," Mr. Brown says. "Everyone take out some paper and start brainstorming topics. Let's hear more talking, less farting."

This gets a chuckle, but the fart noises keep coming for at least another minute.

"Oh," Jamie says, and digs in her backpack. "Here." She slaps a new comic book, still wrapped in plastic, on the desk.

Jaxon's eyes brighten. He puts the wood down. "Whoa." He gently lifts the shiny packet and begins examining the cover.

"It's a *comic*," I say, because seriously. Why is he getting worked up over a comic book?

"It's a first-edition Avengers," Jamie says, raising her eyebrows like this means something. "Jaxon and I were comparing our collections last week and he didn't believe that I had a first edition. It's really my dad's, but still." She holds out a hand—like *Ta-da!* "Do you collect comics?" she asks me.

"No." Who has money for comic books?

"Oh, well," she says, fidgeting with the end of her braid, "my dad and I? We collect them—well, he collected them, and then he let me sort of latch on to his collecting." This girl seems to latch on to anything that passes by. She continues talking. "I've tried to draw my own. I went to a cartooning camp, but my comics are still terrible. I can never come up with a good team. Oh my gosh—we should totally come up with a team name."

"Not Avengers," I say. Cartooning camp? Is this girl for real?

"Of course not Avengers," Jamie says, snorting this little laugh, "though if we were the Avengers, I think Jaxon would be Cap, and maybe you would be—"

"I'm Bruce Banner," Jaxon interrupts, gingerly sliding the comic back toward Jamie like it's made of glass. "My mom called me the Hulk when I was little. She's the one who got me into Marvel."

"No way!" Jamie exclaims. "I can't even imagine you—"

Mr. Brown appears over us. "How are things coming along with you all? Have a topic yet?"

I have never been more relieved to see a teacher. It would have been better to have worked on my own than watch the one person I sort of thought was okay get sucked up by Miss Comic Book Collection.

"I thought," Jaxon says, shoving the whittling into his pocket, "we could maybe do hunting?"

Jamie pales. "I'm a vegetarian."

"I thought falconry," I suggest strongly.

"That's a kind of hunting," Jaxon offers.

"So hunting it is," I say, flashing a triumphant smile at Jamie. She's not a hunter, not like Jaxon and me.

"Maybe there's another group you'd like to join?" I say, but at the same time Jaxon's all, "Hunting isn't just about killing animals and eating meat. It's about wildlife management. My dad says hunting keeps the deer herd at healthy numbers."

"Oh," Jamie says.

I kind of feel bad about how freaked out Jamie looks.

"And falconry's about birds," I add.

"Oh?" Jamie says, and she gives me this little half smile.

Why's she smiling? We're still doing hunting. Maybe it wasn't the topic that was freaking her out. Maybe it was . . . me?

Mr. Brown nods. "We had a hunting group a couple years ago. I think that's a great idea." He hands us a blank assignment sheet, tells us to start outlining what we're going to do for the project and to assign everyone a job, then announces to the class that we'll be in the library doing research for the rest of the week.

"I don't know anything about hunting," Jamie says, tucking a strand of hair into her mouth.

"I hunt," Jaxon says. "And my dad's a game warden with the Fish and Wildlife Department. He can help."

"I've learned a bunch of stuff training a . . . hawk." I stop myself from mentioning Rufus just in time. If Jaxon's dad is with the Fish and Wildlife Department, that means he's in charge of making sure falconers follow the rules. Such as not training owls. The last thing I need is another state agency involved in my life.

Jamie has chewed the strand of hair so it's tight against her head. "I guess the whole point of the project is to learn something." She releases the strand, and it's like a switch flips: she's perky again. "It'll be great."

We're back on track, I guess. "So, Mr. Brown said to assign jobs."

"Maureen should be the leader," Jaxon says.

"Me?" Did he just say *leader?*

"I can see her as our Nick Fury," Jamie says, and I don't know if that's an insult or what.

"She's more of a Tony Stark," Jaxon replies.

"Iron Man?" I ask, finally comprehending something.

"Right," Jamie says, smiling at me like I'm a dog who just mastered *sit.* "Maureen's our Iron Man."

"Iron *Woman*," Jaxon says with authority.

A chuckle escapes Jamie's lips, and this weird smile tickles the corners of my mouth. I write "Maureen L'Esperance—Iron Woman" under "Hunting" on our assignment sheet, and the smile grows. I mean, it's not like I care or anything—this is just a stupid school project—but still, it's kind of cool to be the Iron Woman of any group.

At the end of the day, the teacher lets us spend the last fifteen minutes of the period outside. Jaxon and I are just settling in behind our bush, our whittling wood poised for sculpting, when Jamie comes crashing through the brush.

"Hi," she says, all singsongy. She plops down beside Jaxon and hefts a giant book from her backpack. "I got this history of comic books out from the library. You've got to see the old covers for Captain Marvel."

She opens the book and Jaxon leans in, dropping his whittling in the leaves. "Cool," he says, like we weren't in the middle of something ourselves.

Who is this girl to barge in with her comic book collection when Jaxon and I were perfectly happy whittling together in silence? I shove my whittling into my backpack and pull out the book on owls I took out. I try to flip pages loudly enough so that I can't hear Jamie and Jaxon oohing and aahing over their stupid comics.

"Hey," Jamie says, "Maureen, look! There really is an Iron Woman."

"Rescue," Jaxon says. "One of my mom's favorites."

And a part of me wants to toss my book aside and lean in because I'm Iron Woman, I'm Jaxon's mom's favorite, but then the buzz whispers, *Friends are dangerous.* What happens if they ask about my mom? How do I explain that the only thing I've ever collected was addresses?

"Huh?" I say, like I was so into my reading I didn't hear a word they said, like what they're talking about doesn't even matter to me.

"Oh, sorry," Jamie says, her voice shrinking. "I just thought—"

"I really need to read this," I say. "It's research." I waggle the book so they can see how thick and imposing a tome it is.

Jaxon gives me this confused look, then turns back to Jamie. They go on flipping pages, but there's no more oohing or aahing. The three of us silently flip pages like it's a punishment. I managed to suck the fun out of the entire world. Typical me.

The bell rings.

"See you guys tomorrow," Jamie says, getting up.

"See you," Jaxon says, following her.

"Sure," I say.

The bus can't drive fast enough. The farther I get from school, the farther I am from all the drama. Like I meant to ruin their conversation. Like I even wanted friends.

I get home and burst into the kitchen. Beatrice isn't home yet. I hear Rufus squawking. This drama I can handle.

I drop my backpack, wash my hands, and crack open the door to the bird room. Rufus is chittering and chirping and clacking his beak.

Owls are super noisy. I would not have guessed this going in with the whole rehabilitating-an-owl thing. But I've learned a ton. For example, I know this owl needs to pellet.

I look out the side window, then the front. I have no idea when Beatrice will be home.

Rufus squawks again, louder.

I'm not going to make Rufus suffer.

"All right, buddy," I say, slipping on Beatrice's leather work gloves.

He's shuffled into the center of the crate. His wings are tight against his back and he gives me a slow blink of his yellow eyes.

I open the crate door and slip my hands in to grab his feet. But they're hidden under his long chest feathers. Why bother digging for feet when I can just hold his wings? I get my gloves around him and lift him up. See? Perfectly fine.

I probably should not be doing this without Beatrice

—this is a step beyond feeding. But Rufus has stopped screaming. This is what he needed!

I carry him to the other crate—his "barf- and bathroom," as I'm calling it. I shut him inside, and lo and behold, he shuffles to the back, silently pukes up a pellet, and then poops. Owl poop is called "whitewash." It's still poop.

See? I can do things. I'm a leader. Take that, Tony Stark.

Rufus steps to the front of the crate and stands there staring at me. I open the crate door and get my hands around his wings. I decide to try reaching around his back, so I won't have his talons facing my chest. I can just get my fingers all the way around his wings. Now, I'll just stand and kind of turn Rufus and lift—*careful of the tufts!*—yes, up and out of the crate, and taking a step . . .

My foot hooks the perch on the floor midstride and I'm tripping before I can even process what's happening. My hands drop Rufus to break my fall.

But Rufus doesn't drop.

He flaps and shrieks, then kind of glides to the floor. He begins screeching and pulsing his wings. He gets some air and now I realize why Beatrice has been so careful. Rufus is actually quite large, like an umbrella come to life. An umbrella equipped with sharp and powerful talons.

A distraught owl flapping and squawking and bumbling about a small enclosed space is terrifying. I hit the floorboards and cover my head with my gloves.

"What in the—" Beatrice stands in the doorway.

Oh no.

She quickly closes the door behind her and pulls on a glove.

She warned me . . . *What will she do?* The buzz cranks up to a deafening roar. I should have waited. I'm such an idiot. My eyes sting.

Rufus lands on the arm of the couch and screeches. Did he hurt his wing? He glares at me, and I totally deserve that.

Beatrice pauses against the wall. I am frozen on the floor. A tear drips off the tip of my nose, splatting on the floorboards. This is all my fault. What if Beatrice sends him away? *What if Beatrice sends me away?* The buzz roars.

Rufus turns his head, considers the room, the two humans. He bobs his head a few times. Then he fluffs his feathers out until he looks like an upended dust mop and begins nipping at them with his beak. He slides his beak over each feather, like he's smoothing the seams of his jacket.

He's okay. I didn't hurt him. *He's okay . . .*

"He's preening," Beatrice whispers.

"I dropped him," I confess, still not moving from the floor.

"You should have waited." Beatrice sticks by the wall.

"I know," I whisper, then add, louder, "But he sounded really mad. He cast up a pellet the second I put him in the poop crate."

"You should have waited," she repeats, a bit more sharply.

I bang my forehead on the floor. Of course I should have waited.

Beatrice appears beside me, having tiptoed over, silent as a ghost. She places a palm on my shoulder. "Look."

I drag my head up; it's like hefting a stone.

Rufus finishes his preening and settles into his perch. His lower eyelids slide up—he's sleepy.

"He can perch," Beatrice whispers.

"He's feeling better?" There's a tiny lift inside me.

She gives a little shrug to say, *I dunno*. "But he can perch."

Rufus poops down the arm of the couch.

"And mute. Both good signs."

"I'm sorry," I say.

She nods. "I know."

The buzz inside quiets. We sit there for a while, just watching Rufus snooze. Then Beatrice unfolds her legs. "I should get dinner started."

"What about Rufus?"

"If he's perching, he doesn't need to be in the crate, which means he needs anklets and jesses." She considers Rufus, who twitters softly. "I need to eat before trying that."

We creep out of the bird room together, careful not to disturb Rufus. I sit at the kitchen table while Beatrice throws something together to eat. I can't believe how chill she was about me almost killing Rufus. How cool she *is* about it—no yelling, not even now that we're away from the bird room. I decide to offer her something in exchange.

"I have a project at school," I say. "We're in groups, researching something about Vermont that's important to us. My group is doing hunting."

"But you don't hunt," Beatrice says, shaking some spices into the pot.

"Yeah." Maybe I shouldn't have said anything.

She stirs the whatever-she's-making. Then she puts the spoon aside and comes to the table. "I'm betting your part of this project is about falconry?" She looks me right in the eye. I nod. "I bet there's not one person in your class who's even heard of the sport. It's a great project."

A little smile quirks up the corner of my mouth. It's not like I care what she thinks about the project, but, I mean, it's nice to hear that she—or anyone—thinks it's great.

"You hunt with Red, right?" I ask.

"That's part of my deal with Red. I scare the prey out of the brush so she can catch it."

"Even though you're vegetarian?" I ask, remembering Jamie's complaint.

"Red eats the meat." She goes back to the stove to tip her spoon in and taste her creation. "It's just nature running its course. Bird of prey eats prey."

"Can I interview you?" I say it quickly, forcing the words

out. Asking for favors is not my thing. "It's for the project. I have to interview a hunter."

Beatrice frowns, eyebrows raised. "I've never been interviewed before."

"I've never interviewed anyone before," I say.

She shrugs. "So we'll learn together." Her smile coaxes one out of my own face.

We chow down on pasta and some vegetable sauce. *Human of earth eats plants.*

Once we're done, Beatrice and I head back into the bird room. Rufus cracks open his eyes, sees it's us, and goes back to sleep. Beatrice stops at the little table and begins sorting her tools. She snips leather, picks out some metal rings she calls grommets, then pulls out these long strips with knots at one end—the jesses.

She places her hands on her hips, surveys her collection. "I'm going to need you to hold him."

"I can hold him," I say, my voice a whisper. The buzz rages: *What if I fail again? What if this time, I drop him and he breaks a bone?*

"Hey," Beatrice says, looking straight into my eyes. "I wouldn't ask you to do it if I didn't think you could."

I nod. She thinks I can handle it—maybe I can . . .

"Let's do this." She hands me a towel.

We both put on work gloves and walk calmly over to

Rufus so we don't startle him. Beatrice gently grabs Rufus around the legs and wings. His eyes flash open, the feathers along his back lift, his beak gapes, and he starts hissing like an angry snake. Beatrice jerks her chin, which is my cue to toss the towel over Rufus's head. It lands on him and the hissing stops. His claws dig into the couch, but Beatrice just holds him steady until his talons release, and then she carries him to the table.

"Get a good grip on him," she says, shifting her hold to let me get my hands around his body.

I hold him on his back on the table. Beatrice slips off the bulky gloves and grabs his legs between her fingers to keep from getting slashed by a talon. With a few quick movements, she slips the leather, smooth side in, around Rufus's leg, punches the grommet through the strip and cuts the ends, then does the same thing on the other side. In another thirty seconds, long jesses dangle from the grommets. Beatrice holds them out, judges their length against Rufus's tail, and then snips them.

"I'm done," she says, stepping back and wiping her forehead with her sleeve.

"That was incredible," I say. She moved so fast, like a robot.

"This is not my first bird," she says. She's smiling, though. I think she's a little psyched she did it so well.

Rufus clacks his beak. He probably does not like being on his back. I lift him upright.

"Whoa," Beatrice says. She slides on her gauntlet, gathers the jesses in her glove, makes a fist, and puts the gauntlet right under Rufus's feet. His talons grab on.

I let go.

And it happens. She's holding Rufus on her fist.

"Can I . . . ?" I begin, arm already drifting toward his talons.

Rufus flips out. He drops backwards off Beatrice's fist and starts flapping madly as he dangles from the jesses. The towel falls off and I see his bright yellow eyes and pinhole pupils. He is not happy.

But Beatrice is cool as a creemee. She scoops Rufus up by the chest and sets him back on her fist. "That's called bating. Perfectly normal."

Rufus seems confused but also grateful to be right-side up.

He looks at her, shuffles his feet. Looks at me. Ruffles his feathers. And then just stands there.

Beatrice smiles.

"He's doing it," I say.

And then he jumps off her fist again. And she sets him right again. And I realize that this is going to be a long road that's full of potholes.

10
Rufus

THE FURLESS CREATURES HAVE MADE ME A PART OF THEIR nest. They have tied strips of animal skin to my legs, which I assume is an owl-adapted version of the funny animal skin bladders they wear over their talonless toes. I would have preferred if they had asked me formally, perhaps presented some choice bit of food, but then again, I did roost in the cave they provided for me, so maybe they were confused.

I'm not actually against the little strips, as they do have a shiny bit that sparkles, but I am rather upset about the tails that dangle from the shiny bit. The tails get tangly and then I end up hanging like a bat.

Even the Absolute Worst Great Horned Owl in All of Owldom is above a fruit-sucking, bug-scarfing bat.

At least, I would like to think this is true.

The creature with the brown frizz is asleep on the soft rock-shaped mound near the wall. The Gray Tail put a fluffy skin over her—I have determined that these are female mammalian creatures, perhaps large furless, tail-less descendants of squirrels? Regardless, I would like to run my beak through that fluffy skin covering her, but these tangly tails on my new leg sparkles are tied to an even longer vine, which is attached to this perch.

I tried to fly a little when the Brown Frizz first fell asleep. I ended up beak-first in the dust.

BAH! This is so boring.

The Brown Frizz shifts under her skin.

"Come here and give me that skin!" I squawk.

The Brown Frizz opens her soft, pink, beakless maw and grumbles.

I peck at the perch, try to give her some hints. "Skin!" I hoot. "I want to peck it."

The Brown Frizz shuffles out of the room but leaves the skin on the soft rock.

"You forgot the skin!" I screech.

These furless creatures are not the brightest.

She comes back with a dripping warm mouse. Well, now that food's here, I am up for eating. I chomp that mouse down in one gulp. The Brown Frizz looks surprised. What, she didn't think I could eat a mouse whole? Just because I haven't had many opportunities for such feasting doesn't mean I can't do it.

"Now, about the skin," I chirp, trying a slightly different tone with the creature. "I would like to rip it to shreds. Would you be so kind?"

The creature blows some air at her head fur. That's an odd display.

I stretch my ear tufts. Maybe she's trying to communicate.

The creature's face lights up. She waves her naked little wing-toes up by her head fur.

Is she trying to look like a great horned owl? Because she is failing. Miserably.

I screech for her to stop this silliness. "The skin," I snap. "Bring it here."

The creature looks around the room. How is she not understanding me? I am being very clear! She crawls across the floor to a corner. But wait—are there other skins?

"I am open to an offer of other skins if you would like to keep yours," I chirp.

The creature crawls back. She has a longish, fattish root in her wing-toes that has tufts of fur dangling from either end.

What an odd little root.

The creature waggles the root. It squeaks.

Is there a mouse in that root?

"Creature, give me that root!" I squawk, and then hop off the perch. The creature drops the root and shuffles away from me.

Good — she knows her place.

What a fascinating root! And so wonderful for shredding. I clench it in my talons — it is very squishy, and — ho there! It squeaked again!

I dig into the root with beak and claw. I tear the tiny tendrils that make up its fibers. It is so satisfying to shred.

I am a great horned owl and I shred you, root!

I tear that root to tufts. But there's no mouse in it. The squeaking came from this strange foul-tasting bladder, which I spit out.

The Brown Frizz has fallen asleep again, this time on her featherless wing on the ground. I would wake her up to get me another root with an actual mouse inside, but she does seem like a tired creature.

I hop onto a rock that the Gray Tail placed near my perch and mute, then hop back down and stomp into the little pool of water she left for me to cool my talons. Then I flutter up to the perch. Around me lie the ruins of the root. I have done well.

I fluff my feathers and give them a straightening with my beak, getting everything back in order. Moonlight sneaks in through a crack in the wall of the cave, and I can hear night noises: crickets scratching their legs, bugs buzzing through the dark, a rabbit munching in the grass. And then I hear the call of an owl. Not a great horned, but a big bird, a barred owl.

A threat.

But the threat is on the other side of this cave's walls.

I shuffle my feet to get a better grip on the perch. Warm currents of air flow from the creature, and I concentrate on the thumping pulse of her heart.

I know I'm not supposed to like living here, but an owl has to admit: this nest is snug.

11
Reenie

BEATRICE COMES SNEAKING INTO THE BIRD ROOM TO WAKE me up. My head weighs a thousand pounds and I drooled all over my arm. But then I see my happy owl, perched above the shredded remains of the rope dog toy, sleeping with one foot tucked up under his fluffy chest feathers.

"I thought I left you on the couch," Beatrice says.

"Rufus wanted to play," I say, yawning. But then my heart jumps. "That's okay, right? I didn't touch him. I stayed outside the tether."

She smiles. "It's okay. But you've got to hurry if you're going to catch the bus."

I head for the bathroom, checking the time on the old clock in the living room. Crud, it's almost 7:15! I rush through my routine, toss on whatever's clean, and go to the kitchen in a flash.

"You need to remember that you're not an owl," Beatrice says, handing me a glass of juice. "You have to go to school all day. He sleeps."

"Could *you* resist him hooting at you to play?" I slug down the juice and take the Pop-Tart she proffers.

She snuffs a laugh. "No," she says.

I scarf the Pop-Tart, and a second one, and then go for my backpack, which is still by the door. Did I have homework? Ugh—I'll check on the bus ride.

At school, I pull out the math work sheet I should have finished over the long weekend. The numbers swim on the page, I'm so bleary-eyed.

It's almost a relief when Jamie sits in the desk next to mine. "Hey," I say, pushing aside the paper.

She rummages in her backpack and then pulls out a round box and places it on my desk. "It's an arc reactor," she says. "Well, obviously not a *real* arc reactor, but, um, I made it. For you. Because—"

"I'm Tony Stark?" I ask, picking it up. I've seen the movie.

It's a short metal can with a clear screw-on top that Jamie covered in slivers of silver sticker to make a pattern on the plastic. In the center is a triangle of wires. Jamie reaches over and pokes a finger at the bottom of the box, and the triangle blinks on. It's made of tiny LED lights.

"You made this?" I ask. "For me?" I clarify.

Her mouth shrugs up in a little smile. "I like to make stuff."

I click off the light, then on again. I haven't even been that nice to this girl and she gives me a present? No, *makes* me a present. That lights up. Is she so desperate for friends that she's willing to settle for me?

"I hope it's okay," she says quickly. "I mean, I'm sorry if it's weird."

Maybe only some friends are dangerous.

"I'm the one who's being weird," I say. "I'm sorry. About last week. And yesterday."

"Oh, um, it's okay," she says, fidgeting with the end of her braid.

"It's not okay," I say. I click the arc thingy off and on again. "Thank you. This is awesome."

She's smiling so hard, her cheeks nearly burst.

Jaxon slinks into the room and shuffles to his seat behind me. "I brought in my Fish and Wildlife guide." He slaps an inch-thick slab of paper onto the desk.

Jamie and I are both kind of stunned that there's an entire book of rules about hunting. We all three begin flipping through it, pointing and gasping at how insanely specific these rules are, and I kind of step outside myself for a second. I mean, I'm still sitting at my desk, still pointing at the tiny printed rules—"You can't hunt a half hour after sunset? How do you even know when that is?"—but I'm also, like, three inches above that me, noticing that for the first time in a long time I have . . . friends?

At the end of the day, I see Beatrice is parked outside the school to pick me up.

"I thought I was taking the bus," I say, opening the door of the truck.

"I have to pick up my order of food from the Farm and Yard." She puts down her book and starts the engine. "We have our work cut out for us, prepping it all for the freezer."

"Was that a pun? Because gross," I say, sliding into the passenger seat.

She snuffles a laugh. "Not all of falconry is soaring with a falcon," she says, pulling out of the parking lot.

"Dr. Cho is going to stop by tonight," Beatrice says. "It's time to check on her patient."

"What does that mean?" I ask. "Are we releasing him? What about—"

"Slow down," she says, turning into the store's lot. "I think Rufus is ready to go out to the mews."

"Outside?"

"He's ready to have a little more space to stretch those wings as they heal."

Rufus is screeching when we get home. Red is squawking from the backyard. Beatrice and I throw down our bags and start warming up mice. She hurries out to Red, I sneak into the bird room. Rufus is glaring at me, ear tufts raised. He starts hissing and clacking his beak.

Boy, he's in a crud mood.

I slide on my gauntlet and approach slowly, calmly, quietly, just like all the books and videos say. I get low, stretch my hand toward his dish.

"Let's try something," Beatrice says. She must have snuck in after feeding Red. "Put the mouse on your fist."

The buzz crackles. "But what if—" I'm not even sure what I'm afraid of, just that I'll mess it up, that I'll mess Rufus up.

"No buts," Beatrice says.

I put the mouse on top of my fist between the fingers of the gauntlet. Rufus bobs his head, shuffles on the perch.

I kneel just outside the reach of his tether. I stretch my hand forward. I whistle and flop the mouse around.

Rufus screeches, flattens his ear tufts.

"Come on," I whisper. I whistle again, flip around the mouse. I move my fist closer.

Rufus considers the mouse, considers the fist. He flaps a tiny hop and lands on my glove.

HOLY CRUD, I HAVE AN OWL ON MY FIST!

Rufus pecks at the mouse and twitters and chirps happily, gross morsels of meat going into his beak.

I freeze, too psyched to do anything else. He's heavier than Red but still so light. His talons tighten and loosen as he takes up the mouse and begins choking it down whole. A feeling I can only call pure joy pulses through me with his grip. He trusts me.

"Gather his jesses." Beatrice unhooks the leash holding him to the perch, and then shuffles away, gives me room.

I use my free hand to tuck the jesses into the fingers of the fist with Rufus on it.

"Grip them tight. He's going to bate once he finishes, and you need to hold him."

It's a difficult balance, holding the bird while weaving my fingers around his jesses. And now I have to also worry about him diving off my fist?

"Now sit back."

This is some impossible gymnastics.

"That's it."

I'm sitting. I'm sitting and Rufus is perched on my fist. He swallows down the rest of the mouse and then looks at me. He fluffs his feathers, lifts and stretches his wings. I tense up, ready for him to bate. He glares at me. Can he sense my nerves?

I bet he can. Yes, the books all talked about the need for a falconer to "exude calm." I take a deep breath. Two. Rufus's ear tufts lift. I take two more. My heart rate slows. The ear tufts relax. Rufus squeezes my hand through the glove.

"Excellent," Beatrice murmurs.

I'm not sure how long we sit there. It feels like an eternity and also a single moment. The doorbell rings, and Rufus instantly twists his head and screeches. I startle, shifting my fist. I have pins and needles in my arm from holding it still for so long. And then he bates: Rufus flies off my fist and hits the end of the jesses, and my grip tightens, so he flops down, dangling from the strips.

"Don't panic," Beatrice says calmly. "It's just Lil. She can let herself in." She gently lifts Rufus by his chest and places him back on my fist.

He stamps and squeezes his talons and screeches, and then settles.

Beatrice smiles. "You survived."

I realize I haven't taken a breath since he bated. I suck in a gulp of air.

Rufus bates again.

Beatrice puts him back on my fist. "Now you try," she

says, showing me where my hand needs to go when he's hanging upside down.

When Rufus bates the next time, I brave lifting him myself. I have to do this—for Rufus. For me, too. I tuck my hand on his chest. He's so small and frail and light and I'm totally going to crush him with my gargantuan fingers.

But I don't.

I set him back on the glove. Rufus rouses, settles, then poops.

"That's a good sign." The pride shines off Beatrice's face.

A smile creeps along my lips. I did it. He pooped.

Dr. Cho knocks softly and comes in. "Am I interrupting?" Beatrice waves her in, and together they give Rufus a thorough checkup.

"He's fine to go into the mews," Dr. Cho says. "Though you'll need to keep up the work of manning him if you're going to fly him."

I nod. *He perched on my fist,* is all I can think. *He was comfortable enough with me to poop.* I want to sprout wings and fly with Rufus.

Dr. Cho and Beatrice go into the kitchen to start dinner. I sit on the couch with Rufus. He chirps at me. I stare at his perch area—all the books and webpages told me not to look directly at a predator bird such as a hawk, so I assume the same goes for a great horned owl. I have a lot of cleaning to do. There's a casting and whitewash running down the rock. There are little feathers floating on top of the water in Rufus's bowl.

I catch glimpses of Rufus on my fist. He appears to just be hanging out, looking around the room, bobbing his head at the slightest noise.

Beatrice pokes her head in. "Dinner."

I nod. I walk carefully, crouching low in case Rufus makes a fly for it. Rufus floats across the floor on my outstretched arm. When I hold him next to his perch, he hops onto it and stands there while I fasten the leash to the end of his jesses. Then he rouses and begins to preen. He's happy. He knows he's home.

And we're going to move him outside?

I bring this up at dinner. "Isn't it kind of a betrayal?" I ask nonchalantly, twirling spaghetti onto my fork. "I mean, to get Rufus all fat and happy in the bird room and then toss him outside in an aviary?"

"He's not a pet, Maureen," Beatrice says. "He's going to have to get used to the outside sooner or later. In the end, we're sending him home."

Home. The word lands hard in my gut. She may be talking about Rufus, but I hear the echo of this idea in my own life. Rufus and I are both here on a temporary basis. Only difference is that I don't have a home to be sent to. *Alone,* the buzz whispers. What's the next step for me? What am I going to have to get used to?

"Great horned owls are kings of the night forest," Dr. Cho says, interrupting this terrible train of thoughts. "Don't you worry about Rufus outside. It's the rest of the animal world that will be shaking in their fur." She smiles as she says this, like she's made such a great joke.

"I guess the aviary will keep him safe," I say, reluctantly taking a bite.

"That aviary has withstood ten years of hawks." Beatrice chomps down on a big bite. "It can hold one baby owl."

<hr>

After dinner, we all take Rufus out to his aviary. It's the one right next to Red's. She screeches at us, and Rufus's ear tufts go right up. He spreads his wings, hitting me in the face with his primary feathers, and raises all the feathers on his back, holding them up in a fantastic yet useless show of intimidating size. For extra measure, he begins clacking his beak.

"This is a bad sign," I say, spitting feather fluff. "We should take him back to the bird room."

"He and Red are just getting acquainted," Beatrice says.

"Red will show him who rules this roost." Dr. Cho nods toward Red's mews.

"That's what I'm afraid of," I whisper.

Beatrice opens the door and I see that she's made the

mews all cozy for Rufus. There are two big sticks nailed to the walls forming branches, and a plywood perch up near the roof in a corner. There's a rock on the floor and a bowl of water.

"It looks okay," I say. Actually, it looks a lot better than okay. And a lot nicer than our setup in the bird room.

As if mirroring my thoughts, Rufus spreads his wings. I release the jesses and let him fly off my fist up to the plywood perch, which offers the highest vantage. He looks down at us disdainfully.

Beatrice pulls a tidbit from a pouch and puts it on my fist. "Whistle."

I whistle. Rufus bobs his head. Considers my fist. I whistle again. Rufus launches from the perch and flies straight to my fist and gobbles the tidbit.

Dr. Cho and Beatrice exchange a knowing look. There must be waves of light coming off me from how glowy I feel.

Rufus finishes his meal and sits on my fist. I flick my glove slightly, and he rises into the air and flaps up to the plywood perch. He screeches, rouses, then blinks at us.

"I think he's found a home," Beatrice says, and squeezes my shoulder.

My eyes are watering again. He has, hasn't he? At least for tonight, if not for forever. "Good night, Rufus," I say.

He squawks. I'll take that as a good night.

Upstairs in my room, I take out the little box Jamie gave

me—the arc reactor. Clicked on, it's a decent night-light. I dig out my whittled hawk and put it and the arc thingy on the windowsill near the bed. I drape Mom's string of marabou around them. I never bothered decorating the room I stayed in at Gram's. I lie back on my pillow, staring at the light and the hawk, the marabou fuzz glowing like a furry halo around them. The deep black night beyond sparkles with stars. Sleep just comes, gentle as a hug.

12
Rufus

IT IS ONLY WHEN THEY CLOSE THE WEB OVER THE OPEN-
ing of this new cave that I realize the furless creatures are
not staying here with me. That I am alone in the wild darkness. With a very large and huffy hawk less than a swoop
from where I perch.

I consider hooting for help.

But who in the whole of the wild world would help a
great horned owl?

"So you're the new bird."

It's the hawk. I freeze. Flip up my ear tufts. *Blend in.*

"If you're trying to hide from me, it's not going to work.

You're in an enclosed nest, a small version of what my partner lives in. I'm in the nest next to you."

Nest?

"Meaning I can't eat you, even if I wanted to. Which I don't."

SHE'S THOUGHT ABOUT EATING ME?! The memory of the stabbing pain of the goshawk's talon through my wing nearly causes me to drop off my perch.

"Not the brightest bird in the roost, are you? You're safe. From me and everything else. Stop trembling like a chick."

Is it much of a wonder that owls hate hawks?

"Look, Owl, we're the only two birds around and I haven't had anyone to squawk with in more than a season, so get hooting."

"Was it an owl?" I ask.

"What was that?" Her talons scratch along her perch. She hadn't expected a response.

"Was it an owl who was here in this nest?"

"No," she grumbles. "It was a goshawk that thought he was above talking to a lowly red-tail."

Just the word *goshawk* sends trembles through my feathers. "I do not like goshawks."

"No bird likes goshawks." Her chirp is muffled — she must be preening. "Then again, no bird likes a great horned owl, either."

That just gets me fluffed. "You know, not all great horned owls are bad."

"All great horned owls are large, silent predators that kill you in your sleep and eat basically everything in the forest that isn't a moose, so no, maybe not bad, but certainly not something to be liked."

I bob my head, considering. "You do have a point," I hoot.

"Of course I have a point. I don't bother screeching if I don't have a point."

This hawk is the oddest combination of desperate and standoffish. Not that I have much experience with hawks. This is the first one I've ever squawked with who was not also trying to kill and eat me.

"Why are you here?" I dare to ask. "What are these enclosed nests and what do the furless creatures want with us?"

The hawk rouses her feathers. "Furless creatures? You mean my partner? We hunt food together. She chases rabbits and squirrels from the bushes and I swoop down from the trees and kill and eat them. It's quite fun."

Hunt *together?* That was my idea! "Are you saying that the furless creatures hunt in packs with hawks? Do you think they'd teach me to hunt with them?"

"*Teach* you?" The hawk practically wakes the forest with

that screech. "First of all, no self-respecting hawk hunts in packs like a fur-brained coyote. My partner is a useful assistant on the hunt.

"But more importantly, are you hooting that you don't know *how* to hunt?"

Now I'm fluffed again, and just when I had my face feathers in perfect hearing order. *Pellets*. I must calm down. Breathe in through the beak, let the cool air calm my gizzard . . .

Once my feathers are back in their places and my ear tufts are straight, I chirp back at her, "I have caught a vole. Once."

"Once?"

"Yes," I say. "And it was quite a wonderful kill, if I do say so myself."

"You've caught *one* vole?"

"Yes," I repeat, a little louder. I'm beginning to wonder if the hawk is deaf.

"Only one vole and you're, what, nearly six moons old?"

I tap out the moons with my talons. Great Beak, it has been nearly a full six moons. *Six moons* . . . "My mother," I begin, but can't finish. The hoots catch in my beak like ants in sap.

"Oh, you poor thing." The hawk's tone has changed like a summer's evening: the storm has passed and now it's warm and wet and starry and the crickets are chirruping. "Was it another bird?" she tweets.

She understands . . . "It was a monster. One of the monsters the furless creatures use to roll around the forest."

"Oh, you poor little fledgling!" the hawk screeches. "You didn't see it, did you?"

"I saw everything," I peep.

"Did she hoot at you afterward?" Her tweet is flat.

"She told me to fly away. I didn't. I tried to follow the monster."

"The human took her?" Now her chirp is brighter, her heartbeat faster.

"The furless creature—you call them humans? The human took her. It threw a skin over her and picked her up like a piece of prey and put her inside the monster."

"Oh!" Again, the screech sends the whole forest squeaking and rustling. "What news! That's the best thing that could have happened!" The hawk is flapping around her nest, shrieking with joy. "The human probably brought her someplace like here. Sometimes my partner takes a bird that has been hit by those growling, shiny monstrosities and helps it get better. When it's healed, she lets it go back into the sky."

I run my beak over my hurt wing. It feels better—no stinging, no burning. It's even less stiff. The furless creatures made me better. Could it be that somewhere, a furless crea-ture is helping Mother get better too?

"Do you really think so?" I can barely let myself dream that it's true.

"I do," the hawk says, stamping her talons. "And when you're better, they'll send you out to find her. Hopefully after they teach you to hunt. You can call me Red, by the bye."

At first, hearing those chirps, I'm ready to fly off this very heartbeat. But then somewhere out in the night, the yip of a fox echoes. And I'm reminded of all the terrible things out-side these walls that are waiting for a meal to fly into their snouts. A helpless, hopeless owl of a meal. An owl who's only ever caught one vole in his whole stupid short life.

"Don't get fluffed, Owl," Red twitters. "I'll help you learn how to hunt. My partner will help too, I'm sure of it. We won't send you out to starve and be eaten by a bumble-footed goshawk."

Relief like smooth fur down my gullet calms my feath-ers. "You really don't like goshawks."

Red clacks her beak. "No one likes goshawks. Great big feathers-for-brains bullies." She grumbles softly to herself for a few more heartbeats, and then I hear her snuffling in her sleep.

The furless creatures *are* here to help birds. They help birds get better and then let them fly free. And Red's going to teach me to hunt. I'll catch a vole—no, two voles—no,

THREE voles *and* a mouse and scarf them all down! And then, I'll be set free to find Mother and First and Father. They'll be waiting for me in the branches, wings wide. We'll fly together through the velvet night and hoot as loudly as we want!

HOOT-HOO-HOO-HOOT!

"Gizzards and crops!" Red squawks, sounding completely fluffed. "Please, Owl, do keep it down for us day birds."

"Sorry, Red."

"Blasted owls," she grumbles. "Hooting all night. Waking me from the nicest dream. Here, squirrelly . . . I see your fluffy tail wiggling . . ."

I twitter softly to myself, just imagining her crouched on her perch, ready to pounce on her dream squirrel.

That's going to be me, I hoot to myself. I'm going to learn how to hunt. I'm going to fly free.

I find a comfortable perch in this warm and safe nest and listen to the world of the night—my world, the world of the owl—chitter and snuffle and scrape and chirp all around me.

13
Reenie

"NOW A LITTLE FARTHER FROM THE PERCH," BEATRICE commands. We're back inside the bird room, and Rufus is hopping from the perch to my fist.

Most of the time.

This time, I'm apparently too far for him to bother with flying for the tidbit. He clasps and unclasps his talons, shifting around on the perch. He swivels his head to check out the rest of the room.

"I could move closer," I say. Maybe I'm pushing him too fast. It's Saturday, and we've been working on this every minute I haven't been in school, but still . . .

Beatrice sighs. "No, he's done," she says. "But you got a few good hops in there. I think we can try him on the creance soon." The creance is a long string you tie to your bird's jesses so that he can fly to you from farther away without you having to worry that he's going to fly off entirely.

It's also something you only use outside.

"We're going to fly him outside?" The thought of flying Rufus through the sunset sky, of us soaring through the trees, curls my lips into a smile. But the buzz whispers, *Alone.*

Falconers lose hawks outside. Even on the creance, Rufus could snag the string on a sharp edge and escape, or I could drop the creance and he'd be lost.

"We'll start by just walking him around outside." Beatrice takes off her work gloves. "Then we'll see if he wants to fly."

Panic skitters like spiders underneath my skin. "But he could hurt his wing."

Beatrice looks at him. "He's not even favoring it anymore. I think he's ready."

But what if she's wrong? What if his wing can't take the strain? What if he crashes and it gets worse? *What if I ruin him?* the buzz whispers.

"But it's only been a few days," I say.

"He's a young bird and he's healing well," Beatrice says, standing. "He's got to get back in the air." She folds her arms across her chest. "He has to stay wild, remember. He's not a pet."

"But what about manning him?" I'm ready to scoop Rufus up and hide him in my sweatshirt—I do not want to think about letting him go, not for months, not until the spring. *Not ever.*

Beatrice smiles. "I'm not worried about manning this bird."

I turn around and see that Rufus has hopped off his perch and is pecking at the zipper on my hoodie, which dangles from my waist. I roll onto my butt to get a better look, dragging the zipper across the floor, and Rufus hops after it, grabbing with his talons.

A laugh burbles out from between my lips, the panic scatters, the buzz quiets. "Is he playing?"

"What do you think he's doing?" Beatrice asks.

I untie the sleeves of my hoodie so I can drag it farther and get Rufus to stretch his legs. My wood carving from recess on Friday flops out of my pocket.

"What's this?" Beatrice asks, picking it up.

The buzz whispers, *Dangerous.* Do I tell her? Is it safe to share? I decide to just go for it.

"It's going to be an owl," I say, keeping my eyes on Rufus's silly dance. "My friend—I mean, this kid at school, Jaxon? He whittles. But he can't bring a knife to school, so we're whittling with pens. That's why there's blue smudges."

I glance up, and Beatrice has this queer smile on her lips as she turns the wood over in her hands.

"Huh." She hands it back to me. "I like it."

There's a little release inside, like air from a bag of chips.

"Me too," I say, looking at my owl. The other owl, the real one, has captured my zipper and is ripping his beak through the fabric around it.

"Rufus, no!" I yelp, and go to pull the sweatshirt back.

"Stop!" Beatrice snaps. I freeze. There's that shiver of fear, the crackle of buzz—*I've ruined it, she's had enough of me*—but it fizzles away just as quickly. I get that the yelling is about Rufus; I understand that she's protecting us both.

"Never take prey from your bird," Beatrice—no, Aunt Bea—instructs. She kneels down beside me. "You're building trust here. He's not a dog; he's a predator and you're his partner. He's caught some interesting prey. Now you have to make a switch."

She hands me what looks like an old dog toy with the wings of a dead bird stuck into it.

"That's gross," I say.

"That's a lure," she says. "See if he'll take it instead."

I bend forward, sliding the lure across the floor. I push it right up to Rufus's talons. He's too busy shredding the hem of my sweatshirt. Aunt Bea jerks her hand, and the lure jumps—it's attached to a string.

That got Rufus's attention: the tufts are up.

She jerks it again.

Rufus's ear tufts lie back. His eyes are glued on the lure. His wings droop down, a sign he's ready to fly.

She jerks the lure again.

Rufus is up and pounces on the lure. He screeches and flaps and tears with his talons and then with his beak.

"Get that sweatshirt out of here," Aunt Bea whispers.

I sneak my shirt away and toss it out the door into the kitchen.

Aunt Bea is still jerking and flapping the lure around and Rufus is screeching and lumbering after it, wings wide in an attempt to look big and intimidating. I can tell Aunt Bea is trying not to laugh at him. We have the same smile burning across our faces. Rufus, though, is oblivious, as he's completely focused on attacking the skittering lure.

"Owls hunt with their ears," Aunt Bea says. "We have to figure out how to make a lure that focuses his hearing."

"The dog toy!" I whisper. I creep around to where I found the basket of old dog toys. There are a bunch of thin plastic squeaky things, but I need something that can stand up to a talon. I find a thin rope toy with a tough-looking rubber ball attached to its middle. The ball has a bell buried inside it. *Perfect*. I crawl back, waving it.

Aunt Bea stares at the toy for a second—did she not know they were there?—then shrugs. "Tie a string to it."

I find some twine in the kitchen. I use one of my

loop-knots I practiced for the bal-chatri trap—it's perfect. Aunt Bea has Rufus on the opposite side of the perch. I swing the rope toy slightly, giving off a faint jingle.

Rufus's head instantly swivels. I've got two yellow eyes on me. No, not on me—on the toy.

He screeches and flaps right over the perch, attacking the toy.

"Yes," hisses Aunt Bea. "That's it."

"Did you see that?" I whisper. Rufus is attacking the toy, pulling tufts of string from it.

"We should stop him before he gets to the bell."

"Oh," I say. "How?"

She looks at me, eyebrows raised. She thinks I know the answer? Wait, *do* I know the answer?

A tidbit. What's better than pretend food? Real food. And maybe after all this shredding, Rufus is hungry again.

I pull a scrap of mouse from the pouch I have hooked on my jeans.

Aunt Bea smiles. "You've got it. Now flick it to the side."

I flip it off my finger like a freshly picked booger and Rufus instantly whips his head to follow its flight, his reflexes so fast it's like he knew I would flick it. He flaps and pounces on the meat. Aunt Bea sneaks a hand lightning-fast across the floor and grabs the toy, hiding it in a pocket of her cardigan.

Rufus gulps the tidbit down, turns his big eyes to me.

"Now get him on the fist," Aunt Bea says.

I nod, stick a tidbit on my glove, whistle, shake my fist.

He squawks. And then hops up onto my fist. He gulps the tidbit down, then stands there, chirping and peeping and twisting his head in circles.

Aunt Bea tips her head to us. "That bird is manned."

I manage to do all my reading for English class with Rufus sitting on my fist. Aunt Bea calls me for dinner, and I hook Rufus back onto the leash and let him hop off my fist onto the perch. He squawks, then rouses and begins to preen. He knows he's safe. He knows he's home.

I hunch over my bowl and eat my soup. This isn't Rufus's home, though. At some point, after he's come to love this house, after he feels safe, he's going to get thrown back into the wild to fend for himself.

I can't let him get soft. He can't forget where he came from.

After dinner, instead of working with Rufus on my fist like I'd planned, I put him back in the aviary. I sit at the kitchen table alone and finish my math homework while Aunt Bea reads in the living room.

I haven't written to Mom since Monday. I've gotten two letters from her. She's on a new dose of her medication. She thinks it's helping already.

I want to believe her. I want to trust that it's for good this time. But I want to do that every time.

This golden light floods through the windows and turns the whole house into a honey-scape. The numbers float on the page. I close my math book. Aunt Bea is flipping through her book, which I see now is actually a photo album.

"Are those pictures of your daughter?" I ask, walking over to the couch.

Aunt Bea smiles tightly. "No," she says, moving over to let me sit beside her. "These are pictures of my dog, Buckles." She turns the page and there's this scrawny wirehaired little dog. "He died a year ago. Used to help me and Red hunt."

Gulp. "Are those *his* toys Rufus is destroying?" Now I feel bad.

She snuffles a little laugh. "Yes," she says. "But better he eat them than they be left collecting dust in the corner." She runs her thumb along the edge of a picture of Buckles in the grass, paws down, butt up, ready to chase something. "Buckles would have wanted a raptor to have his toys."

She flips slowly through the pages. There's one old picture with a girl who looks my age. She has stick-straight white-blond hair and holds Buckles like a baby in her arms —the daughter.

"That's Ava," Aunt Bea says, turning the page toward me. "We adopted Buckles together when her father and I first . . . when we divorced. He and his new wife decided to move to St. Louis a year later for some job. Ava went with them."

"She wanted to go?" I ask, because I can't imagine wanting to leave here.

"The judge—" She stops. "Sometimes you don't get to choose."

I didn't choose to come here. It won't be my choice to leave, either. Why would I ever want to leave this place? But then I feel Mom like some ghost limb, a part of me that's been taken. I don't even have a picture of her—no one prints photos anymore. All I have of us is the marabou, and it's lost most of its fluff.

Aunt Bea flips to the next page—Buckles again, this time with Red blurry in the sky behind him. "Ava visited during the holidays and a few weeks in the summer. And we talked on the phone. But she's older now. She's in college, studying to be a nurse. Last time she emailed me, she mentioned a boyfriend she was thinking of moving in with, after graduation." She stares at the picture like she's looking for Ava hovering in the shadows.

Aunt Bea looks so sad. The buzz crackles: *Dangerous.* What if Aunt Bea's like Mom—what if the sadness takes her, too? I can't believe I got her talking about this—typical me. I have to fix this.

"You should invite her back," I say. "I could sleep in the

bird room." I have to force the words out. I don't want to give up my room.

Aunt Bea smiles, closes the book. "Even if Ava did come back," she says, "you'd sleep in your room."

Why does hearing her call it that make me want to cry? Because it's not my room. Not my house, not my homework, not my anything.

And now I *am* crying.

Aunt Bea seems flustered. "Oh, Maureen, I'm sorry. I didn't mean to upset you. I'm just . . . I'm not very good at people." She finds a box of tissues and hands it to me.

My insides roll and twist and the buzz screams, *DAN-GEROUS*, and I have to get away.

"I should check on Rufus," I say, wiping my face clean on my sleeve.

"Wait," Aunt Bea says, placing her hand on my arm.

I sink into her touch, back down onto the couch.

"I meant that about the room," she says. "When they called me about taking you in, they said I had to be prepared for it being for good. I had to agree to that. And I want you to know that. Because I meant it when I said it to the judge, and I mean it now."

The buzz shivers along my skin: *Dangerous*. But it feels wrong. Aunt Bea is not Mom.

"No matter what happens, you always have a place here,

okay, Maureen?" She looks at me straight on, in this way most grownups don't even use with each other.

That look melts the buzz away. I decide to try something different, to try trust. "Okay," I say.

Her lips curl into a small smile, and I know she knows that my whole soul has up and wrapped itself around her.

"Reenie," I say.

"What?"

"Call me Reenie."

She looks confused.

"It's my nickname," I explain. "You can call me it," I add. "I mean, if you want to."

She snorts a little laugh. "Reenie." She chews the name over. "It suits you."

That night, as I sleep, I listen to Rufus hooting like a one-owl rock band out in the night. I know what he's feeling: he's found a home.

14
Rufus

"I HUNTED!" I HOOT TO RED, WHO'S PRETENDING TO BE asleep in her nest. "I heard the root tweeting and I hunted it dead!"

"Gah! Owls! Don't you ever sleep?" Red squawks, snapping her wings and stomping her talons. "That's not hunting, Owl. That's practice."

"What are you talking about?" I chirp. "I heard the root and I pounced. It was in shreds when I finished."

"It was a root, though?" asks Red.

"*Yes,*" I say, restating the obvious. Honestly, this bird listens to less than half of my hoots.

"I doubt it was an actual root," she says, chattering on. "But regardless, if it wasn't prey, it wasn't hunting. It was practice to help you get into your instincts."

Get into my instincts? "No way," I squawk, flapping over to the rock perch to mute. "The root tweeted, and I killed it dead."

"Fine. Seeing as you're the expert hunter of the pair of us," she grumbles, "I'm sure you're right."

"Now, that's just rude."

"Owl, I sleep at night. Please shut your beak."

She rouses her feathers, tromps around her perch, and is silent.

Could she be right? Could my amazing feats of murder and destruction really only be practice?

Of course it's just practice. Obviously only the Worst Owl—no, Worst Bird of Prey—in the Whole Forest thinks hunting a squeaking root is the same as hunting a mouse. Mice are cunning. Mice have legs. Mice are sneaky on their tiny sneaky feet.

I have to practice on living things. But where am I going to find a living thing?

Something small smacks into the wall of my nest. A buzzing thing. A bug!

Yes, perfect. I will hunt bugs.

Now, where is that bug?

I lift my feathers, twist and turn them, sculpting the

sounds the way my wings work the wind. The night around me takes shape. Far away, I hear the leaves of the forest trees rustling. Closer, the blades of grass slipping along the stalks of their neighbors. Heartbeats—hundreds of them, some close, some far—pound out pulses, making the once silent darkness a thrum of noise.

It's too much. I can't hear anything but noise everywhere.

The bug buzzes, flying off, its wing-whipping whir getting softer and softer.

I failed. Again.

I'll never hunt.

I close my eyes, bury my head as deep as I can between my wings, muffling the great roar of noise, that deafening blast of information I have no idea how to pick apart.

◆

The first flicker of sunlight cracks across the stars, and somewhere outside my nest, voices whisper. And then the furless creatures are walking alongside the web around my nest. The Brown Frizz is radiating energy, but the Gray Tail looks half-asleep. They're chirping at each other, and then they split the web.

The Brown Frizz is wearing her paw with meat and chirping, so I flap down as has become our custom. The meat sets my gizzard grumbling, and I decide that even the Most Pathetic Owl Who Couldn't Hear a Bug Unless It Was Buzzing Up His Butt deserves to eat every once in a while.

The Gray Tail slips the little strips of skin into my leg sparkles and the Brown Frizz grabs on to them.

I contemplate trying to fly off and tear those stinking skin strips right off my sparkles, but every time I attempt this feat, I end up in a bat hang, so I decide to give up that particular thought. At least for the moment.

The Brown Frizz begins walking with me through the grass. Red was right: my enclosed nest does look a bit like a smaller breed of the one that the furless creatures sleep inside. The forest I listened to all night looks thick and dark and full of menacing creatures hungry for a bite of owl.

"Brown Frizz," I squawk. "I don't think I am going to be a very good hunting partner. In fact, to be clear, I may never catch any prey that isn't a root."

The Brown Frizz does not seem upset by my hoots. Rather, her beakless maw is twisted into what I've come to understand as a sign of Good Feelings. She growls something and then holds out some meat.

"All right," I say. "I will eat your offering. But I want to be clear—I am not a hunter, and I will only reliably kill roots."

The Brown Frizz mumbles something and keeps making her Good Feelings face. Maybe she only wants to catch roots? No, that can't be it. The Brown Frizz could very well catch a root on her own. No—she must know something

I don't. Or she just trusts that I'm more than just a root catcher . . .

"Well, you are certainly not what I expected."

I whip my head around and there's Red sitting on old Gray Tail's featherless wing. She's quite a big hawk, with a sleek head tapering to a long, sharp, hooked beak. Her red feathers seem to glow in the skinny shafts of sunlight.

"How's that?" I ask, trying to ruffle up my dull tree-bark-brown feathers. I straighten out my ear tufts and fan my tail.

She turns her head, examining the yard around us. "I was expecting a half-plucked hatchling. You're a real bird."

That gets my feathers fluffed. *"Half-plucked hatchling?"*

She flaps her wings and flies to a stumpy tree sticking up in the yard. "With the way you were grousing all night about never being able to hunt and getting eaten by a clutch of field mice? I thought to myself, *No way a full-grown owl would dare to even dream of such a pathetic end.* But I see I was wrong on at least one count." She gives me a long stare over her hooked beak.

She *heard* me? That was a terrible nightmare. How could she have heard anything? Great Beak—was I hooting in my sleep?

This is bad. Even for the Absolute Worst Great Horned Owl in All of Owldom.

"It was just a dream," I chitter. I try to flap over to another one of those stumpy trees in the yard—it appears that the blighted corpses of several trees remain sticking up in the grass—but I hit the end of those blasted leg tails and end up hanging tufts down.

"That's more what I was expecting," Red chirps, her eyes bright.

She thinks this is *funny?!* "DO NOT LAUGH AT ME!" I screech, flapping and thrashing.

The Brown Frizz hisses. Her paw reaches out. Distracted, I forget to thrash and suddenly I'm upright. I grasp the clenched paw beneath me. The Brown Frizz's heart skips along happily and she makes her Good Feelings face.

She helped me. Again. She always helps.

She holds out a little scrap of meat. I gobble it down.

She believes I can be a hunter. A hunter of more than roots. Of mice, of voles—of squirrels, even.

She believes in me.

Maybe I need to give this partnership thing a try.

15
Reenie

"WALK HIM SLOWLY," AUNT BEA SAYS. WE'RE GETTING Rufus used to the backyard. It's a step on the way to flying him on the creance.

"More slowly than this?" I'm barely moving. It's six a.m., so I'm also barely awake.

She shakes her fist. "Follow his cues."

Right. Partners focus on each other. Rufus lifts his tail. I'm moving too fast. I roll my boots through the grass. He settles into a more upright perch.

"Excellent," Aunt Bea whispers.

But I knew that before she said anything. I can do this.

Third period, we're given detailed assignment sheets, with our group and topic printed at the top, that we have to fill out for our project. We march down to the library to begin research on the laptops. Jamie, Jaxon, and I sign out our computers and claim a round table hidden in the stacks. It's like our own private fort.

"I declare this table for hunting," I say, stabbing my pencil—eraser down—in the center.

Jamie whips out her pencil and jams it next to mine. "For hunting!"

Jaxon pulls out his whittling pen, places it next to ours. "Hunting."

"How are you guys doing?" Mr. Brown says cheerily as he appears from between two shelves.

"I'm doing falconry," I announce.

"I hunt deer with my dad," Jaxon offers.

"I'm a vegetarian," Jamie says.

Mr. Brown's face curdles. "Um, okay, well—let's see. Ms. L'Esperance, you seem to have a focused topic. Mr. Doucet, I like your focus on deer hunting."

"I'm doing the rules," Jaxon says. "My dad's a game warden."

"Excellent!" Mr. Brown cheers. "Now you just need a part for Ms. Hendricks by the end of the period. Get researching!" He claps his hands and moves on to another group.

"Maybe I can make the poster?" Jamie suggests. "I can make charts on my computer at home."

"Each of us has to present something," I say, pointing to the assignment sheet's bulleted list of project requirements.

"It's just that, with hunting, all I can think of is the poor deer."

"Deer meat is food," Jaxon says. "You might not eat meat, but other people do." His scowl is the most emotion I've ever seen him show.

Hoo boy. I try the trick I use with Rufus: I exude calm. I open my laptop. "Let's see if Wikipedia has anything helpful."

Jamie ignores me, her eyes focused on Jaxon. "But hunting is different. A chicken on a farm has got to know life is short, but a wild deer?"

"So I can hunt a chicken?"

"Well, no, that would also be awful."

"Now hunting is awful?!"

"Um, I mean, maybe?"

Jaxon's face has knotted into a snarl. He digs out his whittling and gives the wood a violent scrape. Jamie begins chewing her hair like she hasn't eaten in days.

The buzz pops: *Dangerous*. Our group partnership is crumbling. I've seen it too many times with Gram and Mom not to know. It starts with Gram getting on Mom about something small—*You can't leave pans in the sink* or *Any normal person can keep a job at Walmart*—and like a fuzz on a sweater, all it takes is a few prying pokes to start the whole thing unraveling. Twenty minutes later, Gram's slamming drawers and Mom's crying in the shower. I always just want to scream at them, *Stop picking! You love each other! Start there!*

Maybe that's what I need to say here?

"Guys," I say, closing the computer. "So Jamie doesn't like hunting. Remember last week, when you two couldn't stop fighting over whether what's-his-face with a hammer could beat the other dude with a pitchfork?"

Jamie snorts. "You mean Thor versus Aquaman?"

"It's Thor," Jaxon says, repeating his conclusion from Friday's lunch.

Jamie rolls her eyes.

"See?" I say. "Maybe we should do something like that. You could debate the issue." I point to the assignment sheet, which lists "debate" as a possible format for the project.

"Debate hunting?" Jaxon says, dubious.

"Yeah," I say. "Jamie could talk about what she thinks is bad, and you could argue the opposite."

Jamie scrolls through a site. "There's a whole page here on the positive impacts of hunting."

Jaxon glances over at her screen. "I don't see any negative impacts, so there's no debate."

"What about the literal negative impact on the deer?" Jamie asks.

"It's food," Jaxon barks.

"You've already started on your debate!" I say, slapping them both on the shoulders. "You've had so much practice with superheroes, it'll be nothing to switch over to hunting."

Jamie snorts a laugh. "I guess."

Jaxon shrugs. "I bet more of the class agrees with me."

Jamie smiles. "Not after my presentation."

Jaxon half smiles back. "Want to bet?"

Then they both look at me.

"Great idea, Iron Woman," Jamie says.

Jaxon opens his laptop. "That's why I said Reenie should be the leader."

"Actually, I think it was my idea," Jamie says, typing something.

I fill out the assignment sheet while they continue this new debate. A flower of warmth blooms inside me, tickling a smile from my lips. They worked things out—*we* worked things out, together. They think I have great ideas.

The bell rings for lunch. We close up our laptops and I follow them to the caf. I sit at an empty table with my hot lunch and just stir the slimy jumble the lady said was beef stroganoff. Some boys start to sit with me, but I tell them I'm saving seats.

Saving seats. It's weird to even say the words. To be waiting for someone—someone*s*—and know they are going to show up. I have never felt lonely before. You can't feel lonely if alone is your natural state. But just now, watching those boys walk away, looking at the empty seats, I felt lonely. And it felt good.

Jamie and Jaxon sit down.

"Thank you," I say.

"For what?" Jamie says, opening her chocolate milk. She brings her lunch but buys a milk every day.

"For thinking I could be Iron Woman," I say. "For being nice to me in general."

Jamie makes this face like I'm speaking Nepalese. "I thought you were the one being nice to me." She sucks down her milk.

"Yeah," Jaxon adds. He's a boy of few words.

"What's crazy is that anyone would thank anyone else for that," Jamie goes on. "Shouldn't we all just be nice to one another? Shouldn't that be the normal thing?"

I shrug. "But it's not."

She pulls out her sandwich and takes a big bite. "No, it's not."

Daring bubbles up into my throat. "You guys could come

home with me on the bus if you wanted. I mean, if that was something—for the hunting project," I blurt.

Both Jamie and Jaxon look somewhere between confused and worried. I've pushed it too far, too fast. The buzz roars. I should have listened. Friends are dangerous.

"That'd be cool," Jaxon says.

"I can text my mom," Jamie says, pulling out her phone from a pocket.

The buzz fizzles away as quickly as it flared up. My jaw loosens, gut unknots itself, heartbeat slows. They want to come over. It was that easy. Just make the offer.

Of course, it's an easy offer to invite kids to Aunt Bea's house. There's no fear that Mom's crying in the bathroom. No landlord lurking, looking for rent. No Phil. And I saw a box of crackers in the pantry I can offer as a snack. It's easy to invite a friend over when your home doesn't feel like it's perched on a branch that's about to snap.

Jamie puts the phone back in her pocket. "My mom says okay." She continues eating.

Jaxon digs in his bag, sandwich in his other hand, pulls out a phone, texts his mom, then says, "Yeah."

I've got this smile so big, I can barely close my mouth over the spork. "Cool," I say.

The three of us spend the bus ride home coming up with supervillain nicknames for our teachers.

"Ms. Smythe is the Rock," I say.

"No, the Ice Queen," Jamie says, leaning across the aisle.

"The Ice *Cube*," Jaxon says. "For math."

We all agree—Ice Cube it is.

When we get home, I find the crackers and fill some mason jars from the tap. It's kind of cheap, but Jamie and Jaxon don't say anything. We're too busy negotiating a name for Ms. Thomas, the English teacher.

"Something evil," I say, "because she's so mean and yet pretends to be nice."

"*She's* the Ice Queen," Jaxon says, pointing a shard of cracker at me.

"Two-Face," Jamie states.

Jaxon considers the proposal. "The bad guy from *Batman*?" he asks.

Jamie nods, shoving a stack of crackers into her mouth. She glances at my face. "I'll give you an explanatory comic."

"Perfect," I say. Jamie's instructing me in comprehending Jamie-Jaxon-ese.

But the name "Two-Face" claws its way under my skin. I have so many secrets. If I told them even one, would they be here now?

"So your aunt lives here with your family?" Jamie asks. "Your aunt's the falconer, right?"

"My aunt—" I begin. Any answer is either a lie or a risk.

I wait for the buzz, but no hiss rises. "I live with my aunt," I say, testing the truth. "My mom—she's sick."

"Oh," Jamie says.

"That's rough," Jaxon says.

"That's super rough," Jamie adds, like he gave her the right word to use.

"It is," I say. And this relief like cool water fills me to my forehead.

Jaxon grabs another cracker. "These are good."

Jamie crunches a bite of hers. "They're like healthy cookies."

"I wouldn't go that far," I say, checking the ingredients on the side of the box.

And we all kind of laugh. I opened this tiny piece of myself up to them, and they stayed. They think my crackers are good enough to be called cookies.

I put the box down. "Do you guys want to meet Red?"

They both jump out of their chairs.

When Aunt Bea comes home, she kind of freezes when she sees the two additional kids in the yard.

"I wanted to show them Red," I say. "For our hunting project."

She drops her keys into a pocket. "Then I won't take my coat off."

Aunt Bea is a pro; she explains everything step by step to

Jaxon and Jamie. "These buildings are called mews, which is where the birds live. This glove I'm putting on is called a gauntlet."

When she brings Red out, Jamie and Jaxon nearly fall over. Watching Red soar, I feel like a proud mom—as if I have anything to do with her magnificence.

"You want to try calling her?" Aunt Bea asks Jamie and Jaxon.

Jamie nearly faints. Jaxon holds out his arm. Aunt Bea gives him a glove and then puts a tidbit on it and whistles. Red comes soaring down and even Jaxon can't help but laugh and smile like a goof. Aunt Bea shows him how to cast Red, and she glides off into the trees. Jamie regains the power of speech and asks for a turn. She too seems nearly blown over by Red's swoop to her fist.

"Can I show them Rufus?" I can't *not* show him to them. Not when they've seen all this. They'd be missing the most important part.

Aunt Bea's face clouds over. "Rufus," she says. "Well, uh, I guess that would be all right."

"Thank you!" I'm practically popping, I'm so excited. I put on my gauntlet and go into Rufus's mews. "Hey, buddy," I whisper, trying to calm down for him.

Rufus's eyes crack open.

I put a tidbit on my fist, whistle. He swoops down, and my heart jumps and races—every time it's as amazing as the first. As he gobbles the meat, I take a deep, calming breath before tucking his jesses into the fingers of my glove and tying on the short leash from the jesses to my glove. I walk slowly out into the sunshine.

"This," I say, "is Rufus."

Jaxon and Jamie gape at his gloriousness. Aunt Bea nods, eyebrows raised, encouraging me to say more.

"He's a great horned owl," I say. He bobs his head and lifts his ear tufts. "These feathers are called plumicorns."

"Like unicorns!" Jamie squeals.

"They're not magic," Jaxon says.

"How do you know?" I say defensively, smiling at my dragon bird.

"Where'd you get him?" asks Jaxon.

"We're rehabilitating him," I explain.

"Rehabilitating?" Jamie asks.

I tell the whole story—about the bal-chatri trap, the passage hawk, trapping Rufus by accident. My audience is entranced.

"He's a rehab bird?" Jaxon asks. "But he has jesses."

"Part of his rehabilitation," Aunt Bea says quickly.

Why's she so jumpy? "We're getting his wings back in shape," I add.

Jaxon looks confused. What is he confused about?

Rufus's head turns toward the driveway. A car pulls in, sending up a cloud of dust.

"My mom," Jaxon says.

"Can I pet him?" Jamie asks, ignoring the waiting parent, even though it's her ride.

"Better not," Aunt Bea says. "That owl's still a very wild bird."

"And even Red's not a pet," I add. "She's just used to the attention."

Aunt Bea smiles approvingly.

Jamie nods, a little sulky but not angry or mean. "I get it."

"This was awesome," Jaxon says, handing the glove back to Aunt Bea.

"I totally see why you wanted to do falconry," Jamie adds, slipping off hers.

"It's pretty cool," I say, trying to not be too obvious about how much it means to me that they get it. It's like they weren't fully my friends until they also knew about this —my Rufus half. And like Rufus wasn't fully real until I shared him—all this, with them.

Aunt Bea puts Red back in the aviary and goes to introduce herself to Jaxon's mom. I hang on to Rufus while Jaxon and Jamie grab their stuff from the house. I wave with my free arm as they hop into the waiting car.

"See you tomorrow!" I shout.

"Bye, Rufus!" Jamie replies. "See you tomorrow, Reenie!"

Jaxon gives me his signature single wave.

As the car pulls onto the road, Aunt Bea walks back to where I'm strolling with Rufus through the grass.

"Those are some nice kids," she says.

"I know," I say, feeling full up with happiness and afraid of spilling any by talking too much.

Aunt Bea gets it. She doesn't say anything more, just takes Red out. Rufus and I watch her soar over our heads across the brilliant blue sky and pink-tinged clouds.

At school the next day, while we're putting away our laptops in the library, Jaxon sneaks up beside me. "You're not training that owl for falconry, right?"

"Rufus?" I say. "Well, not officially."

"But you're going to let him go back to the wild?"

Weird—why does he care? I mean, we're friends now—there's no way he'd turn me in to his dad. "That's the plan," I say.

Jaxon's face relaxes. "Cool."

Jamie slides her laptop into the slot. "If I had an owl like that, I could never let him go."

Jamie gets it.

"But that owl's a wild bird," Jaxon says. "No one owns the wild."

Jamie shrugs. "I'm just saying, having an owl in your house is too cool."

Jaxon shoves his hands in his pockets. "It's not about what's cool, it's about what's best for the owl."

"I would never do anything to hurt Rufus," I say. Which is true. But there's a part of me that's with Jamie—how is living with me hurting him? And why does Jaxon care?

"I know," he says. "I just . . . it's nothing."

It's weird for a second, but then Jamie whips out her phone and shows us this crazy video she found of a deer jumping on a trampoline and everything is okay again.

When I get home after school, I'm greeted by the alien song of the phone ringing. Aunt Bea got a super basic cell phone that she leaves in the house for me in case of emergencies. Who even knows the number?

"Hello?" I ask, like this is the first phone call in the history of the world.

"Reenie?"

Mom.

"Reenie! It's Mom. I arranged for phone contact. Is this time okay?"

"Uh." It takes me a second to catch up. We've done this before. During the other times. I just have to reshuffle my brain, my life. Readjust. "Hey."

We chat for a couple minutes. She's good, getting help. I'm happy for her—I say so.

"The social worker, Randi?" Mom says. "She's been

really supportive. When I get released, I'm going to start looking at apartments."

"Oh?" I say.

"We can visit again. I miss you, Reens. I miss us."

"I miss you too," I say. And I do. But her doing well is also the beginning of the end of my time here. I've been through this cycle enough times to know. And though I've been reminding myself—I say it every night like a prayer but opposite: *this life is temporary*—it's stopped feeling temporary. This isn't Gram's junk room; this is a whole life. It's stopped feeling like something I can live without.

When we hang up, I say, "I love you too," and I do. But there's also this icy feeling inside, like loving her means I'm halfway out the door of this place, and I can't leave. Not yet.

I sit down to do homework, but my foot starts jiggling, sending mini earthquakes across the kitchen table, which only causes the foot jiggling situation to get worse. By the time Aunt Bea comes in, I'm practically vibrating myself out of the chair.

"Is everything all right?" she asks, face quirked as if questioning a bear sampling her butter straight from the fridge.

"My mom called," I say.

Aunt Bea gives a nod. "You okay?"

I shrug.

"She say something?"

I shake my head no.

"Don't get yourself worked up until you know what it is that's coming," she says, slipping on her falconer's vest. "We have to feed the birds."

The mention of a job helps to pull me back into myself. "I'll get the mice," I say, relieved to know what to do, that there is a right thing to be done.

"*I'll* get the mice," Aunt Bea says. "You can head right out and hook that owl onto a creance."

Just the word sends shivers over my skin and the foot jiggles packing. "We're going to try flying him?" I ask.

She nods. "I think you're both ready."

This warmth spreads through me. *We* are *ready*, I tell myself. And I can feel that it's true. Because even if he doesn't fly to my fist tonight, even if every attempt is a failure, I can always just put him back on my glove. Every failure is just a step in our process. Some night, even if not tonight, Rufus will fly to me.

16

Rufus

"FINALLY!" I SCREECH AS THE BROWN FRIZZ OPENS THE web on my nest. "I've been hooting for food since the last drop of the sun."

"I told you the hooting wouldn't make them come any faster," Red squawks from her nest.

"How do you know it didn't?" I chirp back. "The Brown Frizz may never have returned if not for my hooting."

"The Brown Frizz is your partner." Red rouses, stomps on her perch. "Partners always come back."

I consider the Brown Frizz. She has on her Good

Feelings face, but her heart is not in it. She holds up her big paw and makes her tweeting noise, and I swoop down.

"I can hear that there's something wrong with you," I hoot to her softly, trying to keep Red from listening in. "If it's about what I hooted yesterday, I will make more of an effort to hunt things other than roots."

The Brown Frizz's heart becomes less jumbled in its rhythm, smoothes out, and the Good Feelings face deepens. Perhaps that was all she needed to hear.

"Not that I'm promising anything," I add.

The Brown Frizz remains content. Maybe this is a part of our partnership arrangement. Maybe the only promise she needs is that I'll try.

She puts the odious tails into my leg sparkles, and that just about gets me fluffed because truly those tails are the worst, but then she does something new. She attaches a long, thin vine to the end of the tails. Outside of my nest, she holds her fist near one of the dead trees.

"Hop onto the perch, Hatchling," Red squawks. She's perched right near an opening in her nest. Spying on me.

"I was about to," I snap back. Though I was not. This partnership thing is confusing. One moment, the Brown Frizz wants me on her paw; the next, she wants me on the perch?

Once I'm on the perch, the Brown Frizz takes a step

away from me. I glance at Red, check if she's still spying. Of course she is.

The Brown Frizz whistles. Shakes her paw. She wants me to get back on the paw? But I just got off the paw! Is there meat? There'd better be meat.

I flap off the perch and onto the paw, and thank the thermals, there's meat for my effort. I gobble it down. The Brown Frizz is all atwitter, hooting and trembling like something important is happening.

The Gray Tail appears from the furless creatures' nest. She seems excited by the Brown Frizz's hoots. She hurries toward me and the Brown Frizz, and I see she has a small pile of delicious mice in her wing-toes.

"Give me those mice!" I command. I am the great horned owl around here. I should get first pick. Certainly before the Brown Frizz.

I attempt to lift off the paw and—*PELLETS!* I'm tufts down again and swinging like a bat.

"I just cannot get enough of seeing you hanging from your talons," Red twitters from inside her nest.

"Go stuff your beak in the sap."

The Brown Frizz dutifully sits me back up on the paw. But now I'm fluffed. I'm hungry and Red's a bumble-footed booby and these leg-tails are worse than a midsoar cloudburst. The Brown Frizz tries to get me to go back onto the perch, but I'm not having it.

"There will be mice or there will be no flapping from this owl!" I screech. I stomp on the paw and look everywhere but at the stinking perch and finally the Brown Frizz makes her growling-sigh noise and grumbles to the Gray Tail, who nods her head.

The Brown Frizz takes me back to my nest, removes those terrible tormenting tails, and lifts her paw, and I fly up to my favorite spot, way high near the top of the nest. The Brown Frizz then holds out her paw again, whistles, and — Great Beak, she has a whole mouse?

I swoop down, crash into the paw, and gobble that mouse.

Once I have it down, I notice that the Brown Frizz is staring at me. She is quite fascinated by me. Of course she is, seeing as she is an ugly furless creature and I am quite the great horned owl specimen.

"Yes, fine, admire away," I hoot, stretching my ear tufts and rousing my feathers. She did just give me a whole mouse. I should give her something in return.

"This is another part of partnership, you dud," Red screeches. She's outside now, gliding over the grass and then swooping up onto the Gray Tail's paw. The Gray Tail feeds her a scrap of meat. "The small human is trying to connect with you." Red flaps away and lands on one of the perches and turns her head, basking in the twilight.

So that's what partnership is? Flapping from paw to perch? How is this helping me learn to hunt?

The Brown Frizz grumbles something to me. I turn my head to pay attention. She lifts the little patches of fur that grow above her eyes.

I decide to look at her the same way. Perhaps this is what Red means when she chirps "connect"?

I raise my ear tufts and then sink them down and out, flattish, the way the Brown Frizz has her face furs. I stare deep into her brown eyes, the way she's staring deep into mine. It does give me a bit of a buzz in the gizzard, being this close to a big animal like a furless creature, listening to her heartbeat pound in my ears.

She whispers something to me. Her breath ruffles the feathers along my beak. I don't even need to look to know she's wearing her Good Feelings face; I hear it in her heart, can feel it coming off her in waves.

"I feel it too," I chirp back.

She spreads the pink edges of her beakless maw across her cheeks in a smooth, curving line, wrinkling the skin around her eyes.

I try to make my beak curve, but it's no good. Instead, I do what Mother used to do to me. I knock my forehead against the Brown Frizz's skull and nibble the bridge of her soft nostril tube.

She chirps again, rubs her forehead against my beak. The world feels as safe as when Mother used to tuck me beneath her wing in the nest. This partnership is for more than just learning how to hunt. I get that now. What Red means by partnership is what I call family.

The Brown Frizz's heartbeat is all aflutter and she's cooing like a mourning dove. And I realize my heart is pounding along with the Brown Frizz's pulse. Just like with Mother and First when we were in the nest together. I've missed my family so much — is a great horned owl allowed to admit that? I don't think I'm supposed to feel lonely . . . but I do. I can't wait for night to pass so I can get in a few hoots with Red at daybreak, so I can fly with the furless creatures. I wonder if I'm maybe not cut out to fly alone in the world. I think that maybe I need this partnership as much as the furless creature.

It may not be what I imagined when I thought of hunting in a pack, but maybe family doesn't always look just one way.

"We can be a family, Brown Frizz," I chirp to her.

She growls back softly, our hearts pounding together, and I feel it from talons to tufts: a connection, strange but strong.

17
Reenie

RUFUS IS LIKE A DIFFERENT BIRD THIS MORNING. I WAKE up Aunt Bea at the crack of dawn again and we are out with him on the creance and he flies from the post to my fist not once but four times! He starts getting squawky after that, so we feed him and put him back in the mews.

"We can try flying him from across the yard when you get home from school," Aunt Bea says, whistling for Red, who swoops down from the trees.

Every time Aunt Bea says we're ready to move forward, this double stream of panic and excitement burns up from my belly. "You think he's ready?"

And a part of me knows he is. I knew giving him that pep talk last night would work. I told him that he was a good bird, and more, that he was the best owl ever, and that if he didn't want to flap around on posts, he didn't have to, because we were working on his schedule, and when he was ready, I knew he would fly.

But this other part of me is terrified that the minute I step even halfway across the yard, he'll disappear into the shadows.

"He's ready," Aunt Bea says, closing Red in her aviary. "It's you who needs to know that, though. It's you he's trusting. If you don't believe in him, no way he's going to believe in himself."

"You really think all it takes is my *believing* he can fly to my fist?" That sounds like a load of manure fresh from the cow.

She takes off her gauntlet. "Not all," she says. "But it's not nothing."

Rufus chirps, sounding more like a chick than a full-grown owl—then again, he might not even be full grown. I keep forgetting he's just a baby bird, not even a year old. Maybe the last piece of his recovery is just believing he's recovered?

The sun crests the trees. "You'd better run if you're catching that bus," Aunt Bea says.

I leg it inside and clean myself up, then grab a Pop-Tart

from Aunt Bea's hand as I pass the kitchen on my way out to the bus. I look back through the bus windows toward the house, sending good thoughts to Rufus through the misty strips of sunlight, half knowing that's insane and absolutely not a real thing, but also sure that he hears me and feels loved.

— ❧ —

Jaxon shows up late. "I had an overnight with my dad," he says, sliding into his desk just as Ms. Thomas begins shuffling papers and clearing her throat to signal the beginning of the day. His backpack is bulging—the cuff of a pair of pajama pants dangles from where it's caught in the zipper. He literally had a sleepover with his dad. I guess that's what divorced kids have instead of "visitation."

Not that I've had visitation in a while . . .

Ms. Thomas blathers on about *Dicey's Song*. It's about these kids who go to live with their grandmother because their mom is sick, and they have to start over with this stranger—it's a little on the nose for my life right now. I think Ms. Thomas is trying to *connect* with me: every few pages, she gives me these puppy dog eyes.

Halfway through the period, we break into groups to talk about last night's reading. Jaxon, Jamie, and I turn our desks together. Jamie has this whole theory going about the grandmother and some secret plot to keep the kids from their mom. I let her go on. It's easier to believe the grandmother is the bad guy. It's harder to know that sometimes your mom just can't be your mom anymore.

"I bet the mom was the one who sent that letter," Jamie says, her finger pointing at the book like she's solved the case and everything's going to be all better now—Mom's going to swoop in and take the kids back to some big house complete with playground in the backyard and golden retriever on the porch.

"It's from the hospital," I tell her, because I've seen those same kinds of letters in the mail. "The mom's not coming."

"You read ahead?" Jaxon asks, flipping to the end of the book.

I shrug. "I have a feeling." *I know.*

"I'm sticking to my version," Jamie says as the bell rings. "I believe Mom's going to show up before the end."

I jam my copy of the book down into the bottom of my backpack and zip it closed.

In art, the teacher, Ms. Whipple, has set out on the tables some pieces of paper and coffee cans stuffed with colored pencils. "I'm going to give you the period to draw mandalas," she announces to the class after everyone's perched on stools. There's a circle on each paper.

"A what?" I grumble.

As if answering, Ms. Whipple walks over to one of the posters on the wall. "This is a Tibetan Buddhist mandala." It's a cyclone of color exploding out in patterns and lines, squares inside squares with tiny figures nestled in between. "It means 'circle' and traditionally was meant to represent the universe. I'd like you to think of it as a way of symbolically capturing your personal universe at this moment. If you're looking for where to start, think of it as having a center out of which the rest of the drawing sprouts, like a sunflower or a spinning galaxy."

What a ridiculous project. This is exactly the kind of touchy-feely garbage that guidance counselors always give you.

But whatever. I have nothing else to do.

I pick up a yellow pencil. All I can think to draw is Rufus's eyes. Two big yellow circles inside the black line of the printed circle. Two black pupils at the center of each eye. Then brown fanning out from those circles like scales, like the whorls of fingertips. A sharp jag of beak between them, screaming out red. Red, red, red, like lightning cracking through the circle.

The bell rings.

It's like being shaken awake. I look up from my mandala. Everyone else is already packing up.

Jamie's mandala is a bull's-eye of pinks and yellows. Jaxon drew this incredible green and purple pattern of diamonds swirling out from a sunburst of red.

I look back at my picture. I've drawn a monster. Not Rufus, but some terrible raging nightmare.

Am I that nightmare?

I bring the picture over to Ms. Whipple. "What does this mean?"

She looks at my drawing. "I don't know," she says, handing it back to me. "But it seems pretty intense."

The yellow eyes draw me in, the brown whirlpools around. "It's so angry," I mumble.

She peeks over the top of the paper.

"It's okay to be angry," she says. "Anger is something everyone feels. But sometimes it doesn't feel very safe to be angry. A mandala is a safe place for you to put your anger."

I want to tell her I said the *drawing* is angry, not me, but then I stop because her words are humming inside me, as if answering a call. Everything she said is true and right, but this anger feels so much bigger than any piece of paper can hold. "Oh," I say.

"Here," she says, holding out another page and a new box of colored pencils. "Take this home. See how you're feeling tonight."

I take the paper and pencils. It feels like I've been dropped out of a tree.

Jamie's eyes bug out when she sees me. "What happened? Your face is, like, whoa."

"Do you think I'm angry?"

Now Jamie's confused. "At me?"

"No—just, like, in general?"

Jaxon scrapes a long sliver from his wood with his pen. "I'm angry."

Jamie and I both look at him like he's lying. Jaxon is the calmest and least angry person on earth.

"I am," he says. "My parents had me see the school counselor when they were getting divorced. It took me a while to get there, but I realized I was mad at them. For getting divorced."

"You told your parents you were mad at them?" Jamie's voice is full of awe and wonder, like the concept of being mad at a parent had never occurred to her.

Then again, I'm also kind of like, *Wait, you can be mad at your parents for getting divorced?*

"Yeah," Jaxon says, sliding the pen along the deep groove. "It was hard. But afterward, my parents kind of took their fighting someplace else. They tried to explain things to me, like why they were getting a divorce and how they still loved me."

Jamie's jaw dangles. I peek at my mandala.

"I'm still angry," he says, scraping another piece. "But it helped to say it."

"Is everybody angry?" Jamie asks.

Jaxon shrugs. "Maybe?"

"I'm not angry," Jamie says.

"Maybe you are and you don't know it," I say, thinking back to what she said about the grandmother being the one who should die in *Dicey's Song*. I slip the mandala into my backpack. "Maybe the whole world is actually powered by secret rage."

Jamie frowns. "I hope that's not true."

Jaxon flashes his half smile. "Me too."

I dare to grab both their hands. "Me three."

But during the whole bus ride home, all I can do is stare at the mandala. What am I so angry about? The buzz answers, *Alone*. But I'm not alone—I have Jaxon and Jamie and Aunt Bea and Rufus—and then I remember that I don't "have" Rufus, that he has to leave me and go back to the wild. That I don't have Aunt Bea—that Mom is doing better and soon I'll be leaving everything, though who knows what "better" even means or how long it's going to last this time. And then this guilt for even thinking such a thing, for admitting— even just in my own head—that Mom will fall apart again, floods my lungs and I'm under water, sinking down, down, and by the time the bus stops at the end of my driveway, all I want is to see Rufus, so I stumble through the yard to his aviary, where he's still snoozing, and I collapse through the entry and onto the floor among the feathers and whitewash and just start to cry.

The tears come and they rain down, soaking my shirt.

18

Rufus

THE BROWN FRIZZ HAS COME INTO MY NEST AND APPEARS to be suffering from some fit. She is curled in on herself like a hedgehog and shuddering. Every few heartbeats, she heaves in this huge breath, like she's bobbing up from a deep dive under water. Very odd.

I shall investigate.

I swoop down from my favorite high perch to my mute rock, which is the closest perch to her.

"You have woken me," I begin. "What is wrong with you?"

The Brown Frizz tips her head up and peers at me

through the thicket of her head fur. The whites of her eyes are cracked with red lines. She burbles something from her beakless maw. Great Beak—is the Brown Frizz dying?

"You must go and talk to the Gray Tail," I squawk. "She is very good at fixing things. Perhaps also the small creature with the black head fur. She also seemed rather good with injuries."

The Brown Frizz grumbles softly and curls her head back into her knees.

This is more serious than I thought. It appears the Brown Frizz is giving in to death.

Father said something about this. He had a hatchmate who broke a blood feather. The bird just couldn't recover. Has the Brown Frizz broken some vital part of herself? I bob my head, listen for sounds of injury, check her over for wounds. No—the Brown Frizz is intact.

An *internal* injury. Mother was always going on about that. *First, get off that skinny twig! You'll fall from the tree and get an internal injury!* First was like that. She'd hop onto any branch, no matter how far from the nest, just to make me feel like a dud.

If the Brown Frizz is suffering from an internal injury —to be honest, I really have no idea what that means, but Mother seemed positive that it was the first flap on the flight to death—she must get help. Intervention is necessary.

I adjust my feet on the perch and judge the distance, and with one brief flap and a hop, I land on her knee.

"Brown Frizz!" I screech directly at her head fur. "You may be suffering from an internal injury." No need to upset her further with a clear diagnosis. "You must—I repeat, *must*—go and get help."

The Brown Frizz again tips her head up and sneaks a glance at me through her fur.

"Seriously," I squawk. "Pick up your little tail-less bottom and get help."

The Brown Frizz lifts her head, and I see that her eyes have leaked all over her hairless cheeks. The skin around the eyes is pinkish and the eyes themselves show red still pulsing through cracks in their whites. What strange and wondrous eyes these furless creatures have.

Most bizarre is the fact that she's wearing her Good Feelings face.

The Brown Frizz grumbles something and rubs the feathers on my foot with her little wing-toes.

"That tickles," I twitter, and nibble her wing-toes with my beak.

The Brown Frizz grumbles again, and the Good Feelings face spreads all the way to her eyes.

Perhaps the furless creature does not have an internal injury? Perhaps she is just seriously fluffed? The Brown Frizz tickles my foot feathers again and I nibble at her and she chortles like this is the most wonderful thing. She certainly doesn't seem midflight to death. The Brown Frizz lifts her little paw and runs her wing-toes down my chest feathers. I rouse at her touch—no one since Mother has groomed my feathers. But then again, the Brown Frizz wants to be family. Maybe this is part of the ritual?

"All right, Brown Frizz," I chirp. "You may preen my feathers, but do be careful about the alignment of the barbs." I'm rather particular about my barbs.

The Brown Frizz continues to run her silly wing-toes over my feathers and coo softly. Clearly, she is no longer suffering from whatever had previously ailed her, meaning she had certainly only gotten herself seriously fluffed. Furless creatures do have a dramatic way of getting fluffed, what with the leaky eyes and the shuddering and gasping like a fish dropped in the forest.

"Hey, Red," I squawk loudly. "Look at this! I think the Brown Frizz and I have achieved this partnership you keep screeching about."

Red flaps to the opening in the wall of her nest that looks into mine. She stares down her beak at us, weighing us like prey. "It certainly is an improvement." She glances at the yard and the human nest. "You still can't hunt, though."

She had to bring *that* up.

"But you said the Brown Frizz will teach me," I squawk back. "That's the whole partnership thing."

Red turns her yellow eyes back onto me. "One kill at a time, Hatchling."

The Brown Frizz slides her naked wing-toes into her big paw and I hop from her knee onto the paw, which is clearly her favorite way for me to perch and the way that gets me the most mouse bits per visit.

"On that thought, where is the mouse?" I squawk, because I haven't eaten since sunup and things are getting growly in the gizzard.

The Brown Frizz clearly understands Owlish, because she walks directly toward the human nest, begins barking loudly, and then the Gray Tail comes out bearing a pile of mice.

More owls should look into this partnership business, I think, gobbling down the first scrap she offers. But then I think of First and all her showing off and teasing, and it's clear that certain owls would not make much of a partner for these poor furless creatures. First would have torn the head fur right off the Brown Frizz seeing her so vulnerable and fluffed earlier. No, it is truly only the Absolute Worst Owls in All of Owldom who are fit partners for furless creatures, because only the Absolute Worst Owls in All of Owldom would be desperate enough to discover how nice it is to have a thing like a partner. Only the Absolute Worst Owls would fall so low as to uncover the treasure of friendship.

When the Brown Frizz puts me on the post and whistles, I fly, silent and strong, barely riffling the blades of grass, and land on her paw. Her face is brighter than the moon on a clear night.

19
Reenie

"YOU'RE DOING IT AGAIN." JAXON TAPS MY LAPTOP'S KEY-
board.

The librarian has given us our library period to work on
our Vermont projects. Instead of typing up my brief history
of falconry, I'm doodling owls. But how can I not? Rufus flew
to me from all the way across the yard on the creance. Aunt
Bea can't believe how far he's come, how much he trusts me.
But Rufus and I have come to an understanding: we need
each other. Watching him lift off from the perch, spread his
wings wide, and glide silently, yellow eyes glued on mine,

then flapping once, twice, and swooping up onto my fist—it's like seeing a part of me come back to myself.

In class, Mr. Brown calls for people's attention. "You should have all completed your research at this point and be well on your way to putting that research into your essays as we discussed earlier this week. I want everyone to get into their groups and share what they've written so far. Start talking about transforming your individual pieces into your group presentation."

The room rumbles with the thunderous sound of desks being dragged into new formations. Jamie, Jaxon, and I arrange ourselves into a tight knot.

"I've already finished my essay on the negative impacts of hunting," Jamie says. "But I also found all this stuff on the economic benefits to rural communities. I didn't know if that was okay—I mean, I don't want to step on your toes, Jax." She slides a folder of paper toward Jaxon.

"Step all over them," he says.

A cold sweat prickles out beneath my shirt. She already has a folder of research? Of *extra* research?

"I was thinking for the presentation that maybe I could do some drawings," Jaxon says, pulling out a sketchbook. He's already done three amazing sketches of a deer, men up in a deer blind, and a compound bow.

"Have you finished your essay?" Jamie asks, smiling,

blissfully unaware that I am definitely the weakest link in our chain.

I have not. I still have to do the interview part of the assignment to transition from the history of falconry to what it is today. "It'll be done in time."

Jamie's smile falters. "But you've started, right?"

"Definitely," I lie.

Jaxon's eyebrows launch into the fringe of his hair.

"I'm sorry — Rufus has just been keeping me so busy."

"I thought he was better. You haven't released him?" Jaxon asks.

"He's *getting* better," I say. "He's not one hundred percent."

"The presentation is in a week," Jamie says, eyes wide.

"It'll be done," I promise. Geez, they're touchy about this project.

We spend the rest of the period working in silence on our individual essays, some of us starting from a blank page.

When Aunt Bea gets home, I am ready with my questions. Some of them we just skim over — *how did you get into falconry, what stuff do you need to practice falconry today* — as we've already covered that ground.

"Is falconry in Vermont different than other places in America?"

Aunt Bea nods. "I've met falconers from other places and they all offer me condolences. Vermont's not a great place for falconry. Too many people, not enough open land."

I put my pen down. "Jaxon said the same thing about deer hunting. His dad's always griping about there being too little ground to hunt."

"It's the fight between nature and civilization that humans have been fighting on this land for centuries. You know one hundred and forty years ago, parts of Vermont were eighty percent deforested? It was all cut for timber and sheep meadow. Now we have residential developments and strip malls fighting with farmers and conservationists for land. Sometimes the balance shifts toward one group, then toward another. Unfortunately, falconers are not a loud voice in that fight."

I begin doodling. "I wish everyone would just leave things the way they are, stop making parking lots and garbage piles and just let the animals and trees live."

Aunt Bea smiles, huffs a little laugh. "It can't be all one or the other. But things always change. That, too, is natural." She gets up and grabs a pot to start dinner. "I heard from the social worker today." I stop doodling. "Your mom is doing well."

"Yeah." She has to bring this up? But what's funny is, the buzz doesn't whisper anything. I feel sad. I feel scared. But that's it.

Aunt Bea glances over at me. "You know that even if you go home with your mom, you can still come visit me, right?"

"Yeah," I say, chin on the tabletop.

She nudges my elbow. "Red would miss you if you didn't."

A laugh escapes my lips. "What about Rufus?"

"You and Rufus are both going to have to fly free of me soon. But that's how it's supposed to be."

I lean my head back against the chair. *Is it?* Mom has recovered other times. She would come to Gram's and hug me and we'd be fine for a while, but it never lasted. I don't blame Mom—I've seen how hard she fights the sadness when she can, seen the balance shift to her side. But the sadness is bigger than Mom and me put together.

What if I can have a voice in this fight—a choice? "What if I want to stay?" The words escape my lips before I really understand what I've said.

Aunt Bea gets her flustered face. "Stay? Here?" She picks up my pen, rolls it between her fingers. "Well, of course. I mean, as long as you need to, like I said before. But—Reenie, I—"

I stop her before she can say anything else. "It's okay. I get it." None of us have any choices, not with the state involved.

"But what if it doesn't work out?" I ask. Her face

crumples, her wrinkles getting wrinkles. I don't want to upset her more, especially over a question I know has no answer. "I mean with Rufus. What if his wing doesn't heal completely?"

The switch over to the topic of Rufus seems to calm Aunt Bea, as I'd guessed it would. "Then I petition the falconry school and the state to let me keep him as an education bird."

"Wait." I am all eyes and ears on her. "That's an option?"

Aunt Bea shrugs. "Either that or see if the natural science center will take him. If not either of those, then he'll have to be put down."

My heart rate drops from full-speed excitement to heart-stalled dread. "Put down?"

Aunt Bea rumples my hair. "That's a slim possibility. I think he's going to be ready to go back home.

"Speaking of which," she says, "we have to start getting him hunting."

"But he can't fly free yet," I say. "He might fly off and—"

"Whoa, now," Aunt Bea says, smiling. "You train a bird to hunt with you in stages, same way we manned him for the hunt."

My heart drops back into my chest. "Right," I say. "Obviously."

"Obviously," Aunt Bea says, smirking. "I'll get some things together."

"Okay," I say, but my mind is stuck on the fact that there is at least a chance — a possibility, the merest sliver of a prospect — that Rufus could stay.

20
Rufus

THE BROWN FRIZZ APPEARS AT MY NEST BUT DOES NOT pick open the web and come inside.

Strange.

Instead, she kneels down, pushes open a space in the web, and pokes something inside.

Even more strange.

The something rolls like an egg. Is it an egg? I stretch my wings and drop beside the egg. I snatch at it with a claw. It's hard. My talons slip over it and it hops away, unscathed. The audacity of this egg—scampering off from a great horned owl.

YOU CANNOT ESCAPE ME, EGG!

I am all talons after this egg. It hops and scrambles, but I am fast and cunning and — nope. Got away again.

DIE, EGG!

I pierce it with a claw — nothing.

"Honestly, Owl, did your mother teach you nothing?" Red is glaring down from her perch near the opening.

"That's cold." How could she say such a thing, knowing what she knows?

"I am being serious," she squawks. "Did she teach you anything? Because that is not how we birds of prey hunt. Do you think I stomp around in the grass hoping to pierce a meal on my talons?"

Wait.

Did she screech "hunt"?

Mother never would have sunk so low as to bob along the grass after a meal. No, she dropped down like the night sky itself, her talons invisible until they sliced into their target.

That's it.

I have to smother this egg. That's the trick of it.

I flap up, fix my eyes on the egg, stretch forward with my talons, and dive down onto it. Four toes grip its smooth surface and squeeze. THE EGG IS MINE!

I peck it for good measure.

It is very hard. I will not do that again.

The Brown Frizz is giving off Good Feelings, so apparently this egg hunt is what she'd been hoping for.

"Nice catch," Red screeches from her perch. "Now try it again." She turns her head away toward the space between our nests and the human nest, or the perch meadow, as I like to think of it.

If I can hunt this egg once, I can do it again.

Releasing my talons, I let the egg roll. I hop after it, but my talons keep slipping off each time I reach out to grab it.

Have I learned nothing?

I flap up, sight the egg, extend my talons so they're nearly at the tip of my beak, and crash down on the egg.

IT IS MINE!

I release it again. And smash down upon it. I do it again. And again. I AM MASTER OF THE EGG!

The Brown Frizz is practically buzzing with Good Feelings. She comes inside the web and calls me to her paw with a scrap of mouse, which is just the thing I'm needing about now after all that egg hunting. As I swallow it down, she attaches the infernal tails and vine to my leg sparkles and walks us into the perch meadow. She lifts the paw and I fly to the nearest perch. I glance around the space, taking in the late afternoon light, the rush of the day noises, which are mostly the furless creatures' growling monsters. The Gray Tail has come out of the human nest and walks across the perch meadow. A crow flaps far off, its caw like a talon through my ears.

My ear tufts flatten; I really hate crows. Just hearing them brings back that long-ago day in the woods, the swarm, having to walk, humiliated, through the leaves . . .

The Brown Frizz cries out, interrupting my dark thoughts, and suddenly I see a rustling in the grass.

Is the Brown Frizz warning of danger? Tufts up!

The grass rustles again, and now I see what appears to be a mouse with a large green wing sticking out of its back.

The mouse hops.

If I can catch an egg, I can catch this mouse.

Okay, first steps: prepare for flight, open wings, get some air, take aim, talons out . . . Now DIVE! I am like a bolt of lightning shooting down from the clouds. I stretch my talons wide and smash down onto that mouse and—oh, it's dead.

This green wing is hard and shiny and definitely not a normal part of a mouse. There is a vine coming off the green wing, and—ah, yes. The Brown Frizz is holding the end of the vine.

So, we are both on vines, eh, mouse? But you are dead and I am not, so I'm calling you dinner!

I rip off a beakful, and the Brown Frizz shuffles over in her little toe covers and removes the green wing. Because I know she won't take my mouse, I let her.

After I eat, I flap up to a perch. Red swoops down from a tree. When did she get out of her nest?

"You're catching on quick," she chirps.

"I'm a great horned owl," I say. Even the Absolute Worst Great Horned Owl is a still a great horned owl.

Red raises her crown, feathers fluffing. "Oh, are you, now?"

"I am a GREAT HORNED OWL!" I screech.

The Brown Frizz tweets and holds up her paw, and I soar across the perch meadow. As I pass the forest, I hear the thrum of life — heartbeats in the grass. I could catch them all, I know it. I twist, I flap.

The Brown Frizz whistles again. I glance back at her. She shakes the paw. There's mouse on it.

Ah, the forest can wait.

I bank again, flap, and soar over to her paw. She's giving off waves of fear, her heartbeat pounds. Did I do that?

"I'm sorry, Brown Frizz," I peep, nibbling at her frizzy head fur. "I just heard the call."

"You heard it?" Red sits atop the Gray Tail's paw. Her amber eyes bore into me.

I turn to look again into the deepening black of the forest. The heartbeats pound, the darkness pulls me. "I feel it."

Red fluffs her crown again, then rouses. "That's good," she chirps. "Very good."

The Brown Frizz puts me back in my nest, and I flap up to my favorite perch. Something has changed, though. The roof feels so much lower, like it's pressing down on my tufts. The walls feel so much closer around me, though I can still flap as far.

How can the world change without actually changing?

As the dawn breaks, I hear the sound of squeaking. The Brown Frizz is nearby but outside my nest. The squeaking is definitely *inside*.

Glancing around in the half day, I see movement across the dirt.

I twitch my feathers. The heartbeats sweep and swerve and then stop. The dark patch of dirt below me is no longer a stretch of black: in the corner, the noise of the heartbeats glows slightly. I can *see* the heartbeats, I can see the mouse.

This is just like the egg.

This is *hunting*.

I lift and stretch my wings, and drop silently. I extend my legs forward, talons near my beak.

The mouse scuttles along the wall.

I hear you . . . I see you.

I flap, swerve, and adjust my feet, all silently, like a movement of the night itself. I dive, dropping like rain.

I hit the mouse. Squeeze my talons. The heartbeats stop.

I caught the mouse.

"I did it!" I screech.

Red squawks, flaps loudly. "What skunk! Where?!"

"No skunk, Red—I caught a mouse! Right here! It snuck into my nest!" I grab the meat in my beak and gobble it down in one gulp.

I haven't tasted anything like it since . . . since Mother.

"Well done, Hatchling," Red tweets.

The Brown Frizz is clapping her wing-toes and hooting with joy. The Gray Tail is with her and is giving off Good Feelings.

I did it.

I hunted.

I am no longer the Absolute Worst Great Horned Owl in All of Owldom.

If I can hunt, I've definitely moved up to being one of the Marginally Capable Great Horned Owls Who Probably Still Won't Survive the Winter.

And that's a start.

21

Reenie

HOW CAN SO MANY GOOD THINGS MAKE ME FEEL SO TER-
rible? Mom called this morning to say she's looking at an
apartment and that soon I could start doing overnights with
her at our new place.

Our new place.

A place where I'm going to have to start all over again.

And Rufus caught a mouse on his first try. Aunt Bea
couldn't believe it.

"He's a prodigy!" she cried out.

I knew he was a genius. I've always believed in him. But

to have it be real, to have him be so close to finished with me . . . It's all happening too fast and all at once.

And what if it doesn't work out? What if, when we fly him free, he flies away? What if he's not ready? What if he starves and it's my fault? It's good to know that, worst case, we keep him. Maybe even not just worst case . . .

"Maureen?"

Mr. Brown is standing over me, tapping his arm.

"Um." I have no idea what's going on.

"Your team? How far along are you guys on your project?"

"Um."

"We're going to get together this weekend to finalize everything," Jamie says, nudging me with her foot under the table.

"Yes." Did we actually agree to that? What if I have to do this overnight with my mom?

"Sounds great," Mr. Brown says, walking on. "I'm really looking forward to your presentation."

"We can meet at my house!" Jamie says, practically vibrating with excitement.

"I'm supposed to go to my dad's for the weekend," Jaxon says.

Do I tell them about my mom getting better? About me possibly moving, maybe next week? Before we even get to do the presentation? No. That's just too much to explain, too many maybes. "Can we do it today, after school?" Then, even if I have an overnight, it won't matter.

Jaxon shrugs. "My dad isn't picking me up until six. I could text my mom."

"Can I text my aunt?" I ask, holding out a hand for someone's phone.

Jamie says, "I'll go get my phone from my locker. This is the best day ever!" She heads to the hallway.

Jaxon and I take off for recess and our spot behind the bushes. What if it's my last day? What if this overnight with my mom goes well and the state sends me away from here? Jaxon would be fine. But Jamie? She's already lost two friends . . . but now she has Jaxon . . . Would they even notice I was gone?

I scratch my wood so hard, it splits in two.

Jaxon gasps, his face contorted like he's just witnessed a murder. "We can glue it."

I drop the pieces. "It wasn't working anyway." I spend the rest of recess piling up pebbles and knocking them down.

⬮

Aunt Bea texted back while we were outside that she can pick me up at Jamie's house, and Jaxon's mom offers to give us a ride after school. Jaxon told her we could take the bus, but she insisted. She shows up in scrubs with messy curls springing from her updo. She took a break during her shift at the doctor's office.

"It's great to meet you girls," she says, pulling out of the school's parking lot. "I've heard so much about you."

Jaxon's turning a shade of red last seen on a beet. Jamie and I glance at each other and have to choke down a laugh because just the thought of Jaxon saying anything at all about us—let alone "so much"—is too funny.

"Maureen, Jaxon says you have an owl you're rehabilitating? He helped his dad with a rescued hawk once."

He told her about Rufus? "Um, yeah."

"She's setting him free soon," Jaxon says.

"*If* he gets better," I correct. "If not, we might have to keep him." Perhaps Jaxon is not aware of this fantastic option?

"You said he's hunting," Jaxon says, eyebrows crinkling.

"Turn here," Jamie interrupts—thank goodness for needing to give directions. I don't want to argue with Jaxon about my owl.

We pull into this development where it looks like a giant machine plunked down identical houses *one-two-three* along the stretch of road. Jamie points to one that's sort of bluish, and we pull up to the door.

"Is your mom home?" Jaxon's mom asks.

"She'll be home soon," Jamie says, noncommittal.

"Oh," Jaxon's mom says.

"It's okay," I say. "We have Jamie's cell phone."

Jaxon's mom eyes the house like it's trouble. "All right," she says. "I'm going back to the office, but it's just a few blocks away, so I can be here ASAP if you need anything."

We slide out of the car and walk up the driveway.

"Your mom never leaves you home alone?" Jamie asks.

Jaxon shrugs. "She told me not until I'm thirteen."

"I turned ten and my parents were like, *Here's the key. We'll see you at five.*" Jamie brandishes a key and jams it in the door.

It's funny to think of Jaxon being babied like that. He seems so independent, so self-contained, like a hermit crab. But maybe his mom doesn't see him that way.

Will Mom give me a key to her—*our* new apartment? Will I come home on some strange new bus to some strange new place to wait for her to come home from some job? *If she gets the apartment* . . .

Jamie lets Jaxon and me into the foyer.

"Whoa," Jaxon says. His voice echoes around the cavernous rooms, bouncing off shiny glass and polished wood. Jamie flips on lights as she walks down a two-story hallway into a white and blue kitchen of curving plastic cabinets and glass tile that looks like it was designed for a space station.

We huddle around a massive round white stone table reminiscent of King Arthur's. Jamie grabs a box of cookies from this huge closet full of food and then a gallon of chocolate milk from the fridge and three glasses. I've always wondered what family buys not milk and chocolate mix, but the whole gallon of premixed chocolate milk. Tasting the rich yumminess of it—a fullness of chocolaty goodness that I've never achieved with my powdery additives—makes up somewhat for the imposing, off-putting wealth of the place. I've lived in apartments that were smaller than this kitchen.

"Your house is really shiny," I say. The stone of the table literally glitters.

"My mom has a scrapbook filled with pictures of kitchens like this," Jaxon says, gulping chocolate milk. "Some nights, she takes it out during dinner and pretends."

Jamie runs her fingers over the tabletop. "It's too big. When we eat dinner, my mom and dad and me, we're so far apart, it's like we're eating alone." She hefts her bag onto the table. "But it's perfect for projects. Plenty of space."

She produces a laptop computer and a tablet and her phone from her bag, then goes over and opens another closet, which is stacked with labeled plastic boxes filled with things like "ribbons" and "markers" and "duct tape." A whole box full of different colors of duct tape. When Jamie told me she liked making stuff, I hadn't quite understood the scale of her operation.

She digs a tall trifold presentation board out of a corner. "I was thinking we could put all our research on this." She unfolds the cardboard, spreading it flat on the table.

Jaxon stares into the cavern of boxed craft supplies. "You have a whole box just for buttons?"

Jamie glances back at the closet. "That's old," she says, picking a cookie from the carton. "When I was little, my mom and I used to do crafts a lot. But that was forever ago. The other day I asked her if she wanted to melt some crayons with me, and she said, 'Aren't you too old for that?'"

The hurt and lonely look on Jamie's face is only there for a second, but it's one I know too well. There are so many ways to lose a parent. Even when they still live in the same house.

"I like doing crafts," I say. "I'll melt crayons with you anytime."

"Whittling's a craft," Jaxon adds.

"Maybe that should be our team name? The Crafty Hunters?" I say.

"The Whittling Woodsmen?" Jamie offers, a tiny smile peeking through.

"Perfect," Jaxon says.

Jamie looks like she's about to cry, but instead, she turns on her tablet. "I made this chart to show how many people hunt in Vermont." It's a neat rectangle with different bars for each kind of license: fishing, bow hunting, duck hunting, falconry . . .

"I did these," Jaxon says, laying a stack of drawings on the table: pictures of a kid in hunting fatigues, a hunting rifle, people in a boat covered in grass for duck hunting, with labels for the specific parts of each.

"We can put them on the poster around the chart," I say, holding one up.

"I also made flash cards for the debate." Jamie hands me a stack.

"Did you know that hunters were behind the early conservation movement?" I read. "President Teddy Roosevelt wanted to save the land and the animals, in part so he could keep hunting them."

"Hunters are still a big part of conservation efforts," Jaxon says, sounding defensive already. "And it's even good for the deer. If hunters didn't keep the deer population down, they'd starve in the winter."

"I don't think you can say it's good for the deer who get shot," Jamie says. "The audience has seen *Bambi*."

Jaxon blushes and begins shading a corner of the hunting rifle. "*Bambi* is rough. But it's also a lie. You're not supposed to shoot does."

"Law says you can shoot does." Jamie taps away on her keyboard.

"But isn't that just nature?" I ask, thinking of Rufus and the white mice I'm sacrificing to him. "Hunters eat the deer meat, right?"

"Some do, some donate it to food pantries." Jaxon switches pencils, continues shading.

"But the point is that hunting can be a part of the eco-system," I say. "We don't have big predators, so there has to be some way to fill that role in the food chain."

"So, like, hunters can balance things out? Here," Jamie says, handing me a note card. "Write that down."

"Speaking of food chain," Jaxon says, reaching for another cookie.

"I just can't get past the dead animals," Jamie says, pushing away one of Jaxon's drawings.

"It's not why I hunt," he says, still scribbling on a sketch. "I guess there might be some people who do it for the killing. But my dad and I, we do it to be together in the woods. He hunted with his dad. And it's nice, to be together in the quiet, watching for a lucky shot. And when you do kill something, you don't let it suffer.

"It's why you do falconry, right, Reenie?"

I'm about to blurt, *No, it's because of the birds*, but then I see me walking through the woods with Red . . . and with Aunt Bea. Training Rufus . . . with Aunt Bea.

"It started with Red," I say, "but even that's all because of my aunt."

Jamie begins scribbling on another new card. "Here," she says, sliding it across the table. She wrote, *Hunting is about family*.

Tears squeeze out along my eyelashes. Before reading that, I'd forgotten that Aunt Bea really is family and completely missed that, over these past few weeks, it's what we'd become.

Jaxon peeks at the card. "That's better."

I wipe my face with the back of my hand and nod. "Yeah." I place the card so it's the finale.

⌒

When we get home, Aunt Bea and I rush to feed the beasts. Inside his aviary, Rufus is flappy, hopping from perch to perch. I take him out and fly him across the yard a few times on the creance to let him stretch his wings.

"He's looking good," Aunt Bea says. "I think we should try flying him free tomorrow."

Rufus swoops across the grass, flaps once, and alights on my fist, gobbling the tidbit down and then squawking for more. "You think he's ready?" I rub under his beak and he playfully bites my fingers.

"Do you?" Aunt Bea whistles and Red screeches, then emerges from the trees.

Rufus peeps and twitters, chattering on about something. Most likely, he just wants more food. I place him on the farthest perch and walk back, and then Rufus shuffles around to face me and barks a raspy squawk. I hold up my fist and whistle. He's instantly off the perch, flying right to me, and hits the glove right where I tapped.

He's proud of himself. I can tell by the way he gobbles

down the tidbit and then gazes down his beak at the world. He thinks he's hot stuff.

"He's ready," I say. It's me who's not ready.

Aunt Bea's phone rings inside the house. Rufus and Red both snap their heads in the direction of the noise. Aunt Bea sends Red off into the trees and runs for the phone. Through the glass of the sliding door, I see her glance at the number and pause before answering.

Rufus squawks, nibbles my hair. He can sense when things start going all wonky inside me, and my guts are suddenly boiling.

Aunt Bea sticks her head out the door. "It's your mom," she says, waving the phone.

Mom calls every night now, but usually around eight, before I go to bed. It's not even six thirty.

I start walking toward the house.

Aunt Bea points to my outstretched arm. "You want to leave the bird?"

Rufus swivels his head around.

"No," I say, reaching out to take the cell phone.

"Reens?" Mom's voice is all strangled—ugh, I don't even want to ask.

"Hey, Mom," I say, trying to sound cheerful. "What's up?"

"Oh, Reens, just—gah! I have to blurt it out. We got the

apartment! I can't believe it—there's so much paperwork and I had to talk to all these people to get approved, but it all worked out, just like that!"

Rufus bobs his head, tilts it like he can't quite comprehend what's coming out of the phone.

"Reenie?" Mom asks. "Did I lose you? We got our apartment—did you hear me?"

My brain snags on the word *our*. "Oh, yeah?"

"It's great—two bedrooms. And you can go back to Rutland Intermediate, see all your old friends."

I want to tell her I have no friends there. I say nothing.

"I have the weekend to get our stuff from Gram's, and then we move in next week. Randi—the social worker—she said we could do our visitation on Tuesday at the place. Maybe try an overnight next weekend. What do you think?"

"That's great," I say, because what else can I say?

Rufus digs his talons into the glove. He knows everything's sliding off the rails. I take a deep breath. I have to calm down—for Rufus.

"No, really," I add, projecting calm and control. "I'm sure it's really nice."

"You're going to love it, Reenie-beany," Mom says, though she doesn't sound one hundred percent.

A part of me wants to say, *Of course I will!* But then I look at Aunt Bea and the warm light in the kitchen and Rufus twitters and squeezes my hand through the glove and I can't imagine loving anywhere else on earth.

"Okay," I say.

"I'll call tomorrow to give you an update."

"Great."

We say good night, we say we love each other.

"Everything all right?" Aunt Bea asks.

The buzz has returned like a nightmare, familiar and awful all at once. Rufus must sense it because he bates, flapping and scratching, and I do nothing for a second because I feel exactly like that: caught, frantic, whole world upside down.

I grab him. Set him right on my fist. At least I can save my owl.

"Everything's fine," I tell Beatrice. Because that's just how things always have to be: fine.

22
Rufus

THE NIGHT IS COLD. THE USUAL NOISES ARE SILENT, AS if the summer forest dwellers all as one dug down into their holes or flew off after the warmth. I fluff my feathers, lifting each downy fluff to its fluffiest. This is the first whiff of the winter Mother warned of. This is the bird-killing time.

Father would often hoot about his first winter. "Barely caught a mouse a day," he'd squawk. "And that was a good year."

He'd screech about winds nearly blowing him off his branch, of flying through snow so thick he couldn't see the tips of his primaries, of ice on the lake catching water birds by their webbed feet.

"Easy meals, those birds," he added.

Even First would shudder to hear these stories. I was ready to crawl back into my eggshell. Finally, one night, I asked Mother, "Why does he tell us about this?"

She sighed and then groomed my ear tufts with her beak. "He wants you to be ready."

"How can a bird get ready for rain freezing his feathers into a sheet of ice?"

Mother snuffled through her beak. "I guess there's no getting ready for that." She ran a talon over my skull. "Your father just wants you to know that there's a whole world outside this nest, and it's not a friendly one."

I'd always meant to ask her why we didn't fly away to a friendlier world.

"Were you ever out in the winter, Red?" I hoot softly. I can tell from her heartbeat that she's only pretending to sleep.

"No," she tweets. "And that's a blessing." She rouses, shifts her footing on the perch. "Too many sad stories have come through this place. Broken wings, birds so hungry they lie on their chest feathers and can't lift a talon. Winter is cruel."

"Then why have winter?" I ask.

Red flaps her wings as if shooing my hoots away. "Do you think we have a choice?"

"Why not fly with the warmth? Like the honkers?" Mother hated the honkers, always flying low over our nest like there was something in it for them.

"Honkers? They can't do anything *but* fly after the warmth. It's in their gizzards. Is your gizzard telling you to fly somewhere?"

I turn my eyes inward, dig deep inside. "No," I hoot. "My gizzard isn't pointing me anywhere. But why not? Why is nature like that?"

"Every creature in the forest has its role to play, and every season, too. Winter lets the ground sleep and renew itself. But winter also keeps the balance. Only the strongest can survive."

Meaning winter picks off the Absolute Worst Owls in All of Owldom so that the Absolute Best Owls can find more mice. Meaning winter is meant to cull out . . . *me.*

But I don't want to be culled.

"How will I survive the winter?" I peep, afraid to hoot it too loudly.

"Maybe you won't," Red screeches. "Birds who ask questions like that don't make it too long out in the forest."

That just about gets me fluffed. Here I am, asking her honest questions, and she's screeching back nastiness? Why is she being so mean?

Or is she being mean at all?

Perhaps Red is trying to push me, as usual?

"I will survive the winter?" I hoot, just trying it out.

"You will?" Red squawks. "How's that?"

"I will hunt."

"Hunt how?" She's in the opening now, peering in at me.

"I will listen," I hoot, tipping my head.

"And?" She tilts her head to match mine.

"And I will find the heartbeats," I say. "I will glide between the snowflakes and crash down like lightning with my talons."

Her eyes sparkle. "Perhaps you will survive." She flaps away from the opening, across her nest to her favorite perch near the roof. "Now get some rest, Hatchling."

Warmth unfurls inside me as I picture what I just hooted. I hunch down between my wings, close my eyes, and open my ears. The silence fluffs out into layers: stillness, and quiet, and fullness, all different breeds of silence. And hidden among these are pockets of noise, of life.

I will survive the winter, I promise the silence. *I will live to see the spring.*

◆

The Brown Frizz sneaks out to my nest in the darkness, sending the hidden crickets springing from the stiff grass. I can see her well enough as she stumbles over the tussocks. She slaps her wing-toes against the wall of my nest and crouches down like she's hiding.

"You cannot hide from me, Brown Frizz," I hoot.

She shudders, giving off Good Feelings. And then she toots out her beakless maw an approximation of—Great Beak, is she trying to hoot back to me?

"Brown Frizz, this is embarrassing for us both," I hoot.

"Hoot, hoo-hoo, hoot!" she replies.

Absolute gibberish. Ah, well. She is family, after all. I hoot back at her, mimicking her ridiculous Owlish. She practically explodes with Good Feelings and hoots back at me some more. We go on like this, hooting back and forth, and by the end, she almost has a decent "Get away from my nest, you bent primary feather!"

She plunks her tail-less bottom in the dirt, leans her back against the wall of my nest, and begins growling in Furless Creature–ese, which is truly the ugliest means of communication. I flap down to a lower perch to see if there're any mouse bits coming my way. All that hooting made me hungry. But no, she just sits and grumbles, mumbling on like this is getting either of us anywhere, particularly as regards breakfast, which I'm sensing is due.

"Excuse me, Brown Frizz, but might there be any mouse in your meat pocket?" It's a wonderful thing about furless creatures that they have little pockets full of meat.

She sucks in air and lets out a long breath, then rolls onto her haunch and produces a squeaking something, which she drops in through a space in my nest's wall.

She wants me to hunt.

I am an owl who will live to see the spring. Hunt, I shall!

Bobbing my head, I lock on to the mouse's position, scuttling along the edge of the wall like it can hide from me in the shadows. There is no hiding from a great horned owl!

I flap, twist, dive, and slam down on that mobile meal.

I AM RULER OF ALL I SURVEY!

"For fluff's sake, would you shut your beak!" Red squawks. "Some birds are still trying to sleep."

But the Brown Frizz and I are pumped full of Good Feelings. She's hooting and twittering at me like my hunting has anything to do with her. But that's family, I guess. Mother was always excited to see me hunt. At least now I'm actually catching things.

I gobble down the mouse. The Brown Frizz opens the web and comes in, paw on. I flap up to it and nip at her face to say hello. She sneaks those infernal tails into my leg sparkles, but I don't mind them nearly so much now. I hardly end up tufts down like a bat these days.

We head out into the perch meadow and I see that the Gray Tail is also out in this half day. She grumbles at the Brown Frizz and they have a bit of a hoot about something. The Brown Frizz then swings her paw, which is our signal for me to fly off to the nearest perch. There's a dead tree a flap away, and I land, then turn to look at the Brown Frizz. This next part is my favorite.

Yes—there it is! She gives off a little tweet, smacks a

wing-toe on the paw, and waggles a bit of meat hidden there from her pocket of yummies. That is the signal for me to fly back to the paw for said yummies.

Mmmmm. I gobble that mouse bit right down and squawk for another.

But the furless creatures are chattering to themselves. Something exciting has happened. "What?" I peep.

The Brown Frizz runs a wing-toe over my chest feathers. She is giving off a gust of Good Feelings. Whatever happened, it is good.

She swings the paw and I flap off again, this time to a different perch, just to keep things interesting. Again, I turn, and she taps her paw, and I fly to it and gulp the yummy meat. The furless creatures are practically bouncing on their little talonless toes. And yet none of this is the least bit unusual—we have been doing this every half day and half night for ages!

"What is going on with you, furless creatures?" I squawk.

This only leads them both to start chittering little happy chirps like a couple of squirrels in a tree full of nuts.

"Take a peek at your legs, Hatchling," Red calls from her nest.

I bend over, peck at my leg sparkles—they're still there. And the infernal tails hang down and are gripped in the Brown Frizz's paw . . .

Where's the vine?

Every time we fly out here, there's a little vine on my leg-tails. Now it's gone.

I'm flying free.

I look up. I'm flying *free*.

An instinct to fly high, far, launches me from the paw and I soar up, up, landing on a branch in a tall sugar-sap tree near the furless creatures' nest. I'm dizzy being so far from the ground. I tighten my grip, steady my gizzard.

This is a perch for a great horned owl.

From here, I can *see* . . .

The trees deep into the forest, the twitch of a thousand branches, dry leaves rasping, crunching, whistling through the breeze as they fall to the ground. Songbirds flitting between them, their tiny hearts thrumming. Insects buzzing under the fallen leaves, zipping away from the birds. A moth fumbling through a gust of air. And all the prey I could ever hope to swallow, pulsing beneath the shadows, rustling among the dry leaves, scurrying amid the grasses, digging down into their dens.

Thweet!

The Brown Frizz is holding up her paw. Tapping. Waving the bit of meat from her pocket.

There's a whole wide world out there.

A crow comes cawing out of nowhere, and then another,

and then more, until there's a veritable swarm perching in the nearby trees.

There's a whole wide world full of things that want me dead. But just there, in the perch meadow, is a furless thing that wants to keep me safe.

It's not even a choice.

23
Reenie

"I GOT YOU SOMETHING," AUNT BEA SAYS AT BREAKFAST Saturday.

The plan is to head out around sunset for our first walk in the woods with Rufus. Which means I have a whole day to suffer through. Which is probably a good thing since I still have to finish up my research for the hunting project.

"Is it my essay for school?" I say.

Aunt Bea snuffles a laugh. "Sorry, but no."

Excitement hums in my belly when I see her lift a brand-new falconry waistcoat from a bag. She shakes it out. "There's a real knife in the holster, so don't get silly with it."

"But Mom just called to say—" If I'm leaving, why buy me a whole vest?

"Because you're a falconer," she says, cutting me off, "and a falconer needs the right equipment."

I let her hold it while I slip my arms in. It's heavy canvas, with big pockets covered with thick flaps of material. It fits perfectly.

"Thank you," I manage, tears pricking out from the corners of my eyes.

She smiles. "You've earned it." She stands, collects her dishes. "Now, finish that schoolwork or we're not flying that owl."

I salute her as I get to work, my new vest wrapped around me for good luck.

As the light turns golden, I finish typing up all my notes. Falconry hasn't changed much over the centuries. The ancient kings whose hawks soared over Middle Eastern deserts are kin with King Arthur, whose falcons flew across English moors, and with Aunt Bea and Red. And with me. I'm connected to something deep and true in the world, like I'm part of this thread reaching back through time and stretching forward into the future.

I hunt through the house for Aunt Bea—I've got to show her my finished essay. But she's outside, standing in the yard, flying Red and using a lure—this one meant to imitate a rabbit, but it's really a stuffed sock made of fur. She tosses the tidbit-laden rabbit lure into the grass, then drags it fast across the ground. Red dive-bombs from above, hitting the lure like a missile. I was so into my essay, I'd forgotten that we're taking Rufus to fly.

"Is it time?" I ask, shrugging on a fleece jacket under my vest as I step out the back door and trundle down the wooden steps. "I finished my project."

Aunt Bea calls Red to the fist, and she lands there in an instant. "About," Aunt Bea says, feeding Red her tidbit.

I get Rufus from his aviary as Aunt Bea puts Red back in hers. We're flying Rufus solo in the woods. It's his first time, so we agreed two sets of eyes would work better than one.

"You sure we shouldn't put a radio on him?"

Aunt Bea nods, handing me her pouch of tidbits. "If he flies off, that's how it should be anyway."

Her words bruise my insides. I know she's right; I know that's what we've been working toward; but I can't just yet. I can't even think about it. I tuck the pouch into my vest pocket.

We fly him in the yard a few times, just to remind him about returning to the fist. My confidence builds each time he hits the glove. *We're ready*, I keep telling myself. *You're ready*, I send out to Rufus, as if my mind can penetrate his.

"It's time," Aunt Bea says, checking the sky.

A plume of dust signals a car coming down the road. We'd agreed cars would be bad for Rufus, and we'd wait for any to clear out before heading into the woods to fly him. I call Rufus to the glove, just to keep him focused until the car passes. Only this car—truck, actually—pulls into Aunt Bea's driveway.

I visor a hand over my eyes, try to see who it is, because who would be coming to visit unannounced at sundown on a Saturday? It takes me a second to register the blue lights on top of the truck. And then a man in a uniform—a uniform with the Fish and Wildlife symbol Jaxon's been sketching for our project emblazoned on his vest.

Aunt Bea's jaw clenches. "Stay here," she says, holding up a hand, like I need more than words to comprehend the full depth of her meaning. I am fully aware of that depth. Aunt Bea warned me that first night: *This is a rehab bird. We make him better and then we release him back out to his wild life.* But I wouldn't listen.

"Hello. Are you Beatrice?" says a man's voice attached to the silhouette that steps onto the lawn.

"Hello, Warden," she says, walking his way. Her legs are stiff, like she's being dragged toward him by some tractor beam.

"Jim Doucet," he says, then looks past her, right at me. "I'm here about a rehab owl." His head nods in my direction.

At Rufus.

"I don't have you registered to fly anything but that hawk," he says, examining a notepad in his hand. "And have you signed on for an apprentice this season that I don't know about?"

The laws we've broken flash before my eyes. I can pick out each one from Jaxon's manual. Unlicensed falconer: me. Unauthorized bird: the owl on my fist. The punishments for each: loss of falconry permit. Meaning the loss of the privilege of keeping a raptor.

Of keeping Red.

Aunt Bea seems to shrink as she approaches him. "Well, Warden, there's a bit of a story here."

Bit of a story? No story, just me. Me and my need to train Rufus. And then the name registers: *Doucet*. I look back at the truck. Jaxon sits in the passenger seat.

He told his dad about Rufus.

A black hole opens in my gut and my insides shrivel down into it. I did this. Me. How could I have been so stupid? I knew friends were dangerous. I let myself go for one second, let two people in, and now it's happening all over again—just like with that stupid birthday party I begged my mother to host . . .

The warden holds up a hand to stop Aunt Bea midsentence.

I have to fix this.

"It's my fault," I say, walking straight over toward the warden. "I made—"

"Maureen," Aunt Bea snaps, slicing a hand back at me.

The warden's eyebrows narrow. The notepad in his hand is not a regular notepad. It's a bound stack of citation forms. Citations. For violations of the rules. He's already decided.

I step back.

Aunt Bea will lose everything she loves. Because of me.

I had thought the worst thing that could happen was me being taken away from here, but no—the worst thing is me destroying everything here that I love.

I can't let this happen.

I run headlong into the trees, fist clenched on Rufus's jesses. He's screeching, flapping to stay upright as I barrel through the underbrush. If we're not there, the game warden can't give Aunt Bea a citation. He can't take her license. He can't ruin her life. Not because of me.

My toe hooks on a root and I tumble down. My hands instinctively jerk forward to cushion my fall. Rufus flies off my fist, screeching as he lifts into the net of branches.

"Rufus!" I scream.

I roll over, search the air, but it's just branches and leaves and shadow. "Rufus!"

A twig snaps, a chickadee cries out. I scramble to my feet, rush through the bramble to a clearing.

"Rufus!"

Owls are invisible, designed to blend in with the forest, and silent, with feathers fringed in fluff to keep even the air molecules from giving them away. My eyes scan the tree branches—could that be him? What about that lump in the thicket?

My heart pounds. He's not ready. He hasn't flown alone in the forest for weeks. I'm ruining everything—Aunt Bea's life, Rufus's life, my own life.

Please, no.

"Rufus!"

I run to the next clearing, then to the next, searching the shadows. Branches tug at my pants, my fleece, the vest; I'm streaked with scratches and prickled with burs. I can barely see—thick tears cloud my eyes. I keep going, push farther into the brush. Mud sucks at my boots, splatters my jeans. My gauntlet gets snagged on a pricker vine. I stop to untangle it.

Wings flash.

Could it be? Forget the glove—I wrench my hand free of it and dive through ferns, over fallen logs, my face whipped by switches of yellow leaves. Hidden creatures skitter away from me in a rustle of leaf litter. Good—stay away from me. I'm a hurricane of bad. I destroy every good thing I touch.

A wide stream cuts through the woods, leaving a space in the canopy of leaves. The sky is the deepening blue of evening. The shadows all around me have lengthened into broad strips of black. I'm in a hollow—a dip in the earth, meaning I can only barely guess at what direction I'm facing. And I have no idea where Aunt Bea's house is, even if I could figure out which way is west. A chill creeps over me.

I'm lost.

I fall to my knees.

Rufus is lost.

I slump down farther.

I hear a screech—his screech?—and it echoes from everywhere.

He's really gone.

I sink into the mud at the stream's edge, then lie back in the leaves. I failed my owl. I failed my aunt. It's my fault she did any of this.

It's Jaxon's fault, my anger says.

But I can't even hold on to that anger. I knew the rules. I just didn't like them. I knew what was best for Rufus—it just wasn't what was best for me. This is all on me. It's like I was handed this glass bowl full of everything I ever wanted and I bungled it, let it shatter to pieces. No—it's more that this perfect place was foolish enough to let me into it. I alone am enough to ruin anything.

It's fully dark now. The cold mud along the stream's bank chills the whole of me. Shivers begin shattering my body. I'm so useless, I have no idea how to even start a fire without a match. So much for the *My Side of the Mountain* fantasy. I feel my way away from the water to a tree and hunch my back against it. It's not until I hear sniffing that I remember I'm wearing a vest full of meat. I take the knife from its pocket and then hurl the vest as far from me as I can. I slide my back up the bark to stand against the tree and hit a branch. I should climb onto it. I fold the knife, store it in the pocket of my fleece, and hook my arms around the branch. Years of playground climbing have prepared me at least for this.

I settle on the branch; it's not too far up the tree—if I fall, I'm hoping for a sprained ankle, not a broken neck. Whatever I'd thought was sniffing is either silent as a ghost or gone. I'm not climbing down to find out which.

Who cooks for you? Who cooks the food? a strange owl cries. It's a barred owl's call. Not Rufus. I hold still, listen to hear it again. Barred owls have attacked people who've come too close to their nests. And I know what talons are capable of. As my ears strain to hear the angry owl's approach, the night fills with other noises. A breeze sends the branches clacking, the leaves rustling. A twig snaps somewhere—animals moving. Toads croak in the stream below me. Tree frogs chirp. Grasshoppers buzz. A growl. A snort.

This is the world that injured Rufus. The world we saved him from. A world I've thrown him back into.

If one of us has to be attacked, let it be me. Please, let it be me.

"Reenie!"

It's Aunt Bea's voice.

"I'm here!" I cry, and nearly fall out of my tree leaning toward her voice.

"Reenie!"

A flashlight's beam slices the black. Lands on my vest, which lies across some scrubby plants by the stream. Something's ripped a pocket.

"Oh god—Reenie!" Aunt Bea comes careening down the slope.

"I'm here!" I shout again, and drop down out of my tree—the flashlight's glow shows I was barely four feet up.

Aunt Bea whips the light, catching me in its beam.

The survival terror subsides and is replaced in an instant with horror at what I've done. Tears spring out. "I'm so sorry." A sob bursts from my throat.

Aunt Bea rushes to me, wraps her arms around me. That only makes me feel worse.

"I did this," I wail into her arms. "I'm bad luck."

Aunt Bea strokes my hair. "What are you going on about?" She pushes me off her chest, smoothes a lock of hair from my face.

"The warden," I manage between hiccups of tears. "It's my fault. I'm so sorry." I drop onto my knees.

"Reenie," Aunt Bea says, kneeling beside me. "It was my choice to let you train that owl. My choice to help you."

"But that's not true," I say. "I *made* you train him. If I

hadn't been so stubborn, if I had listened to you, if I had followed the rules—I even know the rules!" I'm screaming now, hitting the dirt with my fist. "That was Jaxon's dad. I brought him here!"

"Maureen," she says. "Any trouble I'm in is my own. You aren't to blame for anything."

"I know it's there in the back of your brain. So just say it! At least you could tell me the truth!"

Aunt Bea gives me a hard look, the look she'd give another grownup. "I'll give you the truth, Maureen. The truth is, none of what you just said is true." She stands up, holds out a hand, and pulls me up from the leaves. "The truth is, none of what that warden said to me is on you. It's *my* license on the line. *My* choices. Any trouble I'm in is mine.

"The good news is, he's not giving me a formal citation. Just an informal probation. I have to fill out some paperwork. Everything's going to be all right."

Her words worm into me, cutting through the walls I've built around my heart. "But I made you," I whisper.

Aunt Bea snorts and wipes her face, and I realize she's crying too. "Girl, you couldn't *make* me do anything." She smiles. "If we aren't both the stubbornest moose in the forest." She hugs me to her, tight.

We walk back up the hill Aunt Bea came down, and she grabs my vest as we pass it. "Barely torn," she says.

"Probably a fisher cat, maybe a skunk. I must have scared it off."

Fisher cats are overgrown ferrets. Skunks are only feared for their stink. Here, I'd imagined bears and catamounts, but the scariest thing that attacked me in this forest came from inside. My own fear was the most dangerous thing hunting me. And it's always on the prowl.

"Your friend was worried when he saw you run off," Aunt Bea says. "I think his dad changed his mind about giving me a citation when he saw how upset his son was."

"Jaxon?"

"I hope you don't blame him. I don't. He was worried about Rufus."

"I should have thought more about Rufus."

"No, *I* should have helped you understand the rules better, kept both of us from having fun we shouldn't have had." She takes my hand. "But I'd wager, what we did—I think you saved that owl's life."

I pick a bur from my vest. "Not tonight. Tonight, I lost him."

"No," she says, holding a dead branch out of the way for me. "He went home. It's where he belongs." She puts her arm around my shoulders as we step over a log.

"I tripped and he was thrown off my arm," I say. "He must think I threw him away."

"He's a bird, Reenie," she says. "He thinks you sent him flying. He's probably out hunting mice and stretching his wings."

"What about the jesses?" I ask. "He'll get them tangled on a branch and die because of me."

"I cut all my jesses so they break if they get tangled in branches."

"He'll be lonely," I say. "And cold."

"He's a great horned owl," she says. "They live alone unless they're raising a family, and he has a coat of downy feathers to keep him warm."

"He wasn't ready." *I wasn't ready*, is what I mean.

She squeezes my hand. "He was." Her eyes hold mine as if to stress how okay he is.

We crunch through the last of the deep leaf pile as we near the house. "You helped that owl more than he'll ever know," Aunt Bea says. "He'll probably live through the winter because of you."

I let the words in, lay them like stones, start to build the foundation of trusting this idea: that Rufus was ready, that I did something right.

"Yeah," I say. I step through the last bush and into the yard. "I just wish I'd gotten a chance to say goodbye."

Aunt Bea stops dead, points toward the mews. "I think you'll get your chance."

I follow her finger and there, perched on the roof of his house, is my Rufus.

Joy explodes through me and every nerve is on fire. A smile erupts—so big it nearly breaks my face—and I can barely get a whistle out to call him to me, but I do. And he soars down through the night, too fast for me to realize I have no glove on, so he hits my arm like a two-ton truck and clenches with his vicelike talons. I grit my teeth, control myself to keep from screaming. At least I'm wearing a thick fleece. Otherwise, I'd have serious holes in my skin.

Rufus is all atwitter. He nibbles my hair and screeches for food. I dig into what remains of a vest pocket and find a tidbit. He gobbles it down.

"My good boy," I whisper to him, tears streaming down my face. "You came home, my dear boy."

We settle Rufus back in his aviary and Aunt Bea tosses in a live mouse, which Rufus hunts like a pro.

"Good night, good buddy," I whisper through the bars, and then I hoot our special hoot, and he hoots back to me, and I know he's as happy to see me as I am to see him.

Inside, Aunt Bea pulls out bread, butter, and cheese, and we start making food.

"He came back," I say as I fry the grilled cheese sandwiches for us.

"That's not a good thing," she says, pouring some milk.

"Of course it's a good thing!" I say, slapping the gooey sandwiches onto plates. "He isn't ready yet. He still needs me."

Aunt Bea takes her plate and begins to eat standing up. "He can hunt," she says. "He can fly, meaning his wing's healed. There's no reason he couldn't have been released today. And he *was* released. But he came back here instead of flying free."

I take my sandwich to the table and sit pertly in my chair. "Which means he isn't ready yet."

Aunt Bea sits next to me. "Which means he's getting too comfortable. Remember the goal here, Reenie. We want him to go away and never come back. He deserves to live a wild owl's natural life."

I stuff a huge bite into my mouth and take my time chewing. What's so good about a wild owl's natural life? The question answers itself: it's the life he's meant to lead. She's right. I know she's right.

"We need to start separating from him," Aunt Bea says, finishing her sandwich and standing to put her plate in the sink. "We need to get him thinking about living on his own."

I take a long sip of my milk. "So, what—I shouldn't go out and talk to him?"

Aunt Bea must hear the abject misery in my voice, because she smiles and says, "How about one more visit? We'll start tomorrow on moving him to more private quarters."

Warmth blooms and fills me, toes to frizz. "One more visit." I gulp down my sandwich and head to the sink to start on dishes.

Aunt Bea shoos me away. "Well, get busy," she says. "I can take on dishes tonight. Feed Red while you're at it."

24
Rufus

WHAT A DAY! I FLAP AROUND MY NEST, LANDING ON EACH perch, letting the place know I'm an owl who flew through the woods and didn't die. I flew past a squirrel's nest—didn't even flinch. Of course, the squirrel didn't come out of the nest, but the important thing to note is the Not Flinching. I even heard a crow somewhere off to the south and didn't fall out of the air with fright.

The Brown Frizz was very sneaky to try out this new hunting technique. Just throwing me into the woods and then hiding in the leaves. Like I couldn't hear her snuffling, let alone the pounding of her heart. But I got the message.

She was testing me. And just wait until tomorrow when I hock up my pellet. She'll see the two voles I caught *all by myself.* HA!

The Brown Frizz appears outside my nest as if called.

"Brown Frizz!" I screech. "Did you see me? I know you were hiding, but please, there is no hiding from a great horned owl. So you definitely should have looked up at me because I FLEW, weaving through the branches and perching and diving, and I caught *two voles!* All by myself, no help needed!"

The Brown Frizz does not seem to be catching on with the Good Feelings in my hoots. She slumps against the wall of my nest and slides like a slug to the dirt. She starts grumbling in Furless Creature–ese.

I land on my mute rock, which is the closest perch to her head. "Brown Frizz, there is no reason to be sulking like a frog in a drought. Focus on the exceptional, exhilarating events of the day. I FLEW!"

The Brown Frizz merely continues her grumbling. She sticks a wing-toe in through the web and I nibble it, trying to get her to scrunch up her beakless maw, which she does, and there's the slightest hint of Good Feelings.

"That's a good furless creature," I chirp.

She cracks open the web on my nest and crawls inside. I don't mind her coming in, especially on a day like today.

She curls up against the wall and continues grumbling. I flap over and perch on her knee.

"Brown Frizz, you are acting like a fly in a web. There is no sense to this moping. You're not giving off nearly the quantity of Good Feelings I would have expected after such a successful test."

She runs her wing-toe over my breastbone, and I fluff my feathers and chirrup at her. I lean in and give her a good nip on the head fur. She chuckles and gives me a nice rub between the ear tufts, which feels quite lovely. I nip at her wing-toes when she looks like she's thinking of stopping such nice rubbings.

We stay there for quite some time, her giving me some excellent rubbings and me giving her some excellent instruction with my beak and talons as to where to rub. But then her beakless maw stretches wide and she sucks in a great gulp of air, and I can see she's half-asleep already.

"You should head back to your nest," I hoot to her.

She hoots back—terribly. She's forgotten everything I taught her.

"Rest up," I hoot to her as she crosses the perch meadow. "There will be more excellent flying tomorrow!" Just hooting about it again brings back the buzz of excitement to my gizzard.

I fly up to my sleeping perch and give myself a bit of

a groom. My feathers are more ruffled than normal, what with all the flying OUT IN THE WILD LIKE A REAL OWL.

I can't keep from hooting softly about it. What a day, WHAT A DAY!

"You're a half dud of a hatchling," Red squawks. She's giving me the Hawk Eye from her perch.

"Shut your beak," I hoot. "I am an owl who can hunt in the woods."

"So what are you doing back here?"

I am on the brink of becoming completely fluffed. "I *live* here."

"No!" she screeches, flapping and footing her perch. "You live *out there*. You are a wild bird."

That's it. Fluffed, I am. "OBVIOUSLY!"

"So I ask again, what are you doing back in *here?*"

My feathers are all out of sorts. I'm practically buzzing with all the hoots I'm holding in. "As I just chirped," I say, beak clamped shut to keep from screeching uncontrollably, "I. Live. Here."

"You are most definitely a half dud." Red flaps out of the opening and into another part of her nest.

That's it. "YOU BEAK-IN-YOUR-BUTT BIRD! I am absolutely sick of you calling me hatchling or half dud or anything! I am a great horned owl, and if anything, you should call me MISTER-OWL-SIR-PLEASE-DON'T-EAT-ME!"

Red flits back onto the perch near the opening. "Oh, should I? Come and get me, *HATCHLING*."

I launch at the opening in the wall, hitting the long, straight branches that cover it and screeching and flapping and putting on quite a terrifying show. I swoop back to my perch. Red is no longer in the opening.

That should shut her beak.

She swoops back to where she'd been, completely unscathed, not a feather out of place. "Huh," she tweets. "Not a very successful attack."

Every feather on my body fluffs out. "If those branches weren't there," I snap.

"Exactly!" she screeches. "That's the entire point. Those branches *aren't* there out in the wild. There are no webs of branches. There's just you and your talons and your wings and the world. And you came back *here*. You chose to close yourself inside this nest."

Ah, now I'm getting my foot around her point. Which forces me to listen to the tiny hoots inside, the ones that told me to come back to this place, the ones that whispered how the woods are full of dangers. The woods are hungry for young owls with no real hunting skills. The woods are cold and unforgiving and snap down like a claw when an owl least expects it. How much better to live in a safe, warm nest with nice furless creatures who give good rubbings and feed me all the mice I can swallow.

And yet this nest is also a trap. This web is not one I can open with my own talons.

"Why haven't *you* left?" I hoot to Red after a while.

Red turns away from me, runs her beak over a feather. "I can't leave," she chirps. "I've never lived in the wild. I was hatched in a nest like this one and taken from my mother as a chick. The only mother I've ever known is the one you call Gray Tail." She turns back to me. "I tried once. I flew far on a hunt, soaring beyond her whistle. Spent a night out in the wild. It rained, and I got soaked on a branch. I flew under the eaves of a human nest and was attacked by a cat. It tore my wing feathers, taking a few primaries in its claws. I scrambled into the sky, flapping any which way to escape the pain. Then I was lost, and scared, and cold, and helpless. But my partner, Gray Tail, found me, crouched in a thicket of evergreens. She brought me back here. I've never tried to fly free again.

"But you," she screeches. "You've lived out there. Your parents showed you how to live in the wild. It may be easier to live in this nest, but it's not the real life of a bird. I failed because I never had a chance. But you. You're choosing to fail.

"Don't choose to be a dud like me."

She flaps up to her sleeping perch. I tuck a foot under my breast feathers and hunker down to think. Is living with the Brown Frizz choosing to fail? Is this life really a failure? And if I leave, will the Brown Frizz be all right?

Of course the Brown Frizz will be fine. Furless creatures are not dependent on birds. Furless creatures help hurt birds . . . hurt animals of all kinds . . . help them and then set them free.

Great Beak, was that what had the Brown Frizz all fluffed tonight? That I didn't fly away? Was today not a test but the end of everything? Was I supposed to fly off?

Wait—does that mean the furless creatures think I'm healed? I stretch my wings. There's no pain, no tightness. I *am* healed. And I can hunt—I caught two voles, all on my own, out in the wild.

I'm here because I'm afraid. But I have nothing to fear.

I am a great horned owl.

Master of the night forest.

Don't worry, Brown Frizz. I understand now. I'm sorry I misunderstood your grumbles. But you furless creatures are so confusing, what with all the very appealing nuzzling.

I am ready, Brown Frizz.

A coyote howls and its warning carries through the trees. *Danger*, it says.

I scrunch down inside my feathers.

Perhaps I am not yet quite completely and *absolutely* ready.

Maybe tomorrow.

Yes, tomorrow.

Or the next day.

25
Reenie

SUNDAY MORNING, I CAN BARELY EAT MY PANCAKES, EVEN
though Aunt Bea went all out and made the amazing ones
with raspberries and buckwheat. Rufus is already hooting
out in the yard, and every cell in my body wants to run out
there and snuggle him and fly together. To have him soar to
me and hit my fist, a part of me stretched far and brought
near.

But that's for me. Those are things I need. And what
I really have to do now is think about what Rufus needs.
What's best for him.

"Did I make a bad batch?" Aunt Bea asks, sitting beside me with her plate.

"No," I say, shoving my forkful through the puddle of syrup.

"Well, eat, then." She shoves a big bite into her mouth. "We have work to do."

I force myself to eat.

Aunt Bea takes breakfast out to Rufus and Red, while I stay inside to do dishes. She found a rat in a Havahart trap in the basement, and every inch of me wants to watch Rufus hunt it, but that's rule number one going forward: no more human contact. As I scrub each dish, I wonder if he's looking for me. I worry he's sad I'm not there, cheering him on. And then I force myself to remember he's a wild bird, and even if he does wish I was there, he needs to get over me. He needs to move on.

Each time I tell myself this, I feel like I'm running my heart over a cheese grater.

After the dishes are done, I throw on work clothes and head for the empty aviaries. Aunt Bea has opened the sides of two that stand near each other. Inside, she's arranging sections of wall. She explains that they can be set together to make a larger flight pen.

"There are preset holes in the grass," she says, lifting a section.

We work together in silence, our only accompaniment Red's and Rufus's screeching and twittering and the *bang-bang-bang* of Aunt Bea's mallet as she pounds down the sections and fastens them together. It takes us until the sun is high over the trees to get the walls up.

Aunt Bea wipes her forehead with her sleeve. "Next, we have to lay these sections across the roof and tie them down, but I need a break before lugging those up there."

Inside, over lemonade, Aunt Bea tells me her plans. "We'll move him to the flight pen this evening," she explains. "I'll do the moving. You prepare the food for their dinner. I'm going to get some live rats in town for Rufus to hunt. He's getting hungrier by the day. If we don't get him rehabilitated, he'll eat all the rodents for a mile in any direction!"

"Can't I release one rat?" I ask.

"We have to break the bond he's formed with you," she says, and then, glancing at me, she softens her voice. "You have to help him find his own way."

I like that idea: that I'm still helping, only different helping. That my giving him the space to trust himself is a job.

I nod, and she nods back, smiling.

After lemonade, Aunt Bea and I get in the truck. We head to the pet store and pick out four rats. As we drive home, I peer into their box.

"Don't get friendly with the food," Aunt Bea warns.

I put the box between my feet, forgetting the shiny eyes, the twitching whiskers. "I won't."

"Sometimes you have to make hard choices," Aunt Bea says, negotiating the truck out of Rutland. "These rats didn't start out this morning thinking they were dinner for a hungry owl. They have as much right to their lives as any creature. But now here they are, because I made a choice, not one I'm particularly happy about, but a choice that had to be made. We made a promise to that owl, and these rats are part of that promise."

"I know," I say, not listening to the little squeaks coming from between my feet.

When we get home, we find Jaxon and his dad parked in our driveway. Jaxon slides out of his seat as we pull in and park. Aunt Bea rolls the window down.

"I recalled you mentioning needing to set up the flight pen," says Warden Doucet, now not in his uniform but jeans and a T-shirt. "My son here thought you might like some help."

Aunt Bea nods. "We could use it."

I get out of the truck and hug the box of rats to my chest. Jaxon comes over to me. "Reenie, I . . ."

A part of me wants to scream at him. To throw the rats in his face and have them scratch him to ribbons.

Then I notice his eyes are red and shiny with tears.

"I was worried about . . . the owl, about Rufus." He kicks a rock at his dad's truck. "I didn't mean to get your aunt in trouble."

I remember what Aunt Bea said, that it was how upset Jaxon was that made his dad decide not to cite her. That he really was worried about me and about Rufus. Maybe this is another part of being friends: Stopping a friend from doing something dangerous, even if they are set on it. Caring enough not to want them to get hurt. I guess Jaxon made a hard choice too.

"It's okay," I say.

"I'm sorry," he says.

I smile. "Want to help me find a place for Rufus's dinner?" I hold out the box.

He half smiles back. "Sure."

It takes the four of us all afternoon to fasten on the roof of the flight pen. Jaxon and his dad leave—their visitation ends at 5:00 p.m. Aunt Bea and I finish tying everything off around sunset and are just climbing down when Rufus starts screeching for dinner.

"He's going to love it," I say, sitting on the grass and admiring our new construction. The flight pen is almost as long as the whole yard. Its walls are made of offset boards, which allow a little air through but don't let the bird see outside the pen. Only the roof is open between the two aviaries at the ends, the plastic-coated wire mesh allowing the bird a clear view of the sky. Aunt Bea is setting perches at different places inside, and there are branches and ropes strung between the walls.

"Hopefully, he won't love it too much," Aunt Bea says, coming out the door of the far aviary. "Hopefully, that view of the stars will make him hungry for freedom."

I sit in the kitchen, allegedly working on my hunting project—I posted my section this morning; Jamie added extensive comments—but actually squinting out into the darkness to catch a glimpse of Rufus moving into the aviary, of Aunt Bea releasing the rats.

I'm having trouble with my new job: helping Rufus find his own way. I mean, there's just so much we don't know. What if he's imprinted on humans? What if he tries to nest on someone's porch and they hit him with a broom? What if . . . what if . . .

When Aunt Bea comes inside, I've worried myself into knots.

"What if it doesn't work?" I ask her the second she's in the door.

Aunt Bea slides off her work boots. "He's going to be fine."

"But why not keep him?" I ask, reminding her that this is an option. "That way he's guaranteed to be safe."

Aunt Bea quirks her face like I'm blubbering gibberish. "That's no life for an owl. An owl needs adventure, needs to stretch his wings. And what about having his own family? Shouldn't he have a chance at that?"

I nod my head, but everything in my body is screaming, *No!* "It's too risky. I mean, what if he gets too friendly with people?"

Aunt Bea nods. "It's a risk," she says. "But isn't it a risk worth taking for the chance to live free?" She lays the remains of Rufus's anklets and jesses on the pages of my book. Then she places a piece of paper with a phone number beside them. "Your mother called. The apartment is ready. She's planning on moving in tomorrow."

It's too much. Losing Rufus, and now this? The tears drop down and smear the ink.

"Call her," Aunt Bea says gently. "Take the risk. Tell her how you feel. I'll be here when you're done." She squeezes my shoulder and places the phone next to the book.

I stare at the paper. Calling isn't the risk. Speaking is. To say what I want—what if it causes Mom to relapse? What if . . . what if . . .

No. I have to do this. Look at Jamie and her parents— living apart in the same house. I don't want that. I want what Jaxon has—I want honesty. I want to have a voice.

Mom answers on the second ring. "Reenie? Hi!"

"Mom?" My voice cracks and then it just rushes out of me. "I don't want to live in Rutland."

"What?" Her tone changes. "Honey, this place is great. And you can go to your old school."

"I don't want to go to my old school. I want to stay at Otter Creek."

I hear Mom breathing on the other end of the line. "Reens, I know it's been hard this past month—"

"But it hasn't," I interrupt. "Mom, I like it here. I have friends."

Mom is silent. Did I push too far? No—I had to say it. She has to know. I don't want to keep hiding myself from her.

"Please, Mom," I say.

"Okay," she says.

"Okay?" I echo, surprised.

"Yes, okay," she says. She's not crying. She sounds . . . like a mom.

"Really?" I ask.

"Yes, really. I want this to be *our* home. I guess I should have checked with you before, but I got so excited, Randi's been so nice—I want you to be as excited as I am about our home. We're partners, right? The two musketeers?"

Inside, this wire coiled around my heart loosens. I hadn't even known it was there. "The two somethings," I manage.

"But two, together," she says. "I'll call Randi. We'll start searching."

"Thank you," I say. My smile shines through my words.

"Don't thank me yet. I have no idea if there're any available apartments in that district."

"Thanks for trying," I say.

"I'll try anything for you, Reens."

We chat for a little longer, and when we hang up, I say, "I love you," and it's different. It doesn't feel like a burden, my loving her, but a gift.

Aunt Bea and I eat dinner, Aunt Bea reading some magazine and me working on a math work sheet. After, we do the dishes and sit in the living room, reading, the silence interrupted every once in a while by a car rumbling past on the road. And then, as if telling me it's time for bed, Rufus hoots his good-night greeting.

Then far off, like an echo, only not, another owl answers.

"Did you hear that?" I ask.

Aunt Bea nods without looking up. "That's what I'm talking about," she says. "Rufus deserves to live with friends of his own kind."

We both sit, silent, waiting to hear if the two owls get their hoot on, but the night remains quiet. Another car rolls by. I decide to head to bed. But just as my eyes are closing, I swear I hear the owls hoot again, first Rufus, then the other.

26
Rufus

I CANNOT BELIEVE MY EARS. IT'S FIRST. SHE'S ANSWERING my hoots. She's coming.

Pellets!

It's not that I don't appreciate a visit, but First, well— after our last hoot, I don't think she's going to be terribly understanding about my partnership with the Brown Frizz. Especially since I am currently ensnared under this web that is awfully exposed in the skyward direction and makes me look disturbingly like prey caught in a trap. Further, given the obscene amount of rat I've just swallowed, any activity beyond perching in the corner and trying not to burst seems ill-advised. Battle, even in defense of my life, appears impossible.

"Second!" First screeches, closer now.

"Red!" I hoot. "I feel I should warn you that my sister is coming and she's possibly going to attempt to eat me. Any advice is appreciated."

Red doesn't answer. She's been quiet ever since our last chat about going wild.

"Seriously!" I call. "Check the walls on your nest. I can't guarantee she won't attack you as well."

Red is silent. Her heartbeat is slow and quiet.

Before I can hoot again, something crashes onto the roof of my new nest.

"Second!" booms First, stomping along the stiff web covering the wide-open part of my nest. "What kind of vine is this? I can't rip it open. You live under here? This is no place for an owl!"

"Go away!" I hoot from under the roof of the north end of my nest. "You can't eat me in here."

"Eat you?" First flaps up and lands above me with a bang. "Why would I eat you? Great Beak, you're not still fluffed about my dropping you in the nest beak-first last time? You seemed to have survived . . . well, lived. Get over it.

"I'm here about Mother."

My gizzard goes cold. "Mother?" I swoop down to a stump situated under the web.

First stays on her new perch on the roof and looks down at me. "Great Beak, you're just like her." Her ear tufts lift straight up. "You're trapped under there, aren't you? Did you get trapped? Why bother even hooting back — of course *you* got trapped."

I feel myself heading straight to fluffdom, but I calm myself, focus on the chill in my gizzard, on Mother. "What do you know about Mother?"

"She's trapped, just like you. But she's in a cave of some sort, like that one there." She juts her beak at the human nest. "I heard her hoots one night as I flew through a thin forest near the lights, the ones we were told never to fly near. What Father didn't tell us was that there's a whole world of rodents living near those lights, all for an owl's easy picking."

"First," I interrupt, sensing her brain flying off into the weeds, "what about Mother?"

First rouses, relaxes her tufts. "Oh, right, yes. She needs our help to escape." She begins to preen. "I came to get you to assist me with the attack. I can see now that was some wishful thinking on my part."

My first instinct is to rip a hole in the web and fly off to save Mother, but then I remember Red's tweets from that first night in my old nest. I remember the last night I had with Mother, the awful monster that came growling out of that blaze of light.

"I don't think Mother is trapped, First," I hoot quietly.

"Of course she's trapped," she replies, finishing her preen and muting on my roof. "I heard her inside the cave."

"She's hurt," I chirp. "She was trying to help me learn to hunt. And she was hit by one of the furless creature's rolling monsters. The furless creature took her inside the monster and the rolling monster grumbled away."

First's eyes narrow to slits. "Furless creatures," she growls. "They are the worst. They're probably fattening her up like a turkey. No way that's happening. I'll perch in a tree right near that cave and swoop down like a fierce wind. I can get into that cave and rescue Mother."

"I was hurt by a goshawk," I hoot. "The furless creatures helped me. And I think the furless creature was trying to help Mother when it took her that night. I don't think Mother's really trapped. Or if she is, it's because she's still hurt."

First's ear tufts flip straight up again. "You *like* furless creatures?"

I pull myself up to my most imposing posture. "I've made a family with one," I hoot. "Furless creatures help owls."

First meanly clacks her beak. "Perhaps it is a good thing you are trapped, Second. You must have been out flying in the sunlight to have been attacked by a goshawk. Didn't you listen to a single one of Father's hoots? You don't fly during the day, and you don't go near the furless creatures.

"The world is not kind to owls who don't follow the rules."

My gizzard sours. "Furless creatures don't eat owls," I screech.

"Maybe not," First screeches back, leaning forward and setting her eyes to glow like stars. "But they have taken shots at me with their fire sticks. And they have chased me from my shadow perches, forcing me to fly out in the sunlight.

"Furless creatures are not friends of owls. They are day creatures. They know nothing of the night."

With that, she lifts off into the black. "Goodbye, my tame brother. If you know what's good for you, you'll stay in there, fat and safe and alone, forever."

I stare after her, listen to her heartbeat become quieter and softer until it is finally just a faint breath on the breeze.

"She's not wrong," Red screeches. "The one you call Gray Tail? She has tried to heal birds attacked by humans and the human things they place in the world. There are bad things about furless creatures. Good, too. But if you want to be free, you should take in her hoots."

"You're not a dud," I call to her.

Red flaps around in her nest. I can only hear her now, not see her. She's near the wall, though. Maybe she's looking at me. "I feel like one some days," she says. "But other days, I listen to all the shouts and cries in the wild and I am grateful for this nest, and for my partner, and for the quiet, safe life we share. Hearing your hatchmate, remembering those injured birds, I feel thankful tonight."

"She's right about furless creatures?"

"She is," Red squawks. "But that is the way with all creatures. There are the kind and the cruel in every form of life."

I knew this, though. Who taught me this better than First herself?

"I wish it wasn't true, though," I hoot.

Red flaps deeper into her nest. "It would certainly be easier if the bad creatures all had bright feathers."

"Bright yellow tufts of feathers," I hoot back. "They would stand out better. A giant plume of yellow feathers sprouting from between their eyes."

"Good night, Hatchling," Red twitters, restored to her usual state of meager Good Feelings. "Dream of dangers, clearly marked."

Night noises crowd around. It's warm, and the last crickets of summer take wing on the dried stalks. A beetle crawls on a starflower just outside my nest. A toad croaks from a mud puddle in the woods, then snaps a gulp of food. A screech owl cries out, dinner in its claws. A fox yips. A bear grunts.

All of them are hungry, or longing, or dying. The wild world is full of dangers, and it is cold and cruel. Even the ones you think you can trust might turn out to be the bright-feathered sort.

Dawn pokes dim talons of light into the darkness. The door of the human nest creaks open. The Brown Frizz's heartbeats warm my gizzard. She stays by the human nest, but I feel her watching me. I pull my feathers in, stretch my wings, and swoop down to a perch. If I tip my head all the way over, I can peek at her through the strips of wood that make up the walls of this nest.

She tiptoes down the steps and turns like she's going to pop into my new nest for a bit of a hoot. But then she stops. Instead, she clambers on top of a perch in the meadow, then stands, wobbling like a newly hatched chick on the strip of wood. She stretches her featherless limbs out like wings, closes her eyes, and tips her head back to face the fading stars.

Little songbirds dart out of the woods. The very air sighs, and droplets shake out onto the leaves. The cool breeze sends a shiver over my feathers.

The wild world is full of life and beauty and surprises. The Brown Frizz feels it. I heard it in First's hoots about hunting near the lights, in the happy screech of that fed owl, in the grumble of the mother bear to her cub, in the fox's joyful pant as it trotted through the tall grasses.

Am I going to hide between my wings, fearing the figments my gizzard conjures, or am I going to dare to fly out into the wild?

27
Reenie

ALL MONDAY MORNING AT SCHOOL, WE PRACTICE OUR presentations in the cafeteria.

We all read our parts. Mr. Brown is totally impressed by Jaxon's drawings. Jamie and Jaxon do the fake debate —he says a good thing, Jamie chimes in with a bad. Jaxon doesn't frown too much. I present my interview with Aunt Bea and talk about falconry and how it helps hawks survive.

"Was that awesome or what?" I ask once we finish and sit down.

"We were awesome," Jaxon confirms.

"I feel like I messed up on my delivery," Jamie says, picking at the sides of the poster board.

Jaxon puts a hand on her arm. Jamie nearly jumps out of her skin. "You were awesome," he says.

Jamie flushes through every shade of pink. "Thanks."

"We are ready for Friday," I say.

"We should celebrate," Jaxon says, pulling back his hand like he just noticed whose arm it was lying on.

"Definitely," I say, trying to help them through this adorably awkward moment.

"My house? After school?" Jamie says, trying to get her blush under control.

"I'm drinking all the chocolate milk," Jaxon says.

"Not if I don't first," I say.

"I don't think we have any," Jamie says, apologizing in advance.

"It doesn't matter," Jaxon says. "We can just hang out."

"Yeah," I say.

"Perfect," Jamie says, grinning brightly.

Mom calls Tuesday. "Randi's working miracles," she says. "I have a few places to check out in Branford."

"That's amazing!" I say.

"It's going to be different this time, Reens," she says.

"I know," I say. Because it already is different. Because I'm different.

On Wednesday, Dr. Cho comes by after dinner to check out Rufus. Aunt Bea throws a towel over his head, less to keep him calm than to keep him from seeing me in the bird room while the doctor examines him.

"You did it," Dr. Cho says, finishing up her exam. She pulls off her gloves. "That's a perfectly healthy owl. Which means . . ." she says, trailing off.

"It's time to say goodbye," I finish for her.

Aunt Bea smiles. "It's time to say goodbye."

Aunt Bea places Rufus inside a cardboard box. The three of us crowd into the truck; Rufus and his box are strapped in the truck bed. The sun is already behind the trees, so we drive through deep shadow beneath a still-bright blue sky decked out with strips of gold and pink clouds. We have to release Rufus as close as possible to where we found him. It will give him the best chance of surviving, of finding his home territory, wherever that is.

I sit between Dr. Cho and Aunt Bea and try to keep from sobbing like a baby.

It's insane to be sad when this is the best outcome possible. When Rufus is healthy and hunting and ready to go back home to the wild.

But how do you let a part of yourself go?

We rumble down the dirt road, the same one we drove

down to set the trap so many weeks ago. Rufus is quiet in the back of the truck. Is he scared? Is he carsick?

Aunt Bea pulls to a stop beside a big tree. "We can walk in a bit from here."

The first star glitters in the sky—not a star, but a planet pretending. Everything wants to sparkle when offered the chance.

Aunt Bea gets Rufus in his box from the truck bed. We walk, her holding the precious cargo, through the brush until we find a meadow. The sky is deep blue now, a rim of gold and pink visible through the trees to the west.

Aunt Bea holds the box out to me. "You should do it," she says.

Dr. Cho nods.

I take the box, careful not to jostle Rufus. I walk with him out into the grass.

"This is it, buddy," I whisper to him. "You're home." My voice chokes.

Rufus scratches inside the box, chirps something.

I set the box in the grass. We watched some videos on YouTube over dinner, to see how it's done, so I know what to do. I just can't do it.

What if he's not ready? What if a giant eagle swoops down and tears him apart before he even gets in one free flap?

Rufus scratches again, screeches.

I choose to believe.

I unhitch the cardboard flaps, pull them apart without looking in, and tip the box forward. Nothing happens. I tip the box farther and Rufus flops out onto the grass.

He stumbles a bit. Looks around. Notices me. He lifts his ear tufts.

I haven't seen him in days. I think he's grown bigger, I think he's gotten more wild. Then it hits me that he's simply returned to what he was, the bird king from weeks ago, all healed up and ready to rule.

"You can do it," I whisper. A smile warms my cheeks, a real smile, because I know he can.

Rufus looks away from me, lifts his wings, and flaps once, twice, rising into the twilight, and then he's a shadow against the stars, a dream.

A hand drops onto my shoulder. "You did good," Aunt Bea says.

I nod, afraid if I say anything I'll explode.

She hugs me to her. The tears come. I'm smiling and crying, happy and sad, so many feelings, all real, all at once. It feels good. The whole world sparkles through my tears.

We turn as one and walk back through the brambles.

Somewhere, deep in the night, an owl hoots.

I like to think it's Rufus, saying goodbye.

28
Rufus

THE FURLESS CREATURES MADE UP THEIR MINDS A BIT
sooner than I expected. I was in a box and now I am in a
field and it is wide open and exposed to all the wild things
of the night forest.

The Brown Frizz stands holding the box. Her eyes
lock on to mine. I lift my tufts. Will she hoot a warning?
Advice?

But she merely whuffles something in Furless
Creature–ese.

She believes I am ready.

I turn my ears to the wild. A map of heartbeats rises from the shadows, life pulsing through the grass, out of the darkness. I *am* ready.

I open my wings, press on the air, and rise up, up, hit a current of heat, and glide into the bent talons of the trees.

"Goodbye, Brown Frizz!" I hoot to her. "Thank you, partner!"

She's already walking away. But that is how it must be for furless creatures. Help a hurt owl, heal it, move on to the next.

I circle the trees, fly higher, higher, and see the perch meadow below, not far in the direction of the sunrise. I swoop down and land on Red's roof.

"Red!" I hoot. "I'm free!"

"Then be free, Hatchling," Red screeches.

Red flaps down to a perch, and I swoop onto one of the dead trees in the perch meadow so we can look each other in the beak.

"I just wanted to say goodbye," I chirp. "And thank you."

"Survive," she says. "Say goodbye to me in the springtime."

I bow to her. "I will," I hoot.

Her eyes gleam in the last glimmers of sunset. "Then go do it," she tweets. "This bird is finally going to be able to get a full night's sleep."

I bob my head, lift my wings, and flap off, hooting as loudly as I can, just so she won't forget me.

The night is cold and dark. I fly high, look down on the rivulets of light that cut the darkness. Somewhere down there is Mother. Only one owl can help me find her.

First.

I swoop through the breeze, my feathers slicing the air currents, splitting them into eddies of silence. I was so afraid to fly high before. What was I afraid of?

The rivulets lead toward rivers of light, which pour into a vast lake of brightness. First will be there, hunting along the shores in the shadows. I glide lower, begin hooting for her. It doesn't take long for me to sense the shadow diving down, talons out.

I dip and swerve to avoid her attack.

"You're out!" First cries, wheeling around.

"Take me to Mother," I screech.

First pulls up in front of me. "You dodged my attack."

"I'm not an owlet."

Her tufts lift. "Oh?"

She swoops toward me and I dive, then twist around, talons out. We lock talons and beat our wings, pulling each other in a circle. Our ear tufts are straight up, our eyes fierce globes glowing.

This is and is not the same game we played in the nest. Now, I'm bigger. And I believe I have a chance.

First releases me. "I guess you have grown," she hoots, ear tufts lowering. She flaps away from me and then glides down into a hummock of trees between the lights.

I follow her into the shadows.

First has set up a perch for herself between the forking trunks of a tall evergreen tree. Discarded remnants of furless-creature stuff tumble across the scrubby grass and dirt below. Furless creatures' monsters roar by, flashing their lights like lightning through the branches.

"Why do you perch here of all places?" I chirp, landing on a small branch above her. We may have made peace, but who knows when First will break it.

"I told you," she says, "the lights attract rodents." She rouses, begins preening her feathers. "Also, I don't have to fight any other owl for the food."

"Did you have to fight other owls in the woods?" This is news.

First finishes her grooming and pulls her feathers in. "Even Father warned me off his territory."

My gizzard turns cold. "*Father* did?"

"I told you to stay where you were. The wild is cold and cruel." First looks away, down at the shadows below.

I want to hoot something comforting to her, but I sense there is no comfort to be had. Father was never a gentle owl, but perhaps that is because there can be no such thing.

"I'm sorry," I hoot.

"I'm not," she chirps back. "Better to have it honest. Better to know the truth. And I have found my own place. I hunt here at night. During the day, I perch near a lake in deep woods.

"You will find your place, Second. If you fight for it, you will."

"I have to find Mother first," I say.

First dives down from her branch, landing like a stone on a tuft of grass. Then she flaps back up, a vole between her claws. She gulps it down whole. "I'll take you," she chirps, wiping her talon across her beak. "But you should grab a meal before we fly."

I raise my tufts. "You don't mind sharing your territory?"

She twitters, tilts her head. "You beat me at Talons," she says. "I'll let you share my territory tonight."

I bob my head. "You're too kind."

"What's a hatchmate for?"

"Apparently, one night of hunting."

"More than you'd get from any other owl."

She has something there. I focus on hunting. It's instinctual now, getting my feathers in line. The heartbeats glow in the darkness. I dive, catch a mouse. Dive again, just miss a vole.

First really has found herself a prime hunting spot. Even if you do have to swoop through garbage to grab your meal.

Once we are both fat and happy, we rest in the tree.

The busy world of the furless creatures slows to a grumble in the deep night, and I close my eyes. When the half day breaks through the darkness, First hoots to me softly, "It's time."

We pellet, then dart beneath the branches and fly out into the dim gray light. First leads me over the black expanses of the furless creatures' paths, over their caves and meadows. I wonder which of them are like my Brown Frizz and the Gray Tail and which have the fire sticks. I wonder which is the kind that has Mother.

First swoops low near a human nest set between thick patches of trees. I follow her and perch in a leaf tree.

"In there," she hoots. "I heard Mother inside that cave." She turns and looks skyward.

"You're leaving?"

She tilts her head to me. "You want me to stay?"

"We have to help Mother escape."

First blinks her eyes slowly. "But I already tried and failed."

"We can try together." I glide down and perch on the branch above her.

First's ear tufts lift, then soften over her brow. *"Together,"* she chirps, digesting the hoot like a morsel of meat. "All right. We shall try. Together." She steps closer to me.

A happy hum warms my gizzard. "Together."

We fly around the place, hooting a greeting to Mother.

She had a special hoot to let us know she was returning to the nest, and we cry this special *Hoot-hoo-hoo-HOOOOOOOOOT!* all around the human nest. A few owls screech or hoot back to us: a pair of screech owls cry for us to go away, that they're not owls but rather bumps on a tree — not a convincing tactic; a snowy owl warns us away from its nest with threat of talon; and a grumpy barred owl chirrups that we're too late.

"Too late?" I perch near where I heard the barred owl. "Too late for what?"

The barred owl is in a small enclosed nest outside the human nest, similar to the one the Brown Frizz let me roost in.

First, always one for direct assaults, slams her talons into its roof. "Where's Mother?" she screeches.

"Get off my nest, you great tufted gizzard." The barred owl flaps down to a lower perch, as if avoiding First's talons.

I raise my ear tufts at First, bob my head to signal her to move off. We need this cantankerous owl's help! Then, lowering my tufts and tucking in all my feathers to create a compact and respectable appearance, I hoot to the barred owl, "You know something of our mother?"

"I don't know if she's your mother," he chirps back. "But there was a nice female great horned here. Her wing never healed right."

My gizzard frosts over and sinks in my gut. "Never healed?"

First is sending off waves of rage. "So the humans killed her?"

The barred owl clacks his beak with disdain. "You fluff-for-brains hatchling," he screeches, "I have a broken wing, and no one killed me. I live here with the humans. These humans take me out and show me off to other, smaller humans. I think it's part of an owl-human alliance they're trying to develop. We've never quite worked out our mutual goals, but they feed me all the mice I can eat without my having to fly on my busted wing, and I let the tiny human hatchlings stare at me and sometimes stroke my chest feathers."

"Owl-human alliance?" First squawks with disdain.

"That sounds right to me," I hoot quietly. "We do live in the same patch of forest. Makes sense we'd want to get to know one another."

"And there is the matter of the food. All I can gobble. Plus, they clean the nest for me. Quite a fine arrangement, if I do say so."

"But Mother is not here," First hoots. "Clearly, she is not a part of this alliance."

"Not this one," the barred owl replies. "But other humans came in one of their rolling hollow rocks, and they took the great horned with them. I believe my humans are trying to spread word of the alliance to other parts of the forest."

It makes quite a bit of sense to me. The Brown Frizz and Gray Tail are certainly the kinds of humans who would support an Owl-Human Alliance. Maybe there are more of their kind of human than there are humans with fire sticks. Or maybe the Alliance is meant to control those fire sticks, at least with respect to owls?

"So you think she's safe?" First chirps. "That the humans mean to take care of her?"

"Of course," the barred owl grumbles. "These humans help owls. At least, they try."

First flaps up and away from the barred owl's nest.

She has absolutely no manners. I bow to the barred owl and hoot, "Thank you," before flying off after her.

"First!" I cry, pumping my wings against an onslaught of icy currents curling down from a nearby mountain. "Slow down!"

"Why?" she hoots back. "We looked for Mother, she's not there, it's over. Go find your own territory."

The air currents push down on me, forcing me to curve around to flap out of their thrust. It's too much pressure. I glide down to the nearest treetop. First fights the currents, burning far too much energy, and then drifts down like a leaf, swerving one way, then the other, and comes to rest in a tree not far from mine.

Half day cracks open into full light. It's too late for us to try to find another day roost. I decide to risk a quick hunt to restore my gizzard. My feathers naturally arrange themselves, and I find a clutch of mice in a nearby tussock of grass. I flap up, silent as a breeze, and glide down, down, and crash into the leaves. My talons squeeze around a mouse and then I fly with it up into the branches.

I find a solid perch and am about to gobble down my kill when I look up and see poor First. I can hear her gizzard grumbling from here.

I flap up to her, present the mouse. "Here," I hoot. "For you."

First cracks open her eyes. "Why would you give me that?" she peeps. "You've got to be as hungry as I am after all that flying."

"I'm hungry," I hoot, "but I can catch another, and you seem in a bad way right now. You need this mouse more than I do." I nudge the mouse toward her with my talon.

"This is not how it's supposed to be," First grumbles. "The rule is *every owl for herself.*"

"Maybe," I hoot, "but I'm not sure those rules apply to hatchmates. At least, I don't think they should."

First fluffs her feathers a bit and raises her tufts. Then they smooth down and she reaches a talon toward the mouse. "Maybe I can agree to that," she chirps. She grips the meat and gobbles it down. "Thank you," she hoots softly.

"You're welcome," I say. "And now, if you'll excuse me, I have a meal of my own to catch."

I swoop down and catch a bite for myself, and when I fly back up to First, she's moved over to make a bit more room on her branch for me.

29
Reenie

IN CLASS THURSDAY, MR. BROWN DROPS A BOMBSHELL: "Instead of doing your presentations in the cafeteria for the other sixth graders, Principal Stanitski wants to have you do them for the whole school at assembly tomorrow!"

Jamie, Jaxon, and I pass the same look of horror among us.

"The whole school?" Jamie whispers.

Jaxon pulls out his wood and starts scraping. The scraping is kind of violent: nervous scraping.

Mr. Brown tells us to get together to discuss how our

practice presentations went on Monday and whether there's anything we'd like to change now that we'll be on stage in front of the *whole school*.

"Our presentation was perfect," Jamie says, flapping a hand as if she can swat away the idea of making any changes. "We'll just do the same thing."

Jaxon flicks off a flake of wood. "We could bring in props. I have a bust of my first deer."

Jamie's lip curls. "No dead stuff."

"You could use it to talk about the economic benefits," I note. "Don't you say something about taxidermy?"

Jamie frowns like she's not quite sold on the concept.

"Aunt Bea," I say, the words emerging as the thought pops into my head.

"We already have the interview with her," Jamie says.

"But she could bring Red."

"She could do that?" Jaxon says, eyebrows tilting up.

"She said she does educational presentations sometimes," I say, shrugging.

"That would be amazing," Jamie says, her body beginning to tremble with excitement.

The same smile appears on all three of our faces.

⌣

When I get home, I see out the back windows that Aunt Bea took down the flight pen while I was at school. Tears prick out along my eyelashes. Every time I remember Rufus is gone, it's as hard as that moment he flew away from me forever.

I leave my bag on a chair and go out into the yard. Red is perched quietly in her aviary, one foot tucked up underneath her. She glances at me, then stares back out her window toward where Rufus had lived.

"I miss him too, old girl."

I wonder what he's doing—he's just waking up, I imagine. Stretching his wings, rousing, preening his feathers. Maybe he scratches an itch on his head with a talon, stretching those ridiculously long legs out before curling back into his stoic stance on the branch. He's got to get hunting—owls are only successful in catching their prey less than half of the time, even on the best days.

My stomach growls. It was loud enough that Red gives me her hawk stare.

"Dinnertime?" I ask.

She steps closer to me on her perch, tilts her head, and then makes a twittering cry.

"I'll take that as a yes."

By the time Aunt Bea comes home, I have started soup on the stove and am cutting up a defrosted quail for Red.

Aunt Bea peeks into the pot. "Smells good."

"Tomatoes, white beans, veggie broth, and some kale I found in the garden."

She nods. "I'll throw in some pasta."

I hold up the box I have ready. "Way ahead of you."

"Should I be worried that you're three steps ahead of where you usually are in the evenings? Don't tell me your homework is done too."

I snort a laugh. "It's still me, Aunt Bea."

She rumples my knot of hair. "Thank the stars."

I shake in the pasta, stirring it into the bubbling red. "You think he's okay?" I ask. The steam stings my eyes.

Aunt Bea places a hand on each of my shoulders, gives them a gentle squeeze. "He was ready," she says. "You helped him get ready. I trust him to take care of himself."

I stir and stir. "I trust him," I whisper into the curls of steam caressing my face.

Aunt Bea gives me another squeeze. "I'll get some milk for us both."

After we eat, we take the filleted quail out to Red, leash her to one of the perches, and watch from the back steps as she feasts. Red plucks little tufts of feathers and flings them aside, then pierces a strip of meat and gobbles it down. She adjusts her grip on her dinner and begins the process again, flinging the feathers with what I can only describe as glee.

"We're doing our hunting presentation for the whole school tomorrow," I say.

"The whole school?" Aunt Bea sips a steaming mug of tea.

"I was wondering if you could come with Red." I glance over at her. "At the end."

Aunt Bea smiles. "I was hoping you would ask."

"Thank you," I say, and give her leg a quick squeeze.

"Your mom talked to me about setting up visitation." Aunt Bea takes a long sip. "She also told me about your request for an apartment in Branford." She looks at me. "That took guts."

I pick up a stick, scrape long arcs in the dirt of the over-grown garden.

"Since she doesn't have a place yet, we talked about doing visitation here at first," Aunt Bea continues. "If things go well, I thought maybe she could even do your first over-night here."

I look up. "Where?" Would Mom sleep in an aviary?

Aunt Bea watches Red rip a morsel free, then mantle over her kill, spreading her wings like a protective wall. As if we would try to steal her dinner. Gross.

"Your mom and I spoke with the social worker," Aunt Bea continues. "I haven't been to see my girl in a while. Red's particular about who takes care of her."

Can she be saying what I think she's saying?

Aunt Bea goes on. "The game warden said he was okay with you taking care of Red while I'm gone."

My heart is thumping against my ribs and the smile on

my face is so wide, it hurts my cheeks. "We'd stay here? With Red?"

She nods, and I see the smile tipping up the edges of her mouth. The porch light sparkles in her eyes. "If you'd like that," she says.

I wrap my arms around her shoulders. "Thank you."

She hugs her free arm around me. "Thank *you*, Reenie."

Sometimes, *thank you* sounds an awful lot like *I love you*.

"I love you too," I whisper.

It's Friday morning and I'm freaking out. "You're sure you have the poster?" I say to Jamie.

"I have the poster." She is absolutely done with my paranoid questions.

"And I have my note cards," Jaxon says, preempting my next question.

I pat my back pocket. I have my note cards. Our group asked to go last because we have a surprise: Red. I now realize this is a terrible mistake.

Morning meeting has never been stressful before, but now, looking out at the whole school packed into the gym from where we're waiting in the wings backstage, stress builds inside me and I feel ready to burst. I pull aside the curtains for a fifth time and peek out. Bad idea. *The whole school* is out there. The gym is packed with eyes staring back at me. And standing against the walls are clumps of parents, invited here to watch the show.

"Okay, Otter Creek Elementary! Let's get quiet!" Principal Stanitski shouts through the mike. Then he does the clap—*clap, clap, clap-clap-clap*—which the whole school then repeats—*clap, clap, clap-clap-clap*—and it's so loud it practically shakes the walls apart, meaning *that's* how many people I'm about to have to speak in front of.

Jamie clamps her fingers around both my hand and Jaxon's. "You guys are so awesome." She's hopping on her toes. And something about the extreme size of her smile calms my nerves. Jamie is just happy to be up here with us, with me. Jamie is happy to be my friend.

Each group goes. I check the clock on the wall. *Aunt Bea said she'd be here.* And then I see the side door crack open, see her head peek in. She waves to me. I wave back, and my smile grows even wider.

We can do this, I remind myself. *I can do this.*

The principal introduces us, and the three of us walk out and face hundreds of bright eyes and open faces.

Jaxon begins, and then Jamie chimes in and they do the debate, and then it's my turn.

"Falconry is another type of hunting," I begin, and I glance off to the side door leading outside from the stage and see Aunt Bea, Red standing tall on her arm. "And we have a special guest to show you."

It's amazing to see this look—the look I remember burning across my face the first time I saw Red—flash on all the faces in the audience. Red, though, is completely calm, a queen surveying her kingdom. Aunt Bea uses her at the falconry school in the summer, so Red knows the drill: perch on the fist, be her amazing self, spread wonder and joy.

All my nervousness disappears because I realize I could just blather gibberish and all anyone would remember is Red.

At the end of our presentation, we get a standing ovation. We know it's mostly for Red, but still, we're pretty psyched.

After a quick group hug, Jamie and Jaxon are pulled away by their families. I wave to Warden Doucet, who salutes back with a single wave—so that's where Jaxon got it. Jaxon's mom smothers him with a hug and flurry of kisses. Jamie's parents pore over our poster board with her like they're the ones who'll give us the grade. Aunt Bea is talking to Principal Stanitski, who seems giddy being that close to a real hawk.

And then I notice, coming up the steps and onto the stage: Mom.

She hop-steps to me, then leans down and wraps me in a hug. "Reenie-beany, that was amazing!"

My arms flap around her. Her shampoo is the smell I've always associated with hugs. "You're here," I manage. "You came."

She strokes my hair. "Of course I did, my girl."

I glance over at Aunt Bea. She's watching us, eyes wary but calm. Red considers us, beak slightly to the side. It's like having my own Secret Service detail, ready to jump in at the first sign of danger.

Jamie places a hand on my shoulder. "Hey, Reenie, is this your mom?"

Mom tenses, like she's afraid of what I'll say.

I see Jaxon watching from over his mom's shoulder as she jostles him with another hug.

I step back, take my mom's hand in mine. "This is my mom," I say. "Mom, this is my best friend, Jamie."

My mom looks at me like I've given her a gift. "Hi, Jamie," she says, voice cracking a little on the "ee."

I'm right about things being different. But it's not just me or Mom that's changed; it's that it's not just me and Mom. I have Mom, and I think I even see Gram trying to make her way through the crowd, but I also have Aunt Bea. I have Jaxon and Jamie.

This is probably not the last reunion scene Mom and I will ever have. I get that. But now, I have many eyes watching over me. I have people I can count on. Now, I know I'm never too far from a safe place to perch.

Rufus & Reenie

"JAXON IS HOGGING THE SEAT," JAMIE COMPLAINS, SHOV-ing Jaxon away from her and thrusting him into me on the other side.

"You said you wanted me in the middle," Jaxon says, readjusting his butt and shoving her back.

They're both smiling like they're hiding a secret in the space between them, but everyone in the car—me, my mom, and even Jaxon's mom, I think—can tell that they like each other. I've talked to them both about it. Jamie could not stop obsessing over whether this was the worst friend betrayal ever, to *like* like Jaxon, and whether I would still be friends with her if she did like him. Jaxon merely asked me if I thought Jamie thought he was cute. I'm not sure which of them was more stressed out talking to me about it. I told them both that maybe they should talk to each other. If I've learned anything over the past few months, it's that talking straight with people is a good thing.

Jaxon's mom worked out this whole plan with my mom last week. It's an early Christmas present, at least for me. We're going to the Vermont Institute of Natural Science in Quechee to see their birds. The Institute, called VINS, is the largest bird rehabilitation facility in Vermont.

It's not that I don't see birds anymore. Aunt Bea got special approval from the Fish and Wildlife Department to let me train as her apprentice with a provisional license, so I'm over at her place three days a week to practice with Red. Aunt Bea trapped a passage goshawk around Thanksgiving, and she's spending all her time trying to train him, so Red needs a little extra love. Plus, Red and I have a "thing" going after my week-long stretch as her hunting partner back in October. Seeing how truculent the goshawk has been, I asked Aunt Bea if she'd rather have kept training Rufus.

"No more owls," she said.

Still, even mentioning his name made me miss him with an ache that cramped my insides. Every time I hear an owl hoot in the woods near the place Mom found for us — it's an apartment in one of the houses near downtown Branford that butts up right against the woods around the old cemetery—I think it's Rufus and run to the window. But it's never him. Or if it is, he never stays for a chat.

That's why I suggested to my mom getting passes to VINS. I saw on their website that they have a new great horned owl that they're using for their raptor shows. A part of me hopes it's Rufus, that he was found by some kindly naturalist and made safe in a cage. But the better part of me hopes it's not. That part of me wishes that he's soaring high over distant pine trees, the cold wind ruffling his feathers.

⌣

"Stop swooping into my current!" I screech at First, who is trying to fly in all the curls of wind at once.

"You're such a hatchling, Second," she chirps, diving at me, talons out, and at the last second peeling away.

I've come to see that heart-attack-inducing, death-threatening dives are First's idea of playful fun. Over the past moon or so, I've come to find them more annoying than petrifying, which is a flap in the right direction. Maybe by spring, I'll actually enjoy flying with her. For now, at least I don't flinch with every pass.

On a positive note, this mad play of hers has made me a more wary flier—I'm constantly scanning with ears and eyes for First, which means I'm also always on the watch for predators, which increases my chances of surviving this blasted winter.

We're taking a chance, flapping in the nearly full day of morning. At least today is cloudy, so we're not as exposed. Our last day-perch was in an evergreen, which got cut down by some cheery furless creatures, all decked out in sparkly clothing, warbling some horrid out-of-tune human song and sipping sticky-sweet steaming liquid from shiny containers clasped in their wing-toes. Truly, furless creatures are the most bizarre creatures in the forest. After we got kicked out of our tree, First and I decided to take advantage of the clouds and head over the mountain pass to see if things were quieter on the sunrise side.

So far, we've only found more furless creatures.

"I'm HUNGRY!" First screeches, swooping right over my ear tufts.

"Great Beak!" I chirp. "Fine, let's find a perch down in those trees over there. There's some open space between the human nests where there's got to be a mouse or two."

"For me!" First tweets, diving toward the trees.

"Not all!" I hoot, swerving midflap. "Not every mouse is for you!" Sometimes First needs reminding about these things.

⌒

It's cold stepping out of the hot, cramped car and into the crisp December air. But I'm so excited, I barely feel the frost. Jamie and Jaxon, however, are instantly shivering.

"Maybe we should have saved this for springtime," Jamie says, her words chopped into syllables by her shivering jaw.

"It's forty degrees—practically spring weather! And there's a new great horned owl," I say, slapping my arm around her shoulders to share some of my warmth. "I have to know if it's—"

"Rufus," she says, snuggling into my side. "I know. But I'm just saying, they could have timed it a little better."

"Here," Jaxon's mom says, handing us each little plastic pouches. "Open these and stick them in your boots and gloves."

We do as instructed—Jaxon's mom, being a nurse, has a very authoritative voice. The little pouches have smaller pouches inside that instantly start to warm up.

"You're a lifesaver, Carolyn," Mom says. They've become friends—Jaxon's mom even helped my mom get a job at her clinic. Mom and Jaxon's mom do this ridiculous special high-five thing. Grownups are so weird.

Then they both slap arms around all of us kids, and we walk into VINS like that, as a single snuggled-up group, ready to see my owl.

⌒

First catches a vole before I even make it to tree cover.

"You really need to pick up your speed on the down-drafts," First hoots once she finishes swallowing the vole.

"I'm working on it," I grumble, flapping to a better perch to watch the open space for a meal.

"Work harder." First glides to perch beside me. "I expect you to still be hunting with me come the summer."

"Then you should leave more prey around."

She nips my ear tufts. "That doesn't help you learn anything."

And then she's off, floating on an updraft and crashing down on yet another yummy morsel.

I adjust my feathers, calm my gizzard, and sight something in a pile of leaves. My ears pinpoint a heartbeat. I'm off the branch and gliding to the perfect dive point, and then I'm dropping like a pinecone from a branch, talons out, and *BAM!* It's dinnertime!

I flap back to the branch with my prize and am midgulp when First lands beside me with not one but two mice in her talons.

"What can I hoot?" she says, gulping the first. "I have a talent."

"For death," I reply.

"We're apex predators. It's the only talent we need."

"What about hooting? I feel I have a slight advantage there." I gently preen my primaries.

First snorts. "Fantastic. You keep hooting over here. I'll go catch my *fourth* niblet."

"Not if I catch it first!" I am right on her tail.

It's agony waiting for the raptor show to start. I mean, all these birds in the exhibits are amazing. I've never been face-to-beak with a real bald eagle before! And yet here I am, looking right into one's eyes, and all I can think about is an hour from now, when I'll be sitting in the outdoor amphitheater and the presenter will come out with my Rufus — or some other owl. I can't get my hopes up.

"I think it wants to eat me," Jamie says, cocking her head at the eagle.

"They don't eat people," Jaxon says, reading the information plaque.

"Yeah, but this one is giving me that look."

"Lucky for you, he's behind a fence," I say, grabbing the links.

The eagle squawks and flaps his wings in response.

"See?" Jamie says, giving me a wide-eyed, eyebrows-up smirk.

"He's just mad about my messing with his fence."

"*She*," Jaxon adds. "It's a girl."

Jamie turns back to the bird, gives her another once-over. "Maybe it's good that she wants to eat me. I mean, she's got to eat. When she goes back to the wild, I mean."

I nod. "When she goes back to the wild." I place my mitten on the railing.

I can barely fly, I'm so full of rodent.

"Get your tail up!" First screeches, swooping by and nipping my feathers.

"We must stop for a break so I can pellet," I manage, diving before First can even give me an answer.

I turn for a clutch of trees—too close to one of the monster pathways and some human nests, but I can't wait for a better perch.

"This is a bad perch," First says, swooping next to me.

"Tell that to my gizzard."

I land on a branch and try to settle before pelleting. It makes the whole process more pleasant.

First flaps down beside me. "We should just perch here for the rest of the day. It's getting too bright and I hear a lot of birds around here. Big birds." She glances around like the branches are packed with hawks, eagles, and vultures.

I'm focused on my pellet, but once that's up and out, my ears pick up distant screeching and squawking.

"There can't be that many hawks," I chirp, mostly to calm my own gizzard. "Not in one place." Hawks are solitary hunters like owls, not flocking featherheads like crows.

"I'll mark this area as our territory." First puffs herself up and then hoots this weak, warbling *Hoot-hoo-hoo-hoooooot!*

It barely echoes around our little tussock of trees.

"Excuse me, sister," I twitter, "but perhaps this might be

my opportunity to render assistance to *you*." I fluff my feathers, clack my beak to loosen my tongue, and then straighten up and give the hoot of my life:

HOOT-HOO-HOO-HOOOOOOOOOOOOOOO-OOOOOOT!!!

It sounds and resounds from far and near, shivering through puddles and ponds so even the fish beneath the frozen rime know that *this* tussock of trees is great horned owl territory.

First's tufts are straight up in shock. "Brother, I did not know you had such hoots in you."

I'm fairly bursting with pride but try to act all calm and nonchalant. "Yes," I chirp. "Well, now you do."

Before she can add something snarky to her compliment, we hear an answering hoot: *Hoot-hoo-hoo-HOOOOOT!*

It's Mother.

❧

Finally, the show is starting. "Welcome, visitors!" the lady begins. On her fist is a red-tailed hawk. Red is a much more impressive specimen, but hey, not every bird can be the most amazing hawk ever.

The naturalist begins telling the audience how grateful she is for our being there and how our entrance fees go directly to supporting the rehabilitation of the birds we've seen at the facility and whom we'll meet in the show.

I hardly register anything she says. My whole brain is

waiting for the owl to be revealed. I'm practically vibrating with excitement.

When the hawk flies over the audience, my brain gets distracted enough to ooh and aah along with everyone else. Even though I've had birds of prey flying around me for months now, it's still a thrill. It's hard to be jaded about something that awesome.

And then it's announced: "And here's our newest arrival in the education wing, a great horned owl we're calling Greta."

It's a girl.

A young guy walks out with this large great horned owl. One of her wings sags, but otherwise, she's a perfect owl.

But she's a she.

She's not Rufus.

What was I expecting? That it would definitely be him and not any other great horned owl? That he'd see me in the audience and flap over for a hoot? How had I let my hopes float so high?

This owl was hit by a car, like so many of the other raptors here at VINS. I never realized that people and their things are the only real predators that birds like hawks, owls, and eagles have to contend with. That even something as simple as not tossing your apple core out the car window could save a bird's life.

"A mouse will come to eat that apple core, and then a raptor will fly down to get the mouse, and then a car comes along and we have what happened to our friend Greta here," the guy says, holding Greta up high so everyone can see her.

And then—it's so weird and I know I'm crazy and already worked up but I swear it's true—I hear Rufus hoot.

But I'm not crazy because Greta totally heard it too. Her ear tufts flip up off her head and then she hoots a quick reply.

The audience claps and burbles excitedly. The naturalist guy looks a little shocked. "Well, we don't normally get a hoot during our shows, but hey! There it is!"

People clap and whisper. My eyes are glued on Greta, whose tufts are lifted even higher now. She bobs and twists her head, listening for an answering hoot.

"Mother!" I hoot, dropping off the branch and flapping blindly through the trees.

"Second!" First screeches, diving after me. "It's bright out! And there are hawks and eagles around!"

But I can't *not* go to her. I can't not see for myself that it *is* her, that she's really here. That she's alive.

I hoot again. Her voice comes to me like a warm breeze. "Second!" she hoots. "Is it really you?"

I follow her voice, flapping down the river of air that leads toward her.

꙳

Even the presenters are befuddled by Greta's excited hooting and flapping about. The guy can barely keep her on the glove. She keeps bating, trying to fly off. But I can tell that she will never fly again—or at least, not well. Her drooping wing can barely flap. But this is not stopping her from trying.

And then two shadows shoot out from behind the roofline of one of the rehabilitation buildings. One's a big owl—a female. And the other—can I dare to even dream it?—oh gosh, I swear it looks like—

"Rufus!" I yell, jumping up.

The two owls swoop right overhead. The big one flaps up into a nearby tree, but the smaller one wheels around, back toward the amphitheater.

꙳

We clear the top of the human nest and there she is: Mother.

"You're alive!" I screech as I fly over her.

Mother tries to fly toward me. "Second! You survived!" she chirps. But then she's tufts down in a bat hang.

"What's wrong with her?" First squawks, flying to a tree. "She's hanging upside down."

"I know all about this," I hoot. "Remember what that other owl said? She's an ambassador now. She's got to have leg sparkles and tails to be around humans."

"What insanity are you squawking?" First looks at me like I'm growing primaries out of my ear holes.

"She's fine," I translate for her.

"Then we should go. This perch is surrounded by hawks!"

"Just let me say goodbye." I swoop back toward Mother. And then—and this is truly bizarre on the one wing but makes complete sense on the other—I see the Brown Frizz standing up in the crowd of furless creatures huddled around Mother.

Of course the humans would send some creature like the Brown Frizz to be their ambassador to the owls. And what a fine ambassador she will be.

I decide to give her a little hoot of recognition. And then I mute on her head. Just to let her know I care.

"Mother!" I hoot, swerving my wings and banking toward her. "I'm so proud that you are an ambassador for owls."

"Second, I'm just happy to see you're alive. And is that First you're with?"

"She's taken me under her wing."

Mother's tufts lower, questioning the truth of this.

"No, really," I hoot. "Her antagonism is forcing me to be the owl you always wanted me to be." I land on the head of this human who's serving as a perch for Mother. He certainly won't mind.

Mother's eyes smile. "I only ever wanted you to be the owl you are, my love."

The human I'm perched on begins twittering like maybe my talons are hurting him. "I believe I might have to be off soon."

Mother bobs her head. "Give my love to First."

"I will. Stay safe, Mother."

"Don't worry about me," she hoots. "These furless creatures have turned out to be nicer than I'd ever have thought them to be."

I glance over at the Brown Frizz, who looks like she's becoming completely fluffed. "They certainly are," I hoot. "Goodbye, Mother!"

I lift off the human perch's head and swoop over to the Brown Frizz, who holds out her arm as always. I perch and give her a nip on the nostril tube. "I did it," I hoot to her. "I am flying free just like you and old Gray Tail and Red always wanted."

She burbles something in Furless Creature–ese. Her eyes are flecked with raindrops—how strange, this thing about furless creatures and leaking about the eyes.

"Don't get yourself fluffed, Brown Frizz. I will fly free once more. I just wanted one final hoot." I give her a bit of a nuzzle and she gives me some excellent rubbings between the tufts.

The other humans step back, like they think I might attack them.

Good.

But the Brown Frizz is all blubbery and drips from her nostrils. What a silly furless creature she is.

"Thank you for all you gave me," I hoot, nipping her fingers, which are in some wonderfully fuzzy paws that, if I had more time, would have made for some excellent shredding, but things being what they are, well, we can't do everything we want whenever we want to. "Goodbye, Brown Frizz! Be a good human!" I screech, flapping off her arm.

She waves her paws at me.

She will continue to be an excellent furless creature, especially to unfortunate owls. She certainly was the most excellent furless creature to me.

When I flap up into the tree, First is practically molting, she's so worked up. "What in the name of all that hoots was that about?! Flying in front of humans?! Snuggling with humans?!"

I tilt my head. "I like humans. At least some humans."

First scowls, tufts flat on her skull. "Inconceivable." She flaps off, sticking low to the tree line.

I catch up to her. "How about you keep me from getting too comfortable with humans and I'll keep you from getting too caught up in your wildness?"

Her tufts lift a smidgen. "We *are* hatchmates," she hoots, eyes shining. "Who better to learn from?"

We glide on a current of warm air toward a thick forest of green in the mountains beyond.

One of the naturalists comes running over after Rufus has flown away. "I'm so sorry, miss! We've never — I've never — I mean, owls don't normally come flapping out of the woods at us!" She's practically shaking from . . . I'm not sure if it's shock or fright or excitement or the fear that I might sue.

"I'm fine," I say, eyes still locked on the gray stretch of sky that Rufus and the other owl disappeared into. "I'm perfect."

Mom grabs my shoulders, checks me for injury before saying, "What was that?"

A smile cracks across my face and this giggling comes out from between my lips. "That," I say, "was Rufus."

"Your owl? The one you released months ago? Honey, I don't think—"

I shake my head. "It was him."

"That was Rufus?" Jamie asks. "*The* Rufus?"

"Yeah," I say, voice all dreamy.

He's alive. He's surviving. He made it. And I had something to do with that.

"He looked good," Jaxon says.

"He did," I reply.

My mom still looks like she might faint.

"They've got hot chocolate in the education center," Jaxon's mom says. "I think we all need some hot chocolate after that excitement."

"With extra whipped cream," I add.

Mom looks at me, shakes her head, and laughs a little. "With lots of extra whipped cream."

And we all go, arm in arm like this weird little family, toward the bright lights of the café and the promise of something sweet.

A Note from the Author

EACH STORY I WRITE STARTS FROM AN IDEA OR TWO THAT hum with possibility. In the case of Rufus and Reenie's story, it began with my daughter and her love of owls. The more we learned together about owls, and visited captive owls, and watched YouTube videos about owls, the more I fell in love with these strange and silent night dwellers. Around the same time, I also happened to read a book about falconry, *H Is for Hawk* by Helen Macdonald, which led me to *The Once and Future King* by T. H. White, both of which got me excited about writing a story with falconry in it. But these two ideas seemed to be singing different tunes, until I brought them together with my work in the foster care system.

When I was a child, I had no idea what happened to children who couldn't live with their families or who didn't have families. I was privileged enough that this didn't even seem like something that happened in the present day; it was an idea reserved for *The Secret Garden* or *Oliver Twist*. After college, I worked for a year in the residential treatment center of a foster agency in New York and learned that I was very much mistaken. Based on the most recent numbers I have, there are 442,995 children in foster care in the United

States, 1,864 of whom are in Vermont. I now work in the family courts here in Vermont and see these families' stories every day.

But this is merely how Rufus and Reenie's story got its start; to turn these ideas into a novel, I had to do research —a lot of research! Researching is not just about hunting down information in books or on the Internet. For this book, in addition to going to bird rehabilitation facilities and talking to rehabilitators about their work (so interesting!) and seeking out live owls both in captivity and online through nest cameras and other videos (so cute!), I took a falconry lesson so that I could experience what the sport was like firsthand.

Even something as mundane as a chickadee on my bird feeder sets me smiling, so imagine the Fourth of July fireworks going on inside my chest when the falconer held his fist beside mine and a Harris's hawk named Monty hopped onto my glove mere inches from my face. At first, I was afraid to even look at him—he was so fierce with his sharp eyes and even sharper talons. But Monty was a friendly guy, as was my instructor, and we got to flying.

It amazed me how I could barely feel Monty's physical weight on my arm and yet was overwhelmed by his physical presence on my glove. Monty is much lighter than a great horned owl like Rufus would be—Monty's flying weight is around 1.5 pounds, and a great horned owl weighs around 3 pounds. Even so, being this close to a real hawk felt like a gravitational force on par with a small planet; I can only imagine what having a big bird like Rufus that close would be like. When Monty glided over the grass and then swooped up to my fist, I was nearly blown over by the magic of his wings beating and how he could land on my glove with such precision, his talons positioning him perfectly to gobble down his tidbit of meat.

As this was a lesson, we weren't hunting, but even if we had been, I was struck by how little my desires played into Monty's behavior. Monty flew where he wanted to fly: if I cast him off toward a tree, he might fly there; or he might change course and disappear among the reeds fringing a pond in search of frogs. He was not like a trained dog, loping happily beside me, and I didn't feel as though he was interested in my affection or cared to please me. Rather, he looked at me as an equal, as if I was expected to pull my weight on this outing and I should not take his presence for granted. This experience helped me in thinking not only about how falconry fit into the book, but how it related to both Rufus and Reenie and what it meant for them together.

Even this is just a tiny fragment of all the information and experiences I dug into to help craft this story. For more information about falconry and bird rehabilitation, please enjoy the following conversations with the experts who helped me!

Falconry Q&A

1. WHAT IS FALCONRY? WHY WOULD SOMEONE TAKE UP FALCONRY?

Falconry is defined as "hunting wild game with a trained raptor." As well as training and hunting, a falconer spends a great deal of time caring for the bird and its needs to ensure that it is healthy and fulfilled. Falconers share a love of birds of prey and nature; the sport brings with it the opportunity to be a part of both.

2. WHAT BIRDS ARE USED FOR FALCONRY? HOW MANY BIRDS CAN A FALCONER HAVE?

Despite the name "falconry," a variety of birds in the falcon, hawk, and eagle families can be used in the sport (examples are the golden eagle, the goshawk, and the peregrine falcon).

Falconers are limited by law as to how many birds they may have, but because it's such a time-consuming pursuit, most work with just one.

3. WHAT IS A PASSAGE HAWK? WHAT IS A CAPTIVE-BRED BIRD? WHAT IS AN IMPRINTED BIRD?

A passage hawk is a raptor that is trapped from the wild at an immature age (younger than a year). A captive-bred hawk is one that is bred in captivity by a licensed breeder.

An imprinted bird is one that is reared by a falconer from a very early age. It will then "imprint" upon (or bond with) the falconer; when done properly, this will make the bird much more at ease around people.

4. IS TRAPPING BAD FOR WILD BIRD POPULATIONS? DOES TRAPPING A WILD BIRD HURT THE BIRD? CAN THE BIRDS EVER BE LET BACK INTO THE WILD?

Falconers are legally permitted to trap only bird species that are plentiful. The process does not harm birds in any way.

Trapping has no impact on wild hawk populations. Studies show that 70 percent of wild hawks die before the end of their first winter, mostly from starvation due to the fact that they have insufficient skills to fend for themselves. A falconer will often choose to release a hawk back into the wild after the winter hunting season has ended. When released, the well-fed and healthy hawk will revert to its wild condition. Plus, it now has more hunting experience than before it was trapped.

5. HOW LONG DOES IT TAKE TO TRAIN A BIRD FOR FALCONRY?

The early training to the point where the bird can be flown completely "free" (untethered) varies depending upon the species, the falconer's experience, and the hawk's temperament. Smaller species tend to take less time than the larger ones. A hawk such as the red-tailed hawk can be flying free in fewer than two weeks.

6. DO FALCONERS HUNT ALL YEAR ROUND OR ONLY DURING CERTAIN TIMES OF THE YEAR? WHERE DO THE BIRDS LIVE WHEN THEY'RE NOT HUNTING? DO THE BIRDS GET BORED SITTING ON THEIR PERCHES?

Falconers have hunting seasons just as other hunters do. These are mostly between the fall and spring; the hawks are not worked over the summer. During summertime, they are placed in their mews and are not kept in hunting condition. This means they are very content sitting for long periods (just as a hawk with a full belly would be in the wild).

7. DOES ONE NEED A LICENSE FROM THE STATE TO BECOME A FALCONER? HOW LONG DOES IT TAKE TO TRAIN TO BE A FALCONER?

Because raptors are so highly protected, a falconer must first become licensed to possess a bird. Age limits and other specifics vary from state to state. There is an exam, a hunters' safety course, an equipment and housing check by the game warden, and then a minimum two-year apprenticeship. The apprenticeship is overseen by an experienced falconer and involves trapping, training, and hunting a wild passage hawk.

Bird Rehabilitation Q&A

1. WHAT IS BIRD REHABILITATION? WHAT DOES A BIRD REHABILITATOR DO?

Bird rehab is the process of helping a wild bird recover from its injuries and releasing it back to the wild. A rehabilitator is someone who has the permits and training required to rehabilitate wild birds.

2. WHAT KIND OF TRAINING DOES A BIRD REHABILITATOR NEED? CAN I REHABILITATE A BIRD IF I FIND ONE THAT'S SICK OR INJURED?

Bird rehabilitators are trained in various ways, from taking online courses to attending in-person conferences. An individual can rehabilitate birds if he or she has the proper knowledge and is licensed. Never try to rehabilitate a bird on your own. Always contact a licensed bird rehabilitator or your state's game warden if you find a sick or injured bird. Many baby birds found outside their nests don't need any help. Parent birds will feed their babies when they start exploring outside the nest or even if they fall out of the nest before they're ready to be completely independent. Always leave a baby bird who has feathers alone until you hear from the game warden or bird rehabber that it needs help; they can advise you on what to do next.

3. HOW MANY SICK AND INJURED BIRDS DO YOU SEE PER YEAR? DO REHABILITATORS SEE MORE AT CERTAIN TIMES OF THE YEAR? DIFFERENT KINDS OF BIRDS AT DIFFERENT TIMES?

The number of birds a rehabber admits varies from year to year depending on the facilities and resources available to them. Admissions peak during times of migration and breeding, which varies with different species but generally is spring and fall. All types of birds are admitted throughout the year.

4. WHAT IS THE CAUSE OF MOST BIRD INJURIES?

Vehicle collisions.

5. HOW DO YOU TREAT BIRD INJURIES? CAN A BIRD REHABILITATOR TREAT EVERY INJURY, OR DO SOME BIRDS NEED HELP FROM OTHER PEOPLE?

Different types of injuries require different treatment. There are some injuries that rehabbers cannot treat, such as traumatic amputations, loss of vision or hearing, and some viral diseases. The number one need for a rehabber is medical support from a veterinarian.

6. CAN YOU RELEASE EVERY BIRD BACK TO THE WILD? WHY DO SOME BIRDS GET CHOSEN TO BE "AMBASSADORS" LIKE RUFUS'S MOM?

In a perfect world, all injured birds would be healed and sent back into the wild, in the safest area closest to where they were found, just as Reenie did with Rufus. Unfortunately, this is not possible for all birds, and some may have to be euthanized because of the extent of their injuries. Sometimes a bird may be able to be rehabilitated to the extent where it no longer lives in pain and can live a healthy, comfortable life with a little help. For example, certain wing breaks may heal but leave the bird unable to fly swiftly and silently enough to hunt efficiently. Or a bird could lose vision in one eye and hearing in one ear after being hit by a car. This bird can continue to live, but it also may have a hard time hunting for itself with limited vision and hearing.

With proper permits, however, the birds can become education ambassadors for their wild-living counterparts. These birds receive food delivered to their aviary, protection from predators, and free health care. In order to be considered for an ambassador program, there would need to be physical space for the bird, a need for that particular type of bird in an education collection (some species are prevalent, and since most facilities already have one or more of those more common species in their collection, a rarer bird may have an easier time being placed), and an educator with time to train and present the bird for programming.

7. WHAT CAN I DO TO MAKE MY WORLD SAFER FOR BIRDS?

Here are a few simple things:

THANK YOU TO ROB WAITE OF THE GREEN MOUNTAIN FAL-conry School, greenmountainfalconryschool.com, who gave me the amazing experience of having a hawk fly to my fist, and to Craig Newman and Cat Wright Parrish of Outreach for Earth Stewardship, ofesvt.org, who gave me the inside scoop on what it takes to help our raptor friends when they need it most.

If you'd like to learn more about owls, check out the Owl Pages at owlpages.com. I also enjoyed reading Leigh Calvez's *The Hidden Lives of Owls,* or for younger readers, Alice Calaprice's adaptation of Bernd Heinrich's *An Owl in the House: A Naturalist's Diary* and Jean Craighead George's *There's an Owl in the Shower.* If you're interested in bird rehabilitation, please contact a local wildlife rehabilitator or natural science center. If you're in Vermont, head to the Vermont Institute of Natural Science, vinsweb.org, or meet the avian ambassadors from Outreach for Earth Stewardship at Shelburne Farms, shelburnefarms.org. If you'd like to learn more about falconry, check out the Modern Apprentice at themodernapprentice.com. You can also contact your state's wildlife agency.

Glossary

Anklet—a little strip of leather that is wrapped around each of the bird's legs like a tight-fitting bracelet. The jesses are attached to the anklets.

Apex predator—a predator at the top of a food chain, with no natural predators.

Aviary—the place where a bird lives; usually a partially enclosed house with barred or mesh windows or walls. This house is also called a *mews*.

Bal-chatri trap—a safe trap used by falconers to catch wild birds. Imagine an upside-down bowl made of metal mesh. Inside the bowl, there's a live mouse. When the hawk flies down, thinking it's in for an easy meal, it feels something on its foot. This is because the upward-facing part of the bowl is covered with little see-through loops that slip onto the bird's toes and tighten, holding the bird to the bowl. When the bird realizes this and tries to fly away, it's held down by the weights along the edge of the bowl.

Bating—an occurrence when the hawk (or owl!) tries to fly off its perch but is held back by a restraint and ends up hanging upside down.

Cast off—the motion that the falconer has to use when a bird is on the falconer's fist in order to throw or push the bird into the air to encourage it to take flight.

Casting—when a bird coughs up (casts) a pellet (also called a casting). This process is also called *pelleting.* The pellet is a lump made up of all the bits of food that the bird couldn't digest. For Rufus, this would be a tightly packed lump of fur and bones, slightly smaller than your fist.

Creance—a long, lightweight string tied to the hawk's jesses. A creance serves the same purpose as a dog's leash: it allows the falconer to fly a hawk without having to worry that the hawk is going to fly away forever.

Crop—the pouch along a hawk's throat where food is stored and digestion begins. Owls do not have a crop.

Crown—the top of a bird's head. Red can lift the feathers of her crown, creating a kind of frill that looks like . . . well, a crown!

Falconry—the sport of hunting wild game with a trained raptor.

Fledged—when a young bird whose wing feathers have developed enough for flight leaves the nest to start life on its own.

Flying weight—the ideal weight for a bird flown for falconry. Think of this the way you'd think of the weight athletes try to maintain to keep themselves at the top of their game.

Gauntlet—a glove made of thick leather worn by falconers, usually on their less dominant hand, that protects them from a raptor's sharp talons.

Gizzard—a specialized part of a bird's stomach with thick, muscular walls used for grinding up food.

Hood—a little leather hat placed on a trained bird's head. The hood limits the amount of sensory information coming at the bird and helps to keep it calm when driving in a car, for example.

Imprinted — when a bird has been raised by humans and not by other raptors. Imprinted birds will often identify with their humans more than with other raptors.

Jesses — a narrow strip of leather, with a knot at one end, that fits through a hole in the anklet and allows falconers to hold on to their birds.

Manning — the process of getting a wild hawk used to the human world so that it can be used for falconry. The hawk needs not only to become comfortable with its partner but also to get used to that person's house, car, and even family, friends, and pets.

Mantle — the feathers on a bird's back right at the start of the wings. This term can also be a verb; raptors *mantle* over their prey, which means that they stand over it with a hunched back and neck and with their wings spread wide to protect their meal from being stolen.

Mews — *see* Aviary.

Mute — when a bird poops. The poop itself is also called a *mute*. Technically, the *mute* includes both pee and poop, in humans' terms. *See also* Whitewash.

Passage bird — a wild raptor that is younger than one year old. In other words, a hawk who has not yet lived through its first winter.

Pellet — *see* Casting.

Primary feathers—the longest feathers on a bird's wing, which are farthest away from the bird's body when the wing is extended. These are attached to the bones at the end of the bird's wing. Think of them as the fingertips of the bird.

Secondary feathers—the slightly shorter long feathers on a bird's wing that are closest to the bird's body when the wing is extended.

Tidbits—small, cut-up bits of raw meat used by falconers as treats for their birds to train them to do what the falconers want. For example, a falconer offers tidbits to get a hawk to hop to the fist or fly to the fist from a perch.

Whitewash—white streaks with brownish clumps "pooped" out by an owl, though the white parts are more similar to human pee and the brown clumps are . . . well, poop. *See also* Mute.

Acknowledgments

THANK YOU TO MY AMAZING EDITOR, AMY CLOUD. I FEEL so lucky that this book found its way to you. You zeroed in on scenes and sentences that I immediately recognized as needing another pass, and you asked all the right questions to help me tell the story I meant to tell on the page. Your support and encouragement inspired me anew for each revision. I am thrilled that you are guiding Rufus and Reenie into the world.

A huge thank-you to my agent, Faye Bender. You saw the potential in this story from the start and helped it grow from a fledgling idea into a free-flying novel in the world. I am so grateful for your support, encouragement, and expertise.

Thank you to everyone at Houghton Mifflin Harcourt and especially to designers Kaitlin Yang and Sharismar Rodriguez, managing editor Mary Magrisso, copyeditor Susan Buckheit, Samantha Bertschmann on the production staff, and the wonderful John Sellers and Lisa DiSarro in publicity and marketing. Rufus, Reenie, and I are lucky to have such a crack team behind us! And thank you, Izzy Burton, for your gorgeous artwork. Your first sketch captured the heart of the story, and everything else has grown beautifully from there.

I am grateful for the support I receive at The Book

Group. Thank you to Lora Fountain and Annelie Geissler for representing Rufus and Reenie abroad.

Thank you to my foreign publishers for bringing this story to readers around the world.

In researching this book, I relied upon the guidance of the following patient and generous people: Thank you to Rob Waite and the Green Mountain Falconry School for introducing me to the real world of falconry and a feisty little hawk named Monty. Thank you, Cat Wright Parrish and especially Craig Newman of Outreach for Earth Stewardship, for helping me understand the hard work of rehabilitating wild birds and the dangers they face in our world. Thank you to the staff at the Vermont Institute of Natural Science for giving me a tour of your facilities and letting me stretch my "wings" in a flight pen. And thank you to Hon. Alison Arms and Gail Straw for letting me bounce ideas off you. Any errors or inaccuracies are my own or represent tweaks made with creative license for the purposes of my story.

It's a rare thing to find critique partners who are not only incredible readers of your work, but who are also wonderful friends and supports in your life. Thank you, Rachel Carter and Margot Harrison, for holding my hands through the years and being the thorough and honest readers I've needed. Thank you, Tui Sutherland, for being there for me always, sometimes literally in the middle of the night, and for pointing out that Rufus's voice should be first. And thank you to Ellen Booraem, Kekla Magoon, and everyone at Kindling Words East for listening to those first words on the page. Thank you to Kate Messner for letting me pester you for title ideas, and to Donna Smith for helping me find the one. And thank you to the fantastic Vermont writers' community for providing such a warm creative home.

Finally, a ginormous thank-you to my family. To my mom and dad, Chris and John, thank you for the years of support and encouragement. To my brother, Jordan, thanks for checking in and pushing me forward. To my kids, Evie and Josh, thank you for inspiring this story and cheering me on as I wrote it. To my husband, Jason, thank you for listening to all my ideas and helping me sort the wheat from the chaff; for reading countless sentences and helping me make them better; for lovingly debating all the issues, large and small; and for supporting me along the way over all these years.